Praise for *Gone to Dust*

"I want more of Nils Shapiro."   —Lee Child,
New York Times bestselling author

"Gotta love it: Spade, Spenser, and now Shapiro. The brilliant Matt Goldman has written the perfect PI novel—smart, spare, sarcastic, and completely heartbreaking."   —Hank Phillippi Ryan,
Anthony, Agatha, and Mary Higgins Clark
Award–winning author

"Blends his storytelling with irreverent humor. His tough yet vulnerable PI, evocative Minneapolis setting, and clever plot, which features a distinctive crime scene and multiple red herrings, will engage and intrigue."   —*Library Journal* (starred review)

"With his wry, observant eye and quick wit, plus a pressing need to follow the truth into dark, uncharted places, Shap is a more optimistic version of Ross MacDonald's Lew Archer. Readers will look forward to his next investigative adventure."
—*Publishers Weekly*

"Clever and compelling . . . Goldman's experience as a stand-up comic, playwright, and TV writer show to advantage in this first novel's wit, the story's pace, and his hero's charm."   —*Booklist*

BOOKS BY MATT GOLDMAN

Gone to Dust

Broken Ice (forthcoming)

MATT GOLDMAN

GONE TO DUST

A Tom Doherty Associates Book / New York

This is a work of fiction. All of the characters, organizations, and events portrayed in this novel are either products of the author's imagination or are used fictitiously.

GONE TO DUST

Copyright © 2017 by Matthew Goldman

A Forge Book
Published by Tom Doherty Associates
175 Fifth Avenue
New York, NY 10010

www.tor-forge.com

Forge® is a registered trademark of Macmillan Publishing Group, LLC.

ISBN 978-0-7653-9130-8

Our books may be purchased in bulk for promotional, educational, or business use. Please contact your local bookseller or the Macmillan Corporate and Premium Sales Department at 1-800-221-7945, extension 5442, or by email at MacmillanSpecialMarkets@macmillan.com.

First Edition: August 2017
First Mass Market Edition: May 2018

Printed in the United States of America

0 9 8 7 6 5 4 3 2 1

*For my farther, Larry, who would have said,
"It's just as good as Grisham!" Even if it's not.*

ACKNOWLEDGMENTS

Jennifer Weltz, my agent, for her editorial contributions and advice and finding a wonderful home for this book. Kristin Sevick, my editor, for championing and improving every aspect inside the cover and out. To everyone at Forge for their outstanding work from copyediting to cover design to marketing and probably a whole mess of stuff I'm not aware of.

My parents and brothers for a lifetime of goodness. My children, their unselfishness and kindness and excellence allowed me to take a risk—they are my favorite reason to get out of bed every day. To all the TV writers who taught me story, the hardest thing to learn. Boredom, coffee, and bad weather, I couldn't have done it without you. Minnesota, I hope this book reads as a love letter because that's what it is. Jacob Gribble, for helping the investigation feel real. Kari Lizer, who brought me to Claudette Sutherland and her table—this is kind of their fault.

1

Minneapolis had a brown Christmas. It happens, sometimes. Store owners complain about not selling sleds, skis, and shovels, but no one else seems to mind. We know what's coming. And just after midnight on January 4 it did, falling wet and heavy. Eighteen inches on an earth frozen stiff by a clear, cold December.

I decided to give myself a snow day and stayed under the comforter to dream in the gray light, but the dreams never came or maybe they did and fizzled out unremembered. Then I woke at the crack of 8:55 to a buzzing nightstand accompanied by a medley of plows scraping streets, snow throwers whining under stress, and tires spinning themselves to nowhere.

I answered my cell. "Hello."

"Shap? You available?" It was Ellegaard.

"Professionally or romantically?"

"Sheesh, Shap. This is serious. East side of Edina near Arden Park. We caught something . . ." He paused. I could tell he was shaken. ". . . something sick."

Ellegaard didn't swear or drink. He wasn't an alcoholic or Mormon or twelve so he had no excuse. "What happened?" I said.

"Dang it, Shap, just get over here."

Anders Ellegaard and I attended the Minneapolis Police Academy together. A week after getting our badges, the mayor, fending off a Republican challenger, made a show of cutting costs. Last hired, first fired. While the other layoffees sat on their pimply ones playing video games until the rehiring, Ellegaard and I got industrious. I went to work for a private-detective firm and started accruing hours toward my license. Ellegaard found a police job across France Avenue in the regal suburb of Edina, where the cops worked the most white-collar job you can while wearing a blue collar. Neither of us put on a Minneapolis police officer's uniform again.

Edina PD spent most of its time camped out at the bottom of a hill on 50th writing speeding tickets to Mercedes and BMWs. The revenue helped pay for consultants when a real crime came Edina's way and apparently one had—the Edina police hadn't worked a murder in over a decade.

"We need you, Shap," said Ellegaard. "Now."

I owned a shitbox one-bedroom near 54th and Drew. A divorce settlement left me with enough money to pay cash for it. The house was more expensive than it looked—good schools and restaurants within walking distance inflated the neighborhood's property values. Every week I received at least one offer to buy it, always from a builder. People saw great value in my home, as long as they could wipe it off its foundation.

It'd take me ten minutes to walk to Ellegaard on the east side of Arden Park or an hour to shovel the driveway so I could back my agèd Volvo out of the garage and get it stuck in the unplowed alley. "I'll walk over," I said. "Save me an acai berry croissant or whatever you Edina hard-asses are eating these days."

I downed two cups of coffee, threw on a jacket, and laced up my Sorels. I opened my front door. A foot and a half of the heavy stuff pressed against the storm door. I wedged it open just enough to slip outside. It was thirty degrees. Compared to the last few weeks of subzero fuckery, it felt like summer. The plows had only scraped the main thoroughfares, leaving most Minneapolis streets rutted and sloppy. I trudged west on the snow-covered sidewalk then hit a stretch some do-gooder had cleared to justify the grand he'd spent on his snowblower. Then I was Ernest Shackleton again until I reached the Edina border where the suburb's streets glistened wet and clean thanks to a battalion of overnight plows.

I turned right on Minnehaha Boulevard which hugged the east edge of Arden Park. A massive house on a hill rose to my right. A sign in the yard read VOTE NO SIDEWALKS FOR—snow covered the remainder of the sign.

On my left, Parks & Rec had already plowed the hockey and free-skating rinks. Shouts and screams and skates and sticks and pucks slapping boards. All comfortable and familiar. Memories of skating with pretty girls with ropey braids and swollen sweaters. It was a youth well spent. I might've become nostalgic if I hadn't seen the flashing police cherries two blocks away through the leafless oaks and maples.

The police gathered outside a gargantuan architectural

mongrel bred of colonial, Cape Cod, and Tudor, all capped off with an English country–style roof of steam-bent cedar shingles that rounded at the edges like mushroom caps. The place looked like a painting you'd see in an art gallery at the mall. A massive red oak, probably older than the state of Minnesota, umbrellaed the front yard, hundreds of dead brown leaves still clinging to its branches in the January air. The wide driveway was clear and dry, evidence of hot water tubes snaking beneath. That's where Ellegaard waited for me.

He told the uniforms to let me through the yellow tape. Whole families stood outside and craned their necks. The watercoolers would be abuzz the next day in the executive wings of Target, UnitedHealthcare, Cargill, and General Mills. A KARE 11 news van pulled up. They're the station that cares. Or so it said on the back of their news team parkas.

Ellegaard looked like a Boy Scout, only he'd traded in his kerchief and merit badges for a Brooks Brothers suit. He was a six-foot-three, blue-eyed blond who either shaved twice a day or didn't shave at all—I couldn't tell which. He had hair like an anchorman on the six o'clock news, and I wanted to slap him for it. "Chief McGinnis," he said, "I'd like you to meet Nils Shapiro."

I pegged the Edina Chief of Police for early-sixties. Craig McGinnis stood six foot five and had the build of a decathlete. He had a full head of silver hair, wore a charcoal suit and a red cashmere scarf. I hoped the scarf was a Christmas present he felt obligated to display rather than an affectation. If it were the latter, he and I were going to have a problem.

"Nils Shapiro," he said. Shaking my hand like it was the love-tester machine at Bennigan's. "That's an unusual name."

"Yeah, but only Swedes and Jews know it."

"I'll bet," he said. He smiled. "Detective Ellegaard says you're the best private investigator in Minnesota. Said you cracked the Duluth murders but didn't get credit for it."

"I don't need a lot of attention."

"I like that in a man. Even more in a woman." He laughed at his joke but the laughter didn't last. I guessed whatever was in that house wasn't going to let him experience much joy for a while. He looked at me and mustered the toughest expression he had in him. "Consultants who work for Edina PD don't talk to the press. They don't talk to Minneapolis PD. They don't talk to the Feds. They don't talk to their wives, their girlfriends, post on the Internet. They don't communicate outside of Edina PD. Period. And even though you're an independent contractor, if you break our chain of command, you're gone. Understood?" I nodded. "How much do you charge?"

"Five hundred a day plus expenses."

"Expensive, but I suppose you're going to tell me I get what I pay for."

"Well, I don't know about that. But the more I charge the less my employer tends to waste my time."

McGinnis looked to Ellegaard for assurance. Ellegaard gave him a nod.

"All right," McGinnis said. "Take him inside."

Ellegaard led me up the walk toward a pair of double front doors. "We're not going in this way," he said, "but I want you to see something." He put on a latex glove and knocked on a massive slab of oak. A voice from inside told him it was okay to open it, and Ellegaard did with a gentle nudge.

I looked inside. A thick coating of grayish dust blanketed the foyer. It didn't look like natural dirt, and any normal human being would have cleaned it up. "Some-one murder the maid?"

"Don't joke," said Ellegaard. "That dirt is why you're here."

"Any idea what that shit is?"

"The consensus at the moment is it looks like what you'd find inside a vacuum cleaner bag—you know, when it's full and you have to change it."

Then I felt it, the lightness, the excitement, as if I'd discovered a sealed box in my basement I'd never no-ticed before. I'd felt it in Duluth. I'd felt it on my first date with Micaela. I'd felt it as a boy the first time I heard Nirvana's "Lithium." And I knew I was about to experi-ence something significant well before I knew what that thing was or whether it would be good or bad.

"The M.E. is upstairs in the master suite with the body," said Ellegaard. "Other than that, CSU has stayed outside. They're afraid they'll make matters worse."

"How could they make matters worse?"

"That dirt or dust or whatever it is, it's all over the house. It continues up the stairs and down a hall and into the master suite and leads right up to the body, which is . . . Well, you'll see. CSU isn't quite sure what to do with it."

I looked over my shoulder and saw the CSU team standing outside their van, sipping coffee and looking uncomfortable and unsure. Each one of them probably had the same expression at prom. "What are you saying, Ellie? The crime scene's so contaminated they're afraid they'll uncontaminate it which will, in effect, further contaminate it?"

"Don't call me Ellie," he said. "That nickname didn't come with me to Edina. I don't want it to start now. And yeah, something like that. We don't even know how to begin on this."

We walked away from the front doors and into the garage, where a dozen paper yard bags sat filled with leaves awaiting pickup in the spring. We entered the house through the garage service door. Ellie hadn't over-sold it—the dusty dirt was everywhere. Gray and fluffy. In the mudroom. In the kitchen. Ellegaard put sanitary shoe covers over his loafers. I took off my boots and put the sanitaries over my socks.

We headed upstairs, looking down on the living room that featured a grand piano. Of course it did. This was the kind of neighborhood where every parent makes their kid take piano lessons but no parent wants their kid to be a musician.

If the fluffy gray stuff hadn't blanketed the master suite, it would have been immaculate. A king-sized four-poster of the Shaker persuasion was the main attraction centered between nightstands and wall sconces. Framed photographs of children, from babies to preteens, sat on the nightstands and floating shelves. A chaise longue took up space, but not enough. The room was so big you had to be in shape to get from one piece of furniture to the next. A wall of windows offered a view of the acre-sized backyard bordered by the Minnehaha Creek, now frozen and covered in snow. You could sit in a cushioned window seat if it was too exhausting to stand while looking out at all that beauty.

Only the mummy-shaped pile of dust on the bed seemed to be at odds with the interior decorator's grand vision. A thermometer stuck out of it at an odd angle, and the M.E. stood over it. Julie Swenson. She usually worked on Minneapolis bodies. I'd met her a few times at the

Hennepin County morgue. She had long gray hair and eyes with a hint of blue. I guessed she was over fifty. I usually stuck to south of forty like myself, but something about the honesty of her hair tempted me to fall in love with her. Maybe I'd tell her one night in the cold room when she wasn't holding the bone cutter.

"There's the body," said Ellie, pointing to the sarcophagus of dust with the thermometer sticking out of it.

"No shit," I said, turning away from the look I knew Ellie was giving me. "Hey, Julie. You moonlighting in Edina?"

"I am while their M.E. is in Fiji. Pleasure seeing you here in the hamlet, Nils." Her eyes didn't mean it though, and I ditched my plans for romance in the cold room.

Julie Swenson pulled the thermometer from the dust-covered body. She tapped her fingers on an iPad then estimated the time of death between 11:30 P.M. and midnight.

A uniform led a neighbor into the bedroom. "This is Beth Lindquist from around the corner on Bruce Place," said the officer. "She can ID the body."

"I think I can," said Beth, small and timid. She sniffled. "But I don't know . . ." She had shoulder-length dark hair, a slender frame, slightly stooped shoulders, and a neck that appeared too thin to hold up her head. I guessed Beth was in her midforties, but she seemed ten years older than that, as if she'd modeled her image on a woman in her mother's generation. No one, I guessed, had ever called Beth Lindquist a firecracker, but plenty of people had called her ma'am. "I don't know if I can handle seeing—" Beth stopped and, for the first time since entering the room, noticed the dust-covered body on the bed. She shuddered.

Ellie stepped toward her. "Mrs. Lindquist, I'm Detective Ellegaard. I know this is difficult. But we'd greatly appreciate your help, so please, take as much time as you need."

Beth Lindquist nodded, shut her eyes and inhaled slowly. She held the breath then exhaled—a move she learned in yoga, no doubt. Then she nodded. Goddamn Ellegaard. His power on women was like a microwave's on a marshmallow—too bad he'd married young.

Beth moved forward in small steps like she was a hundred and two. Julie Swenson brushed away some dust and exposed the gray face of a woman with eyes closed. Wisps of blond hair looked especially yellow next to her colorless skin. Beth Lindquist screamed, dropped to her bony knees, and whimpered, "Poor Maggie. Poor, poor soul."

2

Ellegaard and I left the master suite and explored the rest of the house. The gray fluff was everywhere. On the carpet. On the furniture. Other than that, the place felt more like a five-star hotel than a home—each room looked like it had been professionally staged, even the basement rec room.

An hour later, after compiling information from officers at the crime scene, Ellegaard, Chief McGinnis, and I hopped into a black unmarked Lincoln SUV. We drove six blocks into Minneapolis to grab coffee at Dunn Brothers and review what we knew so far. Dunn Brothers roasts their own beans in a contraption that looks like half a locomotive and occupies a decent chunk of the seating area. It's loud and hot, especially when you're layered up for a winter day, but the androgynous barista with green and blue hair keeps me up-to-date on bands that matter, so I've made it my spot.

Ellegaard read from his notes. "Maggie Somerville, age forty-one, lived in and owned the home. The maid let herself in with a key and discovered the body. We found no evidence of forced entry anywhere in the house. No windows had been left open or unlocked. Same for doors."

I said, "Then the killer is still in the house or has a key."

"He's not in the house and let's not jump to conclusions," said McGinnis, brushing something only he could see from that damn red scarf.

Ellegaard continued. "Maggie had been divorced a year and a half and had two kids, ages eleven and nine. They spent the night at their father's in Morningside. A uniformed officer visited Robert Somerville and informed him that his ex-wife had been murdered. The officer reported that Robert burst into tears when hearing the news."

"That's hard to fake," I said. "Although selective amnesia's not uncommon."

"For a traumatic event, maybe," said McGinnis. "I doubt this murder was traumatic—it was well planned."

Red scarf made a good point.

Ellegaard said, "According to her friend, Beth Lindquist, who identified the body, Maggie had been seeing a man for the past six months. Andrew Fine."

"I kind of know an Andrew Fine," I said. "Where does he live?"

Ellegaard searched his notes. "Indian Hills."

"I bet that's him. I grew up with his younger brother, Stevey."

"In Edina?" said McGinnis.

"How do you know Andrew Fine grew up in Edina?"

McGinnis looked annoyed by my question. "Andrew Fine lives on a five-acre estate with its own bass pond. It's my job, as Chief of Police, to know who's who and where they came from."

"Well, good job then. And to answer your question, no, I didn't grow up in Edina. I grew up in New Hope, a misnamed town if there ever was one."

"Then how do you know Andrew Fine?"

"I said I know his brother, Stevey. I only kind of know Andrew. And I kind of know him because all Minneapolis Jews know each other. It's mandatory. We have to take a test and everything."

McGinnis looked disappointed. I wondered what he'd expected to hear. Or perhaps it was a general disappointment in the private detective he'd just hired.

Ellegaard said, "Two uniforms found Fine at home at his Indian Hills estate. When they told him Maggie had been murdered, he didn't seem too upset. Just said it was a shame."

"Well, we have a clear place to start," I said.

McGinnis dumped a packet of sugar into his latte and stirred without taking his eyes off me. "And where is that?"

"Whoever killed Maggie had a key or at least left the house with one. No dead bolts had been left unlocked. And he—and I am going to assume it's a he for now—knew Maggie well, if not intimately."

"Why do you think that?" said Ellegaard.

"For starters, there was no sign of a struggle."

"We won't know that until we dust her off," said McGinnis.

"Everything was in place. The body was on top of a

perfectly made bed. My guess is Maggie was comfortable with the killer until it was too late." McGinnis stirred his latte as if he was trying to dissolve rocks. "I wouldn't be surprised if the killer rode straight into the garage in the victim's car."

Ellegaard sipped his chamomile tea. He didn't drink caffeine either. I don't know how he survived. Or why, for that matter. "You think Maggie Somerville drove her own killer into her garage?"

"It's possible. If she went out last night. We should have CSU examine her car for hair and fibers." McGinnis looked dubious. "And Chief McGinnis is right—the killer planned the murder well in advance. That dust has to be from a vacuum cleaner bag—nothing else looks like that. But not just one bag. Dozens. Maybe hundreds. It takes time to amass that many vacuum cleaner bags full of dirt."

"Unless he went fishing in a hotel garbage bin," said Ellegaard.

"That's true," I said. "But Dumpster diving outside a hotel is risky. I tailed an unfaithful husband, who frequented hotels, and I had to dig through the Dumpsters to prove what he'd been up to. I avoided video surveillance and hotel dicks who'd been looking for an excuse to kick someone's ass. And even if all that dirt did come from vacuum cleaner bags in a hotel Dumpster—that takes some planning, too."

"And what about getting all that dust in the house," said Ellegaard. "How did the killer do that without anyone noticing?"

"I don't know, but it all points to one thing: the killer was close to Maggie Somerville. So close he gave her a peaceful death—he even shut her eyes. He knew he'd be a suspect. That's why he filled the crime scene with the

DNA and fibers of thousands of people. We could test that house for decades and never isolate forensic evidence that pointed to one suspect. And if the killer is worried about DNA, then chances are his DNA is in the system."

McGinnis stopped stirring. I had his attention.

"And then there's the weather."

"What about it?" said Ellegaard.

"The killer waited for a weather event like last night. The ground was frozen solid. He left on that. No footprints. No indentations. No anything. And he took extra precaution by leaving at the beginning of a heavily forecasted snowstorm. No way in hell can we track his exit out of that house."

McGinnis and Ellegaard looked at each other and communicated telepathically the way cops can after working together for fifteen years. The androgynous barista swooped by and dropped a napkin on the table in front of me. It said EXMAGICIAN.

"Here's how we're going to do this," said McGinnis. "Ellegaard, you question Robert Somerville and Andrew Fine. See if either of them have a key to Maggie Somerville's house. And that neighbor lady . . ."

Ellegaard consulted his notes. "Beth Lindquist."

"Find out everything she knows about Maggie Somerville's personal life. How much she played. Where she hung out. If her child-custody schedule was strict so we can check local spots on her nights without the kids. Follow up with every name you hear about. Family. Friends. And I want a list of all Facebook, Instagram, Tinder, and whatever other connections she has. Get the names and run 'em. See if anything turns up. If Mr. Shapiro here is right, we got to pay attention to anyone whose DNA is in the system."

"Yes, sir," said Ellegaard, just like he did at the academy when some leatherneck told him how to jump over a fence or put on his armor. He was damn close to making lieutenant and he wouldn't stop playing the good boy, and I kind of loved him for it.

"And you might as well hit some hotels," said McGinnis. "See if anyone's noticed full vacuum cleaner bags disappearing from garbage bins or wherever the hell else they'd disappear from. And bring a sample of our dust. See if it looks more like the dust of one hotel over another. Might as well start learning what we can about the stuff."

"Yes, sir."

That sounded like an awful lot of work I wouldn't be doing. But I knew Ellegaard was getting the easy road.

"Nils," said McGinnis, "you're going to attack from another angle. When it comes to our persons of interest, blend in. Observe. Tail. Make acquaintances if you can with the ex, Robert Somerville, and the boyfriend, Andrew Fine, and any other names we get from Detective Ellegaard. Edina PD will apply the heat and draw focus. You slip into their lives when their guard is down. And use those boyish looks of yours to meet Maggie Somerville's single friends." He looked like he was about to take back that idea. He thought a moment, peering down at his stirred-to-death latte then looked back up. "Are you married?"

Ellegaard's cell rang. He answered it.

"I was married," I said.

"I know," he said, as if we had something in common. "Marriage. It's complicated, isn't it?"

"My marriage was simple. My divorce is complicated."

He considered asking more but thought better of it.

"None of this is S.O.P.," he said, "but we're going to have a frightened little suburb on our hands and I want to put this to bed as soon as possible. If anyone asks who you are, tell the truth. You're a private detective investigating the murder of Maggie Somerville. Just don't reveal who you're working for."

"I never do."

"And another thing, Shapiro. Don't get too wrapped up in your theories an hour after we left the crime scene. Keep your ears and eyes open. Follow the trail that presents itself."

I nodded as Ellegaard hung up the phone. "That was CSU," he said. "Maggie Somerville's car is full of gray dust."

3

Ellegaard dropped me at the shitbox around lunchtime then headed out to interview Robert Somerville and Andrew Fine. We planned to meet after dinner so he could fill me in. I made a peanut butter and jelly sandwich and ate it in front of the Bengals/Colts play-off game. I wanted to care about the game but didn't. I'd lost interest in sports, which I chalked up to the general anesthesia I'd mainlined to survive Micaela. Couldn't stick with a game, couldn't get through a book, couldn't give a damn about beautiful women. I'd pissed off more than a few, which was preferable to the others who I had straight-out hurt. At thirty-eight years old, and for the first time in my life, I'd turned into one of those guys.

My anesthetic wasn't booze or drugs or ego or even

sex, not that I didn't partake in a few of those. It was a concoction mixed of equal parts perseverance and stubborn-headedness and garnished with a big old sprig of fuck everything. The humane thing would have been for me to withdraw from everyone female, but that would have infused my concoction with a lethal dose of despair. Because every damn one of them, at least for a little while, gave me hope. Albeit hope at their expense.

I trudged out to the garage, grabbed a shovel, and faced the driveway. It wasn't big but it lay under a foot and a half of heart-attack snow. A plow had pushed through the alley, and now a three-foot-tall wall of dirty ice bordered the driveway. I checked my weather app to see if Mother Nature would give me an excuse to procrastinate. She would not. The temperature had started to drop—every white and gray crystal on my driveway would soon freeze into cement.

I stepped back into the shitbox a couple hours later and tossed my sweat-soaked clothing down the laundry chute. I showered and got dressed and saw I'd missed two calls, one from Ellie and one from Micaela.

Micaela's message said, "Hey, Nils. Wondering if you want to see a movie later. Something art house with powdered wigs, perhaps. Call me."

Then I listened to Ellegaard's message. "I just finished with the husband. You'll want to crash Maggie Somerville's funeral. So get your suit cleaned or, knowing you, get a suit. Meet you at 8:00. Somewhere the good citizens of Edina don't go."

I called Micaela and told her I couldn't see a movie with her because I'd started on a new case.

"It's good you're working," she said. I knew she meant it. I also knew she meant a couple other things.

"Yeah, well. It's been known to happen."

I looked out my front window. Karyn and Alice across the street were shoveling their sidewalk. Together. Why couldn't I find love like that? Their two shovels hung next to each other in the garage. I'd gone to their wedding—a golden retriever bore their rings. A fucking golden retriever named Belvedere. They picked up his shit every day with their bagged hands and still bestowed upon Belvedere the honor of running to the wedding party with a pair of platinum bands tied to his collar. That was a good wedding. They lived a good love.

The only woman I'd had anything like that with was Micaela, who became my wife and then my ex-wife and then lingered like a chronic sinus infection. She'd flare up every once in awhile and ask me to see a movie followed by a few whiskeys at Bradstreet then an hour or so of naked tomfoolery in her big bedroom that looked out on Lake Harriet. Then we'd go our separate ways, but the fever would knock me down for weeks.

"I hope they're paying you what you're worth," said Micaela.

"No need to insult me."

She laughed and we talked about catching that movie another time, though I wondered if there would be another time.

I met Ellegaard at Liquor Lyle's on Hennepin. The walls were covered in sheet paneling, big TVs, neon beer signs, and vinyl wall hangings advertising drink specials during Monday Night Football even though Monday Night Football was over for the season. A dozen tap handles jailed the bartender, including one for Fireball and another for Jägermeister, potions which in some countries were probably sold as cold and flu medicine.

We found a booth in the corner. Ellegaard had changed into something from REI made of zippers and recycled soda bottles.

Sturdy-framed young women who flocked in threes and fours glanced our way. I'd forgotten how it went with Ellegaard and me in a bar. The tall, handsome Nordic guy who attracted most of them and the shorter, Irish-looking guy who attracted one or two of them and didn't have a drop of Irish blood in him unless you counted Jameson.

The sturdy frames probably graduated from high school in Osseo or Fridley and then went to work as cashiers or in low-level office jobs. They dyed their hair at home, took their daily exercise chewing hamburgers, set their DVRs to record UFC, and bought slinky underwear at Target. Most of their friends had married before turning twenty-one. But these women had not, so here they were. I wondered what it would be like to go home with one of them. I didn't expect I would but I ordered a whiskey, neat, to give it a fighting chance.

Ellegaard ordered a soda with bitters. When I pointed out that bitters was alcohol he reminded me that he wasn't a teetotaler—he'd never had a drinking problem. He didn't abstain for moral reasons, he simply didn't enjoy alcohol so he didn't consume it. But soda and bitters calmed his stomach, and his stomach needed calming.

"We ran Robert Somerville and Andrew Fine," he started. "Both are in the system."

"That's a little weird," I said.

"Somerville wrote a not-so-nice letter to George W. Bush. We don't have access to it, but it made enough of an impression that the FBI paid him a visit, swabbed his cheek, and started a file on him."

"Did you ask him about it?"

"He said he was upset about Bush destabilizing the Middle East by going into Iraq. That hundreds of thousands of innocent people would die while creating a more fertile environment for terrorists and eventually terrorist states."

"He should have been a futurist."

"Yeah. Well, Somerville also said something along the lines of if Bush ever came to Minnesota, he'd regret it. That's what triggered the FBI's visit. Somerville told me he'd heard a rumor that Bush was going to throw out the first pitch for the Twins' home opener, and all he meant by the comment was Minnesota fans would boo him off the mound. But the FBI didn't see it that way.

"Other than that, Robert Somerville seems more hippie than anything else. He owns a company that raises sheep on a big spread down in Zumbrota. The sheep run wild and eat organic grass. Somerville's employees milk them to make cheese, shear them to make wool products, and when they die of natural causes they make their hides into boots."

"A whole vertical sheep operation," I said. "Use every part of the buffalo, right?"

"It's strange you say that because now he's doing the same thing with bison. No one wants bison milk, of course, but he's started a renewable fuel plant that runs on bison manure. When the bison die, again of natural causes, he'll make the hides into a new line of winter coats and sell the meat for dog food."

"And he makes a lot of money with the sheep and bison?"

"The bison venture is new. Somerville dropped a ton of cash on land for them to roam. But he does make money on the sheep. Mostly on the boots. A decade or so ago some kids in Manhattan started wearing them and the boots took off. Kids all over the world want those boots."

"Bet he's got those sheep driving without seat belts to keep up with demand."

"He can't meet the demand. That's what makes the business work. He keeps raising prices—people keep buying. Inventory's gone every year before Thanksgiving."

"So Robert Somerville is in the system because he threatened George W., but other than that, he seems clean."

"Yep."

"Alibi?"

"That's not so clean. Said he was home asleep with his kids, who were also asleep. Said he woke up around 8:00 this morning, was making pancakes like on any other Sunday, and got the news when a uniform knocked on his door."

The waitress brought our drinks and asked if we wanted to pay or keep the tab open. I said keep it open and told Ellegaard to give her a card. He shot me a look, and I reminded him this was Edina PD business. He gave her the card, and she left.

"And when I talked to Somerville," said Ellegaard, "he was a mess."

"That could be for a few reasons."

Ellegaard stirred his bitters and soda making it a bubbly, uniform reddish orange. "I agree. But he doesn't seem like the type."

"Well, whoever killed Maggie Somerville isn't the type. That's why he went through all the trouble to cover his tracks. Did you run a search on 'vacuum cleaner–bag murder'?"

"Yeah. Nothing. It's a first. I think Chief McGinnis was disappointed."

"Why's that?"

"I don't know. Maybe he'd hoped we were looking at a serial killer to take the heat off Edina. Like it was going to happen no matter what and it was just bad luck it happened in the bubble."

Half a dozen twentysomethings took their time getting through the front door. A wave of cold rippled to the far end of the bar.

I crossed my arms and said, "And how's Andrew Fine doing?"

"By a lot of people's standards, he's doing well."

"He was a son-of-a-bitch when we were kids."

"He's made the bulk of his fortune in call centers. When the business started going to India, he cut costs. Hires a lot of Somalis and Hmong. Schedules them in a way that doesn't conflict with cultural and religious obligations."

"Nothing wrong with that. I suppose he's got his Jewish mother working on Christmas."

"When he was a student at the University of Wisconsin-Madison, a coed accused him of rape. A medical exam of the coed couldn't find any physical evidence of forced penetration. Fine's lawyer argued that Fine and the alleged victim had consensual sex, but because of the victim's strict religious upbringing, she claimed she was raped."

"Does that make sense?"

"Fine told me the girl was Persian. And when a Persian woman gets married, the couple consummates during the wedding party. Then the old aunts run in to make sure there's blood on the sheets."

"If I ever get invited to a Persian wedding, guess I'm giving them new sheets."

"The jury agreed that the woman hoped to explain the loss of her virginity by claiming she was raped."

"Really. Why would she put herself through a trial instead of sneaking a vial of blood into her wedding bed. It could be any kind of blood—it's not like her aunts were going to test it."

"You think Fine raped her?"

"The Andrew Fine I used to know was a bad dude." I took my first sip of Jameson. They didn't sell the good stuff in a place like Liquor Lyle's, but the cheap stuff could be good, sometimes. That's the thing with Jameson. Some bottles are smooth. Some bottles burn like hell. You don't know which until it's open. I'd caught a bad one and told myself it'd get better with each sip. "Social media makes me tired, but I sure hope to hell people use it to share and find common stories like that one. Get those guys' names out there. That'll be a far better punishment for those assholes than the courts are giving them. And a far better warning to other women."

"I have three daughters," said Ellegaard, as if I didn't already know. "No argument here."

"What about Fine's alibi?" I said.

"He was at home. Alone."

"That's not good."

"Especially if we find out Maggie Somerville was raped."

Ellegaard's phone dinged. He looked at the text.

I took a second sip of Jameson. The second sip is always better.

Ellegaard put down his phone. "Julie Swenson wants to see us in the morgue."

4

Maggie Somerville's skin looked as rosy as the stainless-steel table on which she lay. She'd been vacuumed and washed to reveal a petite blonde with a girlish figure, small breasted with narrow hips. It's impossible to see beauty in dead people, but if she were alive, I imagined Maggie Somerville more cute than beautiful. She had thin lips, a chin just shy of full-sized, and a small, undefined nose. Her face suggested that, somewhere in early adulthood, Maggie stopped ripening and preserved herself in a visually appealing state like a perfect-looking pear that was nowhere ready to eat.

"The cause of death is asphyxiation," said Julie Swenson, whose long gray hair was tucked beneath a green surgeon's cap. Her pale blue eyes remained placid as she snapped on a pair of latex gloves.

"Strangled?" said Ellegaard.

"Nope," said Julie, manipulating the corpse's head to show us the neck. "My guess is she was unconscious then smothered with a gloved hand or pillow. No signs of resistance. No skin under her nails. No bruises."

"Was she drugged?" I said.

"Ding, ding, ding," said Julie, "a hundred points for Nils." She threw a faint smile my way, and I devoted the rest of my life to her. She picked up her iPad and read, "A blood-alcohol level of 1.9 and Rohypnol."

"Rohypnol? She was raped?" said Ellegaard.

"She was not raped," said Julie. "I've found no evidence of any sexual activity whatsoever."

"We'll find out where she drank that liquor," said Ellegaard. "You can slip a woman a roofie, but it's hard to slip her enough alcohol to get her to 1.9."

"So the only reason she was drugged was to be killed," I said. "That is one hell of a non-violent way to kill someone. The killer either cared about her, in his own fucked-up way or barely had the stomach to go through with it. So he rendered her defenseless because, if she fought back, he'd lose his nerve."

"Or . . ." said Ellegaard. He stopped.

"Or what?"

"Men kill themselves with guns and nooses and driving head-on into trees. Women kill themselves quietly— slashed wrists in a tub full of water or, more often, with sleeping pills, which is what Rohypnol was when it was legal in this country. Maggie obviously didn't kill herself. But whoever did—"

"Killed like a woman?"

Ellegaard shrugged. "I'm just saying we shouldn't limit our focus to men."

"Do you mind talking about this on your own time?" said Julie. "There's one more thing. I vacuumed her lungs and nasal and oral cavities and found traces of gray dust. She was still alive when whoever killed her was spreading the stuff around the room."

Ellegaard drove me back to Liquor Lyle's to get my car. We rode in a Ford Taurus that I would have assumed was the department's if it'd had a police radio and a shotgun in back instead of a booster seat. I said, "Why in the hell would you buy a Taurus for your personal car when you have to drive one at work?"

"I like having the same car at home and work so I don't get confused about where the controls are."

"You got to be fucking kidding me."

"I'm not. It's a safety issue."

"It's a something issue."

"If I'm driving to a bank robbery or I got screaming kids in the back, I can't get confused about where the wipers or brights are. It makes perfect sense. There's nothing weird about it."

"There's something weird about a guy driving a Taurus if it doesn't belong to his mom."

Ellegaard smiled and glanced over, "I've missed you, Shap."

I felt grateful for male friendships and their ability to lie dormant for years then pick up where they left off with neither feelings nor egos hurt. "Your family is on my refrigerator. That's a good Christmas card. Only a select few make the refrigerator."

"I'm honored, Shap. But it's all Molly's doing. I take none of the credit."

"Three kids. What's that like?"

"A sadistic sleep and SportsCenter deprivation experiment. But the best thing in the world. You'll see one day."

"I almost did," I said.

"I know, buddy. I know."

We drove along the south side of Lake Calhoun. The Minneapolis skyline on our left peeked down at the mile-wide city lake. It never really gets dark when there's snow on the ground—too much white everywhere for light to reflect off of. Hockey parents had shoveled an oval of snow off the ice, snowbanks substituting for wooden boards. Eight or so teenagers had a game going—I heard their shouts and stick-slapping through the closed car windows. I let the day's events simmer for a few minutes. Something had been gnawing at me, so I flat-out asked Ellegaard. "Why did you call me in on this?"

"What are you talking about? We wanted your help."

"Whose idea was it?"

"Mine. McGinnis didn't know you existed."

"I mean whose idea was it to bring in someone from the outside. I get called in by a police department once in a while, but not until they've hit a dead end or there's some sort of frustration with how the investigation is going. But to call in outside help before CSU works the crime scene, before the body's been ID'd, before time of death has been established—that's fucking weird."

Ellegaard drove without saying anything. I looked at the thermometer on his dash. It was fourteen degrees out. Some warm-up that had been.

I said, "Are you going to tell me?"

Ellegaard squirmed in his seat then exhaled resignation. "McGinnis thought we needed help because of the dust. It's not weird. He asked if I knew anyone. I suggested you. And you, Shap, are welcome."

I said good night to Ellegaard in front of Liquor Lyle's. He went home to his loved ones and I went inside for a drink. I sat at the bar, which had grown more crowded since our earlier visit. I ordered an Irish and made myself invisible. A new bartender worked behind the taps, a skinny kid with long hair. I sometimes play a game where I imagine how a stranger fits into the world of rock and roll. The kid pouring my Jameson likely played "Free Bird" full blast at Guitar Center on a Strat he'd never be able to afford. The sturdy-framed twentysomethings had grown in number, but I'd lost interest. I finished my drink and drove home.

My Nespresso machine made me a cup of whatever the green capsule is. I took it to my leather chair and sunk in. The chair had once been part of a pair that bookended a fireplace in a Kenwood Victorian. Micaela had the other. When we split, she insisted I take both. But when I bought the shitbox, I only had room for one and said she should keep the other. She agreed too easily. So when I sat in my chair, I couldn't help wondering about who might be sitting in its twin. It was an object made of dead cowhide stretched over a wooden frame and foam-wrapped down, but it felt like a portal to Micaela. Furniture shopping was long overdue.

My phone said it was 10:03 P.M. and eight degrees outside. I finished my coffee, left the cup in the sink, visited my coat closet and chose my snorkel parka, a ski hat, a fleece-neck gaiter, lobster gloves, snow pants, and my Sorels. I exited the back door and then the gate that opened into the alley, walked south to 54th then east for four blocks then descended the hill to Minnehaha Creek, which, despite its blanket of snow, was still frozen—the ice thick enough that I couldn't hear the water running underneath.

A jet roared overhead, its engines amplified in the dense, cold air. I started west and followed the snaking creek. Cross-country skiers, snowshoers, and dog walkers had left overlapping tracks which made the walking easier. My heavy rubber-soled boots squeaked on the hardpack as if I were walking on Styrofoam. The leafless trees showed off their web of twigs like capillaries under a microscope. The snow eliminated the cover of darkness—the murderer leaving the scene before it fell made even more sense. I passed a sledding hill on my left where teenagers flew down the packed incline on plastic sheets and tubs and saucers, flasks and wineskins keeping them warm and brave. Windows in homes glowed yellow and cozy. I continued under the France Avenue bridge and into Edina where the yards grew deeper and the homes farther away.

A couple cross-country skiing crossed my path, then an older man walking a Newfoundland, then a young woman skijoring behind her Malamute. I'd forgotten how much this creek is used as a thoroughfare when it's frozen. I reached the pool at the 54th Street falls and heard trickling under the falls' shell of ice. It was the only deep spot on my journey. The ice was untrustworthy. I stepped onto the bank and followed it up to 54th, crossed the quiet street, entered Arden Park, and walked along the creek bank down past the hockey rink to where the ice felt safe.

A wooded hill rose to my left. The flat open field of the park was to my right. Five minutes later, I could see the back of Maggie Somerville's house. It had been built on a hill so what looked like two and half stories from the front revealed itself to be three and half stories from the back, most of which was windows.

Even from a hundred yards away I could see the yellow police tape running across the backyard. If anyone had walked the creek last night, before the snow fell, they'd have seen little to nothing. The police had left lights on in the house. In the windows, drawn translucent blinds created yellow rectangles of nothing.

The puzzle felt muddy. Hard to fit. I stared at Maggie Somerville's house like a mathematician staring at an equation written on a massive board, hoping something would come to me. An answer. A question. Anything.

I smelled smoke. I looked to my left and saw a figure through a clump of naked saplings, a bundled human silhouette and the orange glow of a cigarette. Its head was level with mine so it, too, stood on the creek, just around the bend. I lifted my hood over my hat and pulled the drawstring. It formed a tube in front of my head rimmed with faux fur. Nothing on my face would reflect the ambient light of the snow-covered city. Other than my vibrant personality, I was as invisible as I could get.

I wanted a better view of this person who shared my curiosity for the back of Maggie Somerville's house. I could step onto the frozen creek's bank and approach through the trees, but I'd crunch virgin snow and break the fallen twigs, branches, and dried leaves beneath. Continuing up the creek seemed my only option but my boots made too much noise. So I untied them, pried the rubber shells off their liners, and stood in wool slippers like a fourteenth-century monk, the cold creeping through the felt.

Neither the figure nor its orange glow had moved. I picked up my boot shells then crept upstream, unable to tell if I moved in silence or if my hat and hood prevented me from hearing my own footsteps. I neared the bend and checked over my right shoulder. The person was still there.

I started around the bend and stopped halfway. If I moved forward I'd have a clear view of my creekmate, but he could have a clear view of me, as well.

A car purred along Oaklawn Avenue on top of the wooded hill. A few hundred yards away it stopped. Car doors opened and closed, and the enthusiastic voices of high schoolers rippled through the frigid air as kids descended the path for night hockey or broomball or just to fuck around. If the figure heard the kids, he didn't care. He didn't move. He knew what was happening down at the rink as well as I did. We two strangers, standing thirty feet apart on a frozen creek, would not be interrupted. We two strangers, one of whom had yet to notice the other. All we needed was an introduction.

"Hello," I said.

My new friend took off in a dead sprint. I dropped my boot shells and chased after. He ran upstream, sticking to the hardpack as the creek entered a section of tight hairpin turns. I had canoed it dozens of times. This section of creek is where the amateurs oversteer, get their canoes stuck sideways in the current, and tip over, sending their coolers and oars downstream without them.

I lost sight of the figure when it reached the first hairpin turn. When I came around the bend, I'd made up no ground. The next hairpin bent to the left. When I came around that, I'd lost ground. Whoever it was could run. Maybe if I'd worn trail-running shoes I could keep up. But I didn't and I couldn't.

On the next hairpin turn, I cut up the bank and across an expanse of skinny trees and reeds and ran perpendicular to my creekmate's course, reeds and twigs snapping underfoot. The snow was deep, the ground below it soft and uneven. Every muscle in my legs labored to maintain speed. My chest ached. My lungs fought to suck in more cold air. I angled farther right to cut off the person instead of T-boning him. Or her. I still couldn't identify which. My only intention was to learn who shared my curiosity for the back of Maggie Somerville's house.

A branch scraped across my face. My flesh burned. I looked up to see if I was on course to intercept my friend. But when my foot stretched out for the frozen creek, the creek wasn't there. It had dropped two feet below the bank. I couldn't see that in the flat light and tumbled forward—my head cracked off the hard snowpack. I got back up but the white and gray world blurred and turned and I lost my footing, rolled onto my back, and stared at the night sky. My heart beat in my hooded ears. My breath condensed into icy fog in front of my eyes.

When I was a boy, I'd lie on my back in the snow, bundled like a toddler, looking up at the winter night sky, the heavens framed by the edges of my parka hood. I saw only a small section of sky washed starless by the city lights. Sometimes a plane traversed my view. Less often, a satellite floated through. I have known no greater stillness. I have known no greater peace.

My head hurt. It was 10:30 at night. The temperature was eight degrees and falling. I drifted into half-consciousness and dreamed a dream I knew was a dream in a place I visit in the gray light before color enters my day.

5

I stood on the driveway in February. I was sixteen. The temperature had not climbed above zero in two weeks. My father had just given me the keys to the Honda Civic he'd left idling after his drive home from work. He looked at me through heavy, silver-framed bifocals. His hair was black then, his face clean-shaven. He wore a white shirt with a yellow tie under a wool overcoat. "Be careful," he said. "Don't let some girl ruin your future."

I was his son. If I impregnated "some girl" it would be she who ruined my future, not me who ruined hers. I considered pointing that out, but it was five below and, the truth was, if I had been a girl, it would have been some guy's fault. My dad was just rooting for the home team.

"Thanks," I said. "I'll be careful."

"One more thing," he said. "I don't want you drinking, but if you do, never, and I mean goddamn never, have more than two on a night like tonight. You pass out anywhere out-of-doors and you will not wake up. Do you hear me?"

"I hear you," I said, twenty-two years later, half-conscious on a frozen creek.

Dead leaves crackled and crunched. I turned my head and saw a six-point buck nibbling on a fallen branch. I lived in a metropolitan area of three million people, four major professional sports teams, dozens of colleges, world-renowned museums, and Fortune 100 companies. And through it runs a creek where I'd seen deer and fox and bald eagles flying overhead. I'd seen three-foot-long northern pike in its shallow pools, mallards and wood ducks and blue-winged teal floating on its currents, and wild turkeys along its banks. Sights so common I thought nothing of them, until a deer helped keep me out of the morgue's freezer section.

I rolled onto my stomach then pushed myself up to my knees. The buck looked at me knowing my predator status had been revoked. I got to my feet, and it walked away without concern. The cold had penetrated my wool insoles—my toes stung. I walked back to my boot shells and slipped into them knowing warmth would not return.

I considered calling Ellegaard or Micaela to pick me up but thought the walk home would do me good. My head hurt like hell but my stomach felt fine. I shined my phone's flashlight in my eyes for a few seconds then turned it off and the world got dark again. My pupils functioned. The victim of a head injury probably shouldn't self-diagnose whether or not they have a concussion, but

I was satisfied that I did not. I walked to the area my creek-mate first stood and looked for a spent cigarette butt, but found nothing.

I'd had enough of the creek for one night so I cut across Arden Park to 52nd and back over France Avenue. When I stepped back into the shitbox, I removed my boots and put them on the heat vent. I walked into the bedroom, removed my clothes and dropped them on the floor, then slipped into flannel pajamas with dogs on them. They were Micaela's last Christmas gift to me in lieu of a real dog, which neither of us wanted to bring into a failing marriage. Then I crawled under my comforter. My sleep was filled with the gray winter night sky and gray dust and a deer pulling dead leaves off gray branches.

For the second morning in a row, Ellegaard woke me with a phone call. "We just looked at Maggie Somerville's cell phone records," he said. "The majority of the calls are to one number. And most of her incoming calls are from a blocked number. The outgoing name in Maggie's phone is Bella. But AT&T said the bill is in the name of Ansley Bell."

"Who's Ansley Bell?"

"We have no idea. I just got off the phone with Robert Somerville—he doesn't know who she is, either."

"Lover maybe?"

"Could be," said Ellegaard. "We pulled her DMV records. She lives in Northeast."

"A hipster lover."

"I'm on my way to talk to her," said Ellegaard.

"If she works in vacuum repair, can I take the day off?"

"Get up, Shap. We got a big day."

"We can't joke anymore. What's happened to us?"

"I'm calling back in fifteen," said Ellegaard. "You'd better be out of the shower."

"I'll keep my phone in the soap dish, just in case."

I told Ellegaard what happened on the creek. He thought I probably just scared the shit out of a nosy neighbor who took me for a creep in the night, but he said he'd send CSU over to look for footprints and the cigarette butt.

I took a long, hot shower. The bump on my head wasn't too bad as bumps on heads go. I thought of Ansley Bell, the unknown frequent caller. She was nothing more than a name on a piece of paper, but she was the first real clue the gray dust couldn't cover up.

I knocked on Beth Lindquist's door at 11:30 A.M. It was three degrees outside but the morning sun had created tiny icicles on her gutter. Beth Lindquist lived in a Cape Cod sided with cedar shingles that had been painted instead of stained. Some patches of the previous paint jobs had been scraped away, and other patches had not, making the shingles look like a monochromatic relief map of blue gray. I rang the doorbell. A wreath of fresh juniper hung on the red front door. A moment later, Beth Lindquist opened it. She wore a mint green robe that could have come from her grandmother's closet. Or Sears. She looked like she hadn't slept in days.

"Excuse me, Mrs. Lindquist. My name is Nils Shapiro and I'm sorry to bother you." We Minnesotans are not tough-talking people. It doesn't work here. We sand off our rough edges to play nice and keep our hardness buried deep. "I'm a private investigator looking into the murder of Maggie Somerville. We met yesterday at the crime scene when you identified Ms. Somerville's body."

Beth Lindquist pulled a sodden wad of tissues from her robe pocket and dabbed her wet eyes. "I'm sorry," she said.

"Don't be. I know this is an awful time, but can you spare a few minutes to talk? I understand you and Maggie were good friends."

She nodded and stepped aside. I entered.

The house differed from most in the neighborhood because no one had added on to it since it had been built in the 1940s. Most every other home in the area had grown like cancer. If the Lindquists' house had been remodeled within its existing footprint, the work had been modest and some time ago. For that, the Lindquists gained my respect. A small foyer led to the staircase. I removed my shoes and entered the living room to my left. It was modestly furnished with a couch, two chairs, and a desk with a Dell laptop on it. The couch faced a bay window that looked out on the front yard. The furniture was upholstered in plaids of navy, forest green, and cardinal red. A painting hung on the wall behind the couch. It depicted a fox hunt in the English countryside with horses carrying red-coated English riders flanked by hounds. I was about to look for the fox when Beth Lindquist spoke.

"I have coffee if you'd like some."

"Thank you. Black is great."

Beth Lindquist disappeared into the kitchen. A steady ticking filled the silence. I glanced into the dining room and saw a grandfather clock built of bird's-eye maple, its pendulum swinging back and forth. There was nothing about the woman or her home that tried to be current. The place felt void of desperation, and I found it comforting.

Beth returned with two cups of coffee. I took one and

sat on the couch. She chose the chair opposite me. A robe-wearing woman in mourning doesn't invite idle chitchat so I got right to it. "Mrs. Lindquist, I'm sorry to ask you such a direct question at such a sensitive time, but do you know of anyone who would have wanted to hurt Maggie?"

"The police already asked me that. I told them no, but I never liked that man she was seeing."

"Andrew Fine?"

"Yes. He's quite perverted."

"Maggie told you about their sex life?"

"At first, but I asked her to stop. I didn't want to hear those things." Beth sipped her coffee. The muscles in her pencil-thin neck rearranged themselves to let the liquid pass. "I guess it goes with the territory of getting divorced," she continued. "According to Maggie, it's quite promiscuous out there, people getting out of long marriages, especially when the you-know-what wasn't the greatest."

"The sex?"

She nodded.

"Do you know of anyone else Maggie dated?"

"There was one fellow," said Beth. "Maggie saw him on and off for a short while. He had dark hair and a beard."

"Do you know his name?"

"Maggie called him Slim, but I don't think that was his real name."

"What happened to him?"

"I'm not sure. I didn't see him around anymore so I asked Maggie where he was. She told me she'd ended it. Apparently Slim was fun while he lasted, but he wasn't—what was the word she used?—a 'love match' or something like that."

"So she broke up with Slim because he wasn't the one?"

"Maggie said Slim was too artsy for her."

"What do you think she meant by that?"

Beth checked her robe, pulled the belt tighter and re-tied it. "Well, probably that he didn't make much money."

"Was money important to Maggie?"

"Money's important to everyone, don't you think? Maggie wasn't a snob about it. Perry and I live quite modestly—she couldn't have cared less. Maggie liked nice things, though."

"Did Maggie ever mention a person named Ansley Bell?"

"I don't think so. The name doesn't sound familiar."

"I hope I don't embarrass you with this next question."

"It's okay," she said. "Nothing could be worse than what I had to do yesterday."

"Yes, well. I promise it won't be that bad." I took a sip of coffee. "Did Maggie ever talk about having any female lovers?"

Beth set down her cup and saucer. They rattled and hit the table a little too hard. "No. Lord, no." She began to cry. "I'm sorry. I . . . I . . . I just can't stop seeing what I saw yesterday."

I let her cry for a minute and waited for her breath to even. "Do you think if Maggie was romantically involved with a woman, she'd tell you?"

"She wasn't. I know. I know she wasn't. We talked about everything. Every day. She had no romantic anything with any woman."

"You seem pretty sure of that."

"She would have told me. You know, we had dinner last night."

"Detective Ellegaard mentioned that. You went to Beaujo's on France."

"Yes. They have good food. We had a lovely dinner. She was happy."

"Did she ever talk about even the idea of having a woman lover?"

"Why are you asking me that? That doesn't have anything to do with whoever killed her!"

The front door opened and a man in his midfifties walked in. He, too, seemed older than he was, like the way you saw your father when you were a child. His hair was gray and neatly combed. He wore tortoiseshell horn-rimmed glasses, a camel overcoat, olive wide-wale corduroy pants, and Weejuns with rubber overshoes stretched over them. He carried the torch for the previous generation—old Edina, WASPy, conservative, genteel, and dignified. He was in a race against pluralism, even in this white-bread suburb of a white-bread city in a white-bread state, and he might win if he didn't live too long. I admired his facade of being the most civilized creature on earth. He looked at me and smiled, more out of courtesy than being happy to see a stranger in his home.

"Hello," he said.

"Honey," said Beth. "This is Nils Shapiro. He's investigating Maggie's murder."

"You're not the detective who was here yesterday." He leaned against the foyer wall, lifted one foot then the other to snap off his overshoes. He opened the coat closet, set them inside, then took off his coat and hung it up.

"No, sir, I'm a private detective."

"Working for?"

I smiled. No one liked to hear this. Ever. "I'm sorry. I can't say. Part of the job."

"How mysterious." He smiled and walked into the room. I stood and shook his hand.

"Perry Lindquist," he said. "Nice to meet you." He turned to Beth. "Everything okay, honey?" She nodded. "Please keep it short, Mr. Shapiro is it?"

"Yes."

"Beth hasn't slept in the past twenty-four hours. I'm hoping she gets some rest."

"Of course."

"I'm about to make myself a turkey sandwich. Can I interest you in one?"

"No, Perry. I'm good. Thanks."

"I'm trying a new gourmet mustard. Let me know if you change your mind."

He walked through the living room and the dining room then into the kitchen.

"I'm sorry for those last questions," I said to Beth. "I'm just trying to narrow down who possibly could have killed Maggie."

"Who is that Ansley you mentioned?"

"I have no idea. Just a name that's been tied to Maggie. One other thing. The medical examiner said Maggie had quite a high blood-alcohol level last night. How much did she drink at Beaujo's?"

"Well, it's kind of embarrassing, but we drank two bottles of wine, which is an awful lot. We were just having so much fun. I know. We shouldn't have driven home."

"Whose car did you take?"

"Maggie's. She drove."

"And you didn't stop anywhere else on the way here?"

"No, it's just a few blocks away. The end of the evening is a bit fuzzy. I'm sorry. I barely remember going to bed. I do remember us talking about how it was good we beat the storm."

"And what time was that?"

"Oh, golly. Not too late. Maybe 9:30."

I stood. "Thanks, Mrs. Lindquist. I don't want to take up any more of your time."

She nodded and followed me into the foyer. As I slipped back into my shoes, I glanced into the open coat closet and saw two pairs of running shoes. A pair of men's and a pair of women's.

"I hope I was of some help."

"You were quite helpful." She smiled. "Um, I'm so sorry to ask you this, but I left my cigarettes at home. You wouldn't happen to have one around, would you?"

"No. Neither of us smoke."

"No one does anymore. It's become quite a sign of weakness. It's embarrassing, really. I'm down to about four a day and was hoping to avoid making a trip to the store. By the way, here's my card. Please call if anything else comes to mind."

I turned toward the door and saw a key rack. Two hooks. One labeled PERRY. One labeled BETH. Both labels made with a label maker. I once dated a woman who I now call "the mistake." She labeled everything with a label maker. It only took once for me to learn never to date a labeler again. *Do not ask for whom the label maker tolls, it tolls for thee.*

"One more question, Mrs. Lindquist. Do you have a key to Maggie's house?"

"Oh. Of course," she said. "I'd keep an eye on her place when she was out of town. She did the same for us."

"Thank you."

I called Ellegaard from the car and asked him to run a check on Beth and Perry Lindquist to see if their DNA was in the system.

"Anything suspicious?"

"No, but they have a key. And I still think our killer is in the system, so let's eliminate people as we go."

"On it."

"I have another call. Gotta go." I looked at my phone. It was Micaela. "Hey."

"Are you working the Somerville murder?"

"How'd you know?"

"The paper quoted Ellegaard and I figured he may have hired you. Be careful. Whoever killed that woman is smart."

"Don't worry. If I end up covered in dust, it'll be because I cleaned under my bed."

"I'm serious, Nils."

"So am I."

There was a long pause. The silence lasted so long I thought the call might have dropped. Then she spoke. "Call me if you need anything."

"Okay."

"Promise?"

"Promise."

"All right. Well. I'll talk to you soon, Nils."

"Good-bye, Micaela."

"Good-bye."

6

_____

Stevey Fine managed the Hyland Lakes Office Park near the Hyland Lakes Recreational Area where highways 100 and 494 intersected in "prestigious" West Bloomington, which was dubbed by realtors and wasn't all that prestigious unless you liked McMansions, draconian homeowners' associations, and people who looked as similar to one another as their houses did. The north end of the office park is bordered by Highway 494 and the south end is bordered by Normandale Lake, the Hyland downhill-ski area, and a ski jump because ski-flyers need somewhere to practice before going to the Olympics. Paths for running and, during winter, Nordic skiing crisscross the recreational area, bending to accommodate lakes and ponds connected by Nine Mile Creek,

which held trout in the days before mowed-down prairie and chemically fertilized lawns.

I parked in the ramp and took the skyway to the 400
Building. Stevey Fine's name was on the directory as
Steven Fine-Bldg Mgmt. I climbed the stairs to the fourth
floor and stepped into the lobby decorated in postmod-
ern corporate bland, boasting neutral walls and carpeting. The art looked like it had been commissioned by a
can of beige paint. I followed the signs to suite 428
where an assistant sat behind a modular desk with its
own built-in wall and filing cabinets.

The woman was young and pretty but looked like her
mom had dressed her from the "You're a Grown Up
Now" collection, with hues as neutral as the rest of the
place. Within five years she'd cut her hair to a more prac-
tical length, have a ring on her finger and a three-year
plan to bring two babies into this world. She was a
young Beth Lindquist, anxious to put her youth behind
her and get on with sensible living. When I approached
she smiled. "Hi. May I help you?"

"I'm here to see Mr. Fine."

She looked at her computer screen, her forehead wrin-
kled. "Do you have an appointment?"

"I do not. Tell him Shap is here."

"Shap!" said a voice from inside 428. "I'm on the
phone. Get your ass in here!"

A pained disappointment betrayed the assistant's
sunny facade. Her boss had taken away her raison d'être,
but she pushed the disappointment down with an impres-
sive force of willpower. She stood. "Hi, I'm Kelsey. Can I
get you some coffee or water or pop?"

"Hi, Kelsey. Nils. Thanks, but I'm good." She threw
me a Minnesota-nice smile and pushed Stevey's door
open. I walked through it.

Stevey Fine had dark curly hair and dark eyes that were always smiling even if his mouth wasn't, but it usually was. He sat at a desk littered with so much shit I couldn't see the desktop. Papers and envelopes, some opened, some not, a house made out of Legos, pencils and pens, a dog leash, an Uglydoll, a sweater in a bag from J.Crew, a box of Asics Gel-Kayanos, a windup toy robot, a wad of bubble wrap, a juicer, and that was just the visible layer. A phone cord connected him to the pile. He smiled when he saw me and held up his finger to tell me it'd be a moment.

"I can't give you the entire eighth floor," he said, "unless you commit to a three-year lease." He lifted his eyebrows to tell me he was just as surprised he was playing the part of a businessman as I was.

Stevey and I met in Hebrew school at Temple Israel when we were eleven, then spent the next seven years going to bar and bat mitzvahs, confirmation class, youth groups, and working at Camp Teko, the synagogue's camp on the North Arm of Lake Minnetonka. I still saw him as the sixteen-year-old boy who once stood with a can of beer in one hand and a lit bottle rocket in the other before throwing it into the air where it launched itself over the bay and exploded with a weak pop.

He was a happy kid with little ambition other than to ride the sound waves of Radiohead, Nirvana, and Minneapolis musicians—the Jayhawks, Semisonic, and Paul Westerberg—all of whom he befriended working part-time at Willie's American Guitars.

I slept over at his house at least a dozen times during our middle-school years, where we were exposed to the dickheadedness of his older brother, Andrew. Andrew Fine liked to fire projectiles at us while we played on the Sport Court in the backyard. These came in the form of

chipped golf balls or hurled snowballs. Sometimes he'd
shoot BBs at us with an air rifle. They'd usually bounce
off, but one time he lodged a BB in Stevey's forehead
and when Stevey ran toward the house crying to tell his
parents, Andrew intercepted him and said if Stevey told
his parents he would kill Stevey and it would look like
an accident. He said it with such calm intensity that Stevey believed him. I did, too. Stevey pulled the BB out
himself and told his parents he'd run into the end of a
branch.

The worst projectiles came from Andrew's tennis-ball
bazooka. It was a contraption made of three tennis-
ball cans, held together with duct tape and hollowed out
at both ends, except for the bottom can, which only had
airholes punctured into each end. Andrew would soak a
tennis ball in lighter fluid and drop it into the open end
of the bazooka. The butane from the lighter fluid collected in the bottommost can. Andrew would then point
the bazooka in our direction and hold a flame to the bottom can. The gas ignited and shot out the tennis ball at
a frightening velocity. I don't know how fast, but when
he shot the tennis ball straight up, it went out of sight.
He never hit either of us, which I'm pretty sure was on
purpose, but it scared the shit out of us and sent us running inside and eventually led us to sleep over exclusively
at my house.

The former tennis-ball-bazooka-wielding Andrew Fine
dated Maggie Somerville until she was murdered the
night before last. I hated to gather intel from Stevey
before reconnecting with his douche bag of an older
brother, but I didn't hate it enough to prevent myself
from doing it.

Stevey hung up the phone. "Shap, good to see you!
What are you doing here?!"

"I just met someone for coffee at Parma and remembered you told me something about managing this utopian office park, so I thought I'd stop by. Hope I'm not interrupting."

"Fuck . . ." said Stevey. "Can you believe I'm doing this?"

"I cannot. That's why I had to see it with my own eyes."

"Goddamn money. It fucks everything up, doesn't it?"

"I wouldn't know. I don't have any."

"That a boy. Keep it simple." He grabbed the windup robot off his desk and turned it over in his hands. "So what's new? How're things on the lady front?"

"Not great."

"Yeah, I hear you, man. We should get together."

"We'll grab dinner."

"You got a date Friday night?"

"Is that any way to ask a fellow out?"

"We'll go to the Bachelor Farmer. Maybe meet some women."

"I'm all for that. But if we do, we're not bringing 'em back to your place. I'm still afraid Andrew will jump out of a closet with his tennis-ball bazooka."

Stevey laughed. "Fucking Andrew. Unfortunately, he hasn't changed much."

Kelsey stuck her head in. "Steven, I have Shelly Shultz calling from that recruiting company."

"Ah, shit," said Stevey, "I got to take this." He looked at Kelsey like she'd just told him he had to do his homework. "Tell her I'll be there in a minute."

Kelsey smiled her smile and left.

"Looking for a new job, Steven?"

"No. A recruiter wants to lease space here."

"You're the man."

"Oh, don't say that."

I stood. "See you Friday."

"Yeah, looking forward to it."

"Oh, hey. I almost forgot. Edina PD called me. Apparently your brother was dating that woman who was murdered in Edina. They asked if I knew him."

Stevey looked directly at me. The smile had left his eyes. "Why would they call you?"

"I got a buddy who's a detective over there. We were cadets together at the Minneapolis Police Academy. He's the one who called me. Anyway, you know, it's Edina. They think all us Jews know each other."

"What'd you tell them?"

"I said I knew you, but didn't really know your brother."

"Jesus Christ," said Stevey, more to the world than to me.

"I'm not implying Andrew had anything to do with it," I said. "I don't even know why I mentioned it."

He nodded. "I'd better take this call. See you Friday."

"All right, man. See you Friday." I left feeling confident Stevey Fine's older brother hadn't changed much in the past twenty-five years. It was time to pay Andrew Fine a visit.

7

I grabbed lunch at Chipotle near Lake Calhoun then drove east on Lake Street to the Midtown Global Market. It had once been the iconic Sears building, with a sixteen-story office tower standing over the store, a monument glorifying the great Sears Roebuck, which wasn't so great anymore. The building had decayed to the point of demolition only to be saved by a nostalgia for recent history and a deluge of urban-renewal tax credits. The retail space now housed an open market that catered to Minneapolis's growing Latino, African, and Asian populations. Andrew Fine's call center occupied the entire eighth floor.

I pulled into the parking lot and noticed a black Lincoln SUV idling in a spot far from the building, the same

Edina PD vehicle I had ridden in yesterday. It was parked next to a white Porsche Cayenne. I found a space toward the front of the lot, reached under the passenger seat, and pulled out my Nikon with its 800mm zoom lens. A client gave it to me as a bonus after I used a less sophisticated rig to photograph her husband facedown in his assistant's lap. The husband was a professional photographer and had made the mistake of leaving the Nikon at home in his wife's care. He may have been a terrible husband, but I had grown to appreciate his insistence on buying the finest equipment.

Looking through the telephoto lens, I saw Chief McGinnis sitting behind the steering wheel wearing that stupid red scarf. Andrew Fine sat in the passenger seat. Blond hair and broad shoulders. He wore sunglasses and a shearling coat and took a hit from a nicotine vaporizer that looked like the handle of a lightsaber.

McGinnis and Fine's conversation appeared calm. I looked at my watch. 12:47. I snapped off a dozen pictures. Maybe McGinnis was telling Fine he was a person of interest in the murder of Maggie Somerville. Hell, I'd done the same thing just to see the reaction on Stevey's face. And Stevey's reaction verified our interest in his brother was warranted. He did not scoff. He did not use the word *outrageous*.

Or maybe McGinnis was interrogating Fine. Maybe he was warning Fine about my involvement in the investigation. Maybe he was asking Fine if he could fish Fine's bass pond come May. Maybe, maybe, maybe. Whatever they were talking about, it was in a car in a parking lot without witnesses. Or so they thought. A while later, Fine got out of the Lincoln and into the white Cayenne. I looked at my watch. 1:33. Forty-six minutes wasn't a short conversation, and who knew how long they'd been there before I arrived. McGinnis left. A moment later, Andrew Fine drove off. I followed.

Fine drove west on Lake Street to the split at Lake Calhoun, where he forked left onto Excelsior Boulevard. I got caught in the left lane and was forced to pull ahead and front-tail him. If he turned off, it wouldn't be hard for me to circle back unless he got onto Highway 100. But he passed over the highway then pulled into Bunny's, a sports bar popular with the over-thirty crowd from Edina and St. Louis Park. I drove around the block, giving Fine plenty of time to find a parking place and go in. Ten minutes later, I walked into Bunny's and sat at the bar.

Weekday lunchtime was a mix of blue and white collars. Most consumed noon beer, which I've never been able to manage without a nap. My intolerance for alcohol earned me the reputation of a lightweight, particularly in college when I was nicknamed Two-for-one Shapiro, because anyone who drank with me would get my barely touched drink in addition to their own. Not since I split with Micaela did my consumption pick up, and that never topped three drinks an evening, rarely two, and most often one or none. I am hardly a PI of detective novels, and that has disappointed more than a few people.

I ordered some fries I didn't want and the Ellegaard Special—a soda with bitters. The McGinnis–Fine powwow in the Midtown Global Market parking lot had sent my stomach tumbling. I took my drink and swiveled around to face the tables where Fine sat with half a dozen other guys his age. They laughed and talked over each other. I guessed they were friends from high school or golfing buddies relegated to Bunny's because their golf course was under a foot and a half of snow. I don't know what I was hoping to discover when tailing Andrew Fine, but it was something more sinister than sweater-clad suburban dads laughing it up over beer and onion rings.

I turned my stool back toward the bar and glanced up at the English Premier League soccer game on the TV. Two women, who appeared to be in their midtwenties, sat at the bar next to me. They suckled noon beers and ate burgers. One talked too much and the other listened, or at least pretended to. After a little eavesdropping, I learned they were nurses at Park Nicollet and had just got off their shifts.

"Hey, what kind of beer is that?" said the talker who sat next to me, a recovering towhead with blue eyes wearing one of those turtlenecks where the neck is so big it looks like a scarf. She wasn't exactly pretty but was attractive in the way most twenty-five-year-olds are—she still had hope. And hope is drop-dead gorgeous.

"It's not beer," I said. "I can't drink until it gets dark out. Kind of like a vampire, but without the blood."

She looked confused. "Then what is it?"

"Soda with bitters."

"Can I taste it?"

"I guess, if you like to taste strange men's drinks."

She stood on the footrest of her stool, leaned over the bar, and grabbed a straw. "No offense. I'm a nurse. I know about germs." Apparently she didn't know that much about germs because a new straw didn't change what was in the glass, but I pushed the drink over to her, she inserted her straw and tasted it. "That's good. That's really, really, really, really good."

"Can I try?" said the listener, who had long, straight black hair, emerald eyes, a roll of baby fat on her neck and a BMI in the red zone, none of which stopped her

from carrying herself like the beauty she was. Since
Micaela, I'd vowed to stay away from twentysomethings
and had done a damn good job. I considered breaking
my vow for Emerald Eyes when I heard a voice boom
behind me.

"Little Shap! What are you doing in here?"

I looked over my shoulder and saw the big smile of
Andrew Fine that showed off teeth whiter than they
should have been. He wore a blue button-down oxford
under a dusty rose cashmere V-neck and jeans. Up close
I could see he hadn't shaved in a few days and his hair
looked a mess, but I couldn't tell if that was from neglect
or expensive hair products and an embarrassing amount
of time in front of the mirror.

"Hey, Andrew. How's it going?"

"Not bad. Not bad at all. Just catching up with some
buddies over there." He motioned over his shoulder then
looked at the nurses and back at me with an expectation
I didn't catch. I lost it sifting through his facial expressions as I tried to figure out if McGinnis had tipped him
off about my involvement in the investigation. A moment later, I realized the only reason Andrew Fine came
over is because he saw me talking to two women and
wanted an introduction.

"Oh . . ." I said. "I'm here alone."

"Thanks for the taste test," said Emerald Eyes, and she
slid the drink back to me. "That's delicious. Did you say
it's soda and bitters?"

Andrew caught the bartender's eye. "Two sodas
with bitters for the ladies. And another for my buddy,
Shap, and one for me." They swiveled around on their
bar stools. "Hope you don't mind," said Andrew. "I
saw you talking to Shap here and thought you were all
friends."

"We are friends," said the loquacious blonde. "We just met and hit it off right away." Emerald Eyes smiled but seemed tired of her bar mate. "I like your name, Shap. It's cool."

"Thanks," I said. "And you are . . ."

"Kallie."

"Lauren," said Emerald Eyes. She extended her hand and I shook it.

"Kallie and Lauren, I'd like you to meet an old friend, Andrew Fine."

They said hellos and shook hands and said thank-you when the bartender set down four sodas with bitters. Andrew helped himself to the open bar stool next to Emerald Eyes, and I felt a twinge of jealousy followed by a wave of disappointment in myself. He asked what they did for a living and told them what he did and within ten minutes had invited them to a party at his Indian Hills estate. It would involve broomball on his frozen bass pond, and they should bring bathing suits because the hot tub would be "cranked up." And while trying to process what it might mean that Andrew Fine so blatantly hit on two women in public knowing he was a person of interest in the murder of another, I'd lost track of their conversation until the blond windbag slugged me on the arm and said, "You are not!"

I had no idea what she was talking about. But Emerald Eyes did and saved me. "Are you really a private investigator?"

"I am."

"Are you carrying a gun?" said the blonde.

"Not at the moment. But don't tell anyone. Edina's a rough town."

"Yeah, right!" I wished she would go away.

Emerald Eyes said, "Are stakeouts as boring as they seem?"

"Worse."

Kallie said, "What do you drive, like, a Ferrari or Lamborghini?"

"That would make it kind of obvious when I'm following people, don't you think?"

"God, you're right," said Kallie, as if I'd just revealed a great truth.

"Come on, Shap. Tell 'em about Duluth." Andrew placed his hand on the motormouth's back. "Shap's good. The real deal. Solves the ones the police can't."

"That's not true. I got lucky once."

"Modesty," said Emerald Eyes. "It only attracts a certain kind of girl." She smiled and those green eyes glistened something Irish. "Shap, are you going to Andrew's broomball party?"

"I sure as hell hope so!" said Andrew. "I saw Shap sitting at the bar here and came over to invite him." Andrew threw me a look that suggested something in the neighborhood of I should be a good pal and go on a double date with him so he could get laid. I hadn't seen that look in over a decade, but spending a night at Andrew Fine's party would be a night on the clock and there was nothing wrong with that.

I said, "When is this party and would I have to bring my own broom?"

"Thursday night because the weekend is for amateurs and you do not have to bring your own broom. Just bring yourself." He leaned toward my ear. "I got to talk some business with you, too. May need your help on something. I'll call you."

I nodded. Phone numbers were exchanged. Andrew

Fine returned to his friends. The blonde excused herself to hit the head, and I offered Emerald Eyes cold fries and the bartender my credit card. I wanted to get the hell out of there before yackety-yak returned.

"Well," said Emerald Eyes, "I hope we're on the same broomball team Thursday night."

"So do I," I said. "And I hope we're not skins."

She laughed and I was grateful Kallie wasn't there to tell me there's no such thing as shirts and skins in broomball because it's too cold.

After I left, I called Ellegaard from the car and told him I'd bumped into Andrew Fine and got myself invited to his broomball party. I skipped the part about seeing Fine talk to McGinnis and me then tailing Fine to Bunny's. I was pretty sure Ellegaard had no idea McGinnis and Fine were in contact. If he found out, his good-soldier complex would jam him into a bad spot. I didn't want McGinnis to learn I'd seen him with Fine, not yet anyway, and I couldn't ask Ellegaard to keep that from his boss.

Ellegaard said both Beth and Perry Lindquist were clean—not even a parking ticket between the two. CSU had combed the creek behind Maggie Somerville's house—they found no cigarette butt or discernible footprints. Ellegaard had no luck finding Ansley Bell, the mysterious frequent phone pal of Maggie Somerville. Ansley wasn't home and no neighbors who were home knew where she worked. I got Ansley's address from Ellegaard and told him I'd take care of it.

8

I drove east on Excelsior Boulevard and, a few minutes later, turned south on France Avenue. The monotone on the radio said it was ten below zero and the temperature would plunge to twenty below after midnight. You can't stake out anything when it's ten below. You can sit in front of a place with your car running, the tail pipe churning out a cloud of condensed exhaust, but stealth is not an option. I'd need another tactic for Ansley Bell and delayed that task until most people get home from work.

Maggie Somerville's ex-husband lived in Morningside on a street with backyards the size of football fields. The homes, at one time, had all been hobby farms. They were old and modest and no one had gargantuanized them like the homes in Maggie Somerville's neighborhood.

Solar panels sat on Robert Somerville's roof. River birch grew from the low spots in the undulating terrain of his prairiescaped front yard, and I could see the tops of golden, dormant grasses poking up through the deep snow. Several other cars were parked out front or in the driveway. I got out of the Volvo, walked up to the door, and rang the bell.

A woman in her sixties with a tear-stained face answered the door.

"Oh, hello. You must be from the funeral home."

Wearing a thick down puffer coat is as good as being naked. You're a blank canvas. "No, I'm sorry. I'm here to see Robert."

"Sure, of course," she said without concern, assuming Robert was expecting me. "Come right in, and I'll get him."

Robert Somerville's home was everything his dead ex-wife's wasn't. The furniture was old and eclectic and looked more found than purchased. Large, worn oriental rugs covered hardwood floors that were in need of refinishing. Photographs, European posters, and the kids' artwork hung on the walls. And there were plants. In pots and planters and vases. Green leaves flowed and fell in corners, on tables, and from the ceiling. The air felt warm and humid, impossibly humid considering the temperature outside. And there were windows everywhere. All without muntins. Just big sheets of glass, triple paned with insulating layers of air between. I felt heat in my feet. No forced air or radiators anywhere. The only similarity between Robert Somerville's home and dead Maggie's was the same photographs of children were displayed in each.

Robert Somerville approached with a face of kindness and curiosity. He had shoulder-length brown hair, blue eyes, and a wide jaw like a Kennedy. He wore crystal acrylic framed glasses, a wool sweater, and rust-colored cords. Either he or his sweater smelled a bit ripe. He looked the type to use an ineffective deodorant rock rather than laboratory-tested chemicals. He was barefoot with a dark purple toenail on the second toe of his left foot. Another fucking runner—this town was full of them.

"Can I help you?" he said.

"I'm sorry to bother you, Mr. Somerville. My name is Nils Shapiro. I'm a private investigator looking into your ex-wife's death. My condolences. It's a terrible tragedy."

"Thank you. But one of your people was here yesterday."

"My people?"

"From the insurance company? The kids are Maggie's life insurance beneficiaries."

"I'm not with the insurance company," I said.

"Then who are you working for?"

"I'm not at liberty to say."

"Then I don't need to talk to you, right?"

"Not at all. It's your choice." I took out my notepad and wrote, "Robert Somerville refused to be interviewed . . ."

"What are you doing? Why are you writing that?"

"In case I'm called to the witness stand. I want to accurately record what happened here."

"You can't do that. They'll think I'm trying to hide something."

It was a cheap trick but it worked. "I know it's a terrible time, Mr. Somerville. I just want a few minutes."

"All right," he said. "A few minutes."

I shed my down puffer and removed my shoes, then Somerville led me toward the back of the house and into a sunroom that was more of an attached greenhouse. The walls were made of glass and covered in foggy condensation—I couldn't see outside. Plants poured out of their pots. Lettuces, tomatoes, peppers, and onions grew in raised planting beds. A hot tub made of wood that looked like half a barrel simmered in the corner. Steam swirled off the water's surface—the humidity suddenly made sense. Somerville sat in a wicker chair and invited me to do the same.

"What can I help you with?" he said, not friendly, but not unfriendly either. I just seemed to be another piece of business Maggie's death had forced him to deal with.

"Listen," I said. "I know this sucks. You've probably already been questioned and re-questioned by the police and then the insurance company, so some of this is going to be a repeat. I'm just trying to find out what happened, and I know you want that, too."

He nodded.

"Do you have any idea who could have done this?"

"No," he said. "Maggie was friendly and likable. We had our differences, mostly on how we chose to live our lives, but she was a good person and a good mother. She was easygoing and liked everybody and everybody liked her. That's what's so shocking. Some people have a hardness to them, you know? They take themselves too seriously and get worked up about this or that and you can at least imagine how something could have escalated. But not with Maggie. If anything, she erred on the side of not taking enough seriously: politics, the environment, our kids' education. She was happy going with the flow, not questioning anything. Kind of like she was along for the ride."

"I'm sorry to ask this, but when you're married to someone like that, how does the marriage get strained to the point of divorce?"

Robert Somerville looked down at his bare feet. "It got strained because I wanted something she didn't care about."

"Which was?"

"A loving marriage." He looked back up but not at me. "I don't tell many people this because it doesn't make me look good, but I married a woman who didn't love me."

"Did you know it when you married her?"

"Not at the time, no. I just assumed she loved me because she said she did. I didn't look at the relationship with a critical eye. I guess when I was twenty-two, I was so happy to be with Maggie I didn't want to see the facts right in front of my face."

"Which were?"

"What I said. Maggie wasn't in love with me. She never called me. I always called her. She never wrote me a note. She never initiated sex. She never bought me a serious gift. I didn't give a shit in a materialistic way, but, you know, it is the thought that counts. And she expressed her thoughts by buying me gag gifts."

"That's strange."

"Right? A ridiculous sweater I'd never wear or an incredibly ugly painting I'd never hang up."

"Like a velvet Elvis?"

"Close. A velvet clown. And a velvet dog wearing a tuxedo. And stupid desk accessories like a mug that said 'You don't have to be crazy to work here but it helps!' I own a fucking company—there is no scenario where that mug's going on my desk."

Robert Somerville wanted to talk. I wasn't about to get in his way.

"And the real kicker was when the kids were born. That's when it hit me because then I saw Maggie love someone. You know, real love. And even though romantic love and how you love your kids is different, it shouldn't be *that* different. When she was away from the kids, Maggie thought about them. They were in her heart. When she was away from me, it was like I didn't exist. And once I realized that, I guess I just stopped trying. And got resentful. And then it was like every other shitty marriage where you choose to see the bad in the relationship instead of the good."

"Yeah, I know," I said, even though I didn't. That wasn't my marriage or anything close to it. My marriage ended like Romeo and Juliet's but with self-preservation and independence substituting for the poison and rapier.

"I thought Maggie might not be capable of romantic love—it just wasn't in her DNA," he said. "Maybe I was rationalizing—I don't know. . . . But I think she fell pretty hard for that guy she was seeing."

"Andrew Fine?"

"Yeah. She was in love with him. Or his money. But she was in love. The kids definitely felt it. They were like, 'What's up with Mom? She's all happy and doesn't listen to us anymore.'"

"Do you think her love for Fine was really about money?"

"Maggie liked nice things. Things I've never cared about. Not that I don't spend money, I just care more about how energy-efficient my house is rather than who designed the fucking couch."

"She liked expensive furniture?"

"Very. She asked for twenty grand for a couch. Ten for a chair. Another ten for the only painting that could possibly pull it together. It looked like regular Room & Board stuff to me. You know, good. But not over the top. It seemed to make her happy, though, so I gave her what she asked for."

"Do you know anything about Maggie seeing a man named Slim?"

"No," Robert laughed, "I'd remember that name."

The tear-stained woman poked her head in. "Robert. We can't choose the flowers without you."

Robert said, "Be right there."

"I don't want to take up any more of your time," I said.

"I appreciate that. We have a lot to do before the funeral on Thursday."

"Just a word of advice, if that's cool."

"Of course."

"The Edina police are in way over their heads on this. Be careful around them."

"What do you mean?"

"I don't trust them. Not that they're dirty or anything, they're just little kids playing a big-kids' game. They may push you hard or they may back off and watch you from afar. You know, just because of the statistics."

"What statistics?"

"When a woman Maggie's age is murdered, the murderer almost always turns out to be the husband or ex-husband or boyfriend. Edina PD is such a straightlaced actuarial bunch, you know, like stockbrokers with guns, they're going to play the numbers rather than intuit anything intelligent."

"I know the type," said Robert. "I got some of those guys on my board."

"If you don't mind me saying so, you don't seem like a business guy."

"I'm in the business of making the world a better place."

I liked Robert Somerville until he said that, but I'm glad he did. It made my job easier.

"Well, like I said, just be careful around Edina PD."

"I will, thanks. I actually know one of them," he said.

"Which one?"

"The chief. McGinnis."

"No shit. How do you know McGinnis?"

"He's been hitting up all the money in town for contributions."

"For what?" I shifted in my wicker chair. It squeaked.

"Eleanor Nordahl. She's going to run for governor. Wants to anyway. And she's running as an independent so she'll have to raise a ton of money."

"But she was elected Hennepin County Attorney as a democrat."

"And apparently she's been a little too law-and-order. McGinnis says Nordahl doesn't want to compromise her tough-on-crime stance to appease the DFL. That's why she's going to run as an independent."

I said, "McGinnis doesn't seem like an independent kind of guy."

"No, not at all. There's got to be something in it for him."

"My guess is Commissioner of the Minnesota Department of Public Safety."

"What is that," said Robert, "like head of the state patrol?"

"Head of all state law enforcement. Alcohol, gambling, traffic, licensing, everything. Minnesota's top cop. It's the governor's most powerful appointed position. Even the state supreme court justices are elected."

"Sounds like McGinnis," said Somerville, "securing himself a nice step up from Edina Chief of Police."

"So he's hitting up everyone in town for money?"

"Yeah. Really playing the independent card. Says Nordahl is a socially liberal financial conservative who's tough on crime."

I smiled. "She wants to cut taxes and spend more on education, right?"

"They're all so full of shit," said Robert. "Every damn one of them."

We shook hands, I bundled up and left Somerville's rain forest and reentered the arctic. I jumped onto Highway 100 for a few miles, then drove east on 394. It was just after 3:30, but the afternoon sun had set low in the western sky and reflected orange and red off my rearview mirror. I snaked through Spaghetti Junction to 35W and, a few minutes later, exited on Stinson. Northeast Minneapolis is full of artists and musicians and wannabes. You can't rent a place there without showing two forms of ID and three tattoos.

Ansley Bell lived on the second story of a stucco upstairs-downstairs duplex on 3rd Street. I drove by it once and spotted someone sitting in a Camry with the motor idling, a huge cloud of exhaust condensing in the cold air behind him. I drove off, zig-zagged through the neighborhood, and returned fifteen minutes later. The man in the Camry was still there. Apparently, I wasn't the only person wanting to talk to Ansley Bell.

9

The idiot in the Camry had no idea what he was doing. If Ansley Bell didn't want to be found, he was helping plenty.

I called Minneapolis PD and reported a suspicious-looking man idling in a Camry near a school bus stop. I had no idea where the school bus stop was, but I knew they were every few blocks so I couldn't have been off by too far. Twenty minutes later, the man handed over his license to a cold and pissed off Minneapolis uniform while I walked unnoticed into the alley behind Ansley Bell's duplex.

I'd been in my share of prewar, two-story duplexes in this town. Most had one front door and one back door. Inside each door was a small foyer and in each foyer a door led to the downstairs unit and a staircase to the upstairs unit. I opened the rear exterior door—it was unlocked. I took off my shoes, left them in the foyer, then climbed a narrow staircase that had been retrofitted with a vinyl floor of raised dots so it appeared to be made of giant Legos. At the top, I faced Ansley Bell's rear door. I knocked. No one answered.

I don't have a college degree but I've made up for it by studying a rare field called Useful Shit. First my police-academy training and then, during my business's slow times, I completed my imaginary degree with courses in digital photography, emergency medical response, and the fine art of locksmithing. All useful in the course of doing my job but none more than the latter. Ansley Bell's back door was protected by Kwikset locks, one in the door handle and one dead bolt. They should be called Kwikpick locks—I was inside in under a minute.

The back door led into the kitchen, which was lit only by the bulb in the range hood. The place didn't look like the home of a twenty-six-year-old. Nothing from IKEA. Nothing visibly secondhand. A Wolf four-burner range. Mauviel copper pots hanging from a rack. A full block of Wusthofs on the counter. I continued into the dining room. A solid walnut dining table with matching chairs sat under an art deco chandelier made of hanging crystal prisms, the bulbs of which were dimmed and glowed an orangish gold. In the living room, a deep leather sectional faced the fireplace and a sixty-inch flat-screen TV hung over the mantel. The area rugs were newer and expensive looking. Something felt familiar but I couldn't peg what.

A radiator knocked and steam pulsed inside it. I checked the thermostat: seventy-two degrees. Not the setting of someone sticking to a tight budget, especially in an old building with single-paned windows, leaky storms, and poor insulation. Seventy-two degrees meant that either Ansley Bell could afford to keep her apartment warm while she was away or she left in a hurry or she hadn't left at all.

I heard the front door open downstairs and then footsteps. They seemed to be coming from below me rather than heading up the stairs. The old wooden-framed building, with its winter-dried tongue-and-groove flooring, creaked when you looked at it. I walked close to the walls to minimize the sound of my own footsteps and paused when reaching the hallway. I poked my head in and looked each way. There were two bedrooms, one on each end, and a bathroom in-between. The doors were closed, and no lights were on. I stepped into the hallway when a phone rang. It sounded like a cell phone from the bedroom down to the right. It rang three times, then stopped.

"Hello," said a raspy feminine voice from behind the closed door. "Yeah, but that's okay. What time is it?" Sheets and blankets ruffled. "Shit. I slept for twelve hours." I heard a click and a creak, then a wedge of light slipped under the bedroom floor.

I backpedaled along the wall. I was almost all the way through the living room when the voice said, "I'll jump in the shower and meet you at six." I hastened my pace as I neared the dining room. "No, no. That's plenty of time. See you there." I continued into the kitchen and heard footsteps in the hall. The footsteps stopped. The shower started then a toilet lid flipped up. Half a minute later it flushed, then I heard metal rings dragging on a metal rod. She was in the shower.

I darted along the baseboards back through the dining room and living room and peeked into the hall. The

bathroom door was open—the light from within flooded
into the hallway. Water hit the tile in uneven waves and
slaps. I knew I had a few minutes so I slid into the hallway and down to the bedroom. An iPhone lay on the
nightstand. It hadn't put itself to sleep so I grabbed it,
opened the settings app, and went to the Phone icon and
found the item "My Phone." Using my iPhone, I took a
picture of the phone number, navigated to the Facebook
app, and went to the phone owner's page.

Ansley Bell. An olive-skinned beauty with pronounced
cheekbones, caramel eyes, twenty-eight friends, and her
privacy settings cranked to invisible. A selfie of Ansley
and Maggie Somerville. A picture of Ansley standing
next to a red Subaru Outback with a giant green bow
on the roof. I closed Facebook and opened her e-mail.
ansley.bell@umn.edu. E-mails from professors and students with the same @umn.edu. Ansley appeared to be
studying medicine at the University of Minnesota. The
other e-mails were the usual blast of ads. Williams-
Sonoma, Anthropologie, Groupon, and a deluge from the
Minneapolis Star Tribune. She had several recent missed
calls and voice mails, a couple from Edina PD. How come
no one under thirty answers their phone? I took a picture of her Favorites in Contacts. The top name belonged
to Maggie Somerville. I opened the Find My Friends app
on my phone and added Ansley's e-mail address. Her
phone received the request to let me find Ansley and I
accepted it. I went to the home screen, set down her
phone, and crept back the way I'd come.

A garage in the alley behind Ansley's duplex had a service door with a joke of a lock. Ansley's red Subaru was
parked inside. It was free of snow but the garage floor
was wet.

I walked around front. The man in the Camry was still

parked in the same spot where the police had questioned
him. That confirmed he was a private investigator, and a
lazy one at that. I didn't know who he worked for and I
didn't really care. I just wanted him out of my way. I
walked back to the Volvo, opened my glove compart-
ment, and grabbed a little brass contraption that looked
like a tire valve stem. It cost three bucks but made me
feel a hell of a lot less guilty than slashing rubber. I knelt
by the dick's rear passenger tire and, hidden by the
Camry's exhaust cloud, removed the tire's valve cap and
screwed on its replacement. I returned to my car and
drove around back to the alley and waited. Twenty minutes later, Ansley Bell pulled out of her garage. I tailed
her out of the alley, around the corner, and down 3rd
Street where she drove right in front of her duplex. The
dick must have had a description of her car, because as
Ansley drove by, he pulled out to follow but stopped after twenty feet. In my rearview mirror, I saw him get out
of his car, run to the back passenger side, and throw his
arms in the air as if he were in a comic-book panel.

I tailed Ansley into the North Loop District downtown. She valeted her car at the Monte Carlo across from
the Colonial Warehouse. I found a meter around the
corner on Washington—tail jobs and valet parking
don't mix.

The Monte Carlo is deep and narrow with a high ceiling finished with tin tiles. The bar sits in front where you
enter, the dining room behind it. Behind the bar, six glass
shelves filled with liquor bottles rise to the ceiling. The
liquor bursts with color from a backlit glass wall. The
dining room boasts red leather booths, dark floral wall-
paper, and sconces. It's the kind of place you go for an
old-fashioned and chicken potpie on a cold winter night.
The menu says it opened in 1906 and, over a hundred

years later, the place feels old and new at the same time. It's as if when they first decorated they bought ten of everything, and each decade, instead of remodeling, they just replaced every leather booth, light fixture, the wall-paper, and the carpet with a brand-new version identical to the last.

The hostess grabbed two menus then walked Ansley Bell and her friend to their booth. The friend was a tiny woman, about thirty years old and four-feet-ten-inches high. She had short brown hair and wore cat-eye glasses and a short-waisted, vintage baby blue cardigan with something pearly embroidered into it. I hung up my coat and found a seat on the near corner of the bar so I faced the dining room. Until then, I hadn't seen Ansley Bell's face in person. I doubted my earlier assumption that she was olive skinned. From thirty feet away, she appeared half Caucasian, half African-American. She had long, curly dark hair, a narrow nose, and full lips. I only took my eyes off her to meet the bartender's. I ordered a Red-breast neat and a New York strip with garlic mashed potatoes. My phone buzzed. It was Ellegaard.

"Hey," I said. "Anything new?"

"No, but I just got a call from Gabriella." Gabriella Núñez attended the Minneapolis Police Academy with Ellegaard and me. Now she was a big deal in the Min-neapolis PD with her own office and parking spot and a golden eagle on her dress blues. "She said they got a call from a private investigator. Wouldn't say who he was working for. He was staking out Ansley Bell's apartment, and thought the police might want to know that some-one called Minneapolis PD to harass him, and then someone else, or maybe the same person, let the air out of his tire. Said he spotted Ansley Bell's car but couldn't pursue because of the flat. This someone had screwed a

tire deflator onto his rear passenger tire. He also mentioned that someone following Ansley in an old Volvo
didn't seem to have his troubles."

"That's a coincidence."

"Oh, no it's not. Where are you, Shap?"

"Let me do my job, Ellie."

"You're working for Edina PD. Your job is to keep us
informed."

"You'll get what you're paying for. Just give me some
breathing room."

"Liquor Lyle's at 9:00. Don't be late." Ellegaard hung
up, and I took my fist sip of smooth Irish, courtesy of the
Edina PD.

Ansley Bell and the Tiny Woman drank red wine and
ate something from a basket I couldn't identify from the
bar. They seemed to be having a good time. From where
I sat, it appeared Ansley was either a cold-blooded killer
or wasn't aware of her friend's death. Maggie Somerville
had kept Ansley a secret. No one seemed to know about
Ansley, so it made sense that no one would call her about
the murder. If Ansley hadn't paid attention to local news,
a real possibility for a medical student, then she probably didn't know. Unless she was a cold-blooded killer.

I finished my whiskey and ate my steak and, when
I thought of Chief McGinnis meeting with Andrew Fine
in the Global Market parking lot, ordered a piece of
flourless chocolate cake to pad my bill.

On ridiculous television shows, I've seen it suggested
that if a man wants to break up with a woman, he should
take her to a nice restaurant so she won't make a scene.
I don't know why anyone would want to drop a buck
fifty on a woman who was about to hate his guts. And if
she wants to make a scene, a nice restaurant provides an
excellent stage. But nice restaurants do serve a purpose

on the other end of the spectrum—they're a good place to introduce yourself to someone without them making a scene. I closed my tab with the bartender and walked into the dining room.

I look back on a handful of moments in my life as if they were traffic circles. I didn't know I was driving into one, but once I realized I had, it was too late. Whichever direction I drove out would send me in a direction I hadn't intended to go. Ansley Bell was one of those traffic circles.

"Excuse me. I'm sorry to bother you. My name's Nils Shapiro. I'm a private investigator."

Ansley Bell and the Tiny Woman looked at each other for a second too long, then burst into laughter. Big, loud, wine-fueled laughter. The kind that makes you feel like an outsider, like other people know something you don't, like you want to ask what's so funny or just walk away and leave those nuts to it.

"I'm sorry, I'm sorry, I'm sorry," squeaked Ansley. "We were just talking about . . ."

Another wave of laughter crashed onto shore and took them out to sea. When they washed back up, the Tiny Woman tried to talk. "We were just discussing the worst . . ." And out they went again.

"Maybe I should come back in a few minutes."

"No, no," said Ansley. "We were just telling . . ." She took a couple of deep breaths and wiped the tears from her eyes with the white hand towel the Monte Carlo thought made a cute napkin. "Okay . . ." A breath. "Sorry . . ." A giggle. "We were just telling each other the worst pickup lines we've ever heard. And then you walked up and . . . and . . . and said, 'I'm a private investigator.'" Another wave swept them away.

"Looks like this could take a while. Mind if I sit?"

They shook their heads and laughed some more at what they obviously interpreted as another pickup line. When the laughter passed, I handed a business card to each, and the laughter drained out of them.

"I truly am sorry to bother you," I said. "I have a private matter I need to discuss with Ms. Bell."

"How do you know who I am?" said Ansley.

I said nothing and let the silence hang over the table.

The Tiny Woman looked to Ansley, who nodded. "Well," said Tiny, "I got a bladder full of cabernet. I'll be back in a few minutes." She slid out of the booth with her purse in tow, and I sat down.

Ansley looked concerned. "What's this about?"

"Would you be more comfortable talking somewhere less public?"

"I can't do that. I don't know you."

"I understand."

"Is this about Maggie Somerville?"

"Yes, it is."

I saw fear in her caramel eyes. Her sculpted face tensed. Her full mouth shrank into something small and defensive. "I've called and texted her but she hasn't responded. That's never happened before." The waitress approached, then saw Ansley's face and backed off. Ansley said, "Is Maggie okay?"

"I'm sorry, Ms. Bell. She's not. Maggie's dead." Ansley Bell hung her head and wept. "Have you seen the news in the past forty-eight hours?" She shook her head. "I've been hired to investigate Maggie's death. It wasn't an accident. She was murdered."

"Oh, God. Oh, God. No . . ."

"You can verify the news on your phone if you want. And please check the State of Minnesota Board of Private Detectives Website so you know I'm legit."

Ansley Bell placed her hands over her face and lifted her head. When she took them away, her wet, dark eyes shined like polished tigereye glinting gold and brown. That's when I knew I was in the traffic circle.

10

Ansley and the Tiny Woman paid their check, then I followed Ansley to her place. She parked in back, and I approached the Toyota Camry idling in front of her house. I rapped on the driver's side window, and it went down.

A pencil-thin man with a pencil mustache, who looked like he'd been rejected by every police department in the country, sat behind the wheel surfing porn on his Samsung tablet while sucking on a piece of hard candy that clicked around in his teeth. He made no effort to hide his tablet, as if he was proving how badass he was by looking at naked women in two dimensions. A bag of groceries sat on the passenger seat and a royal blue water container sat on the passenger-seat floor. It was, no doubt, full of piss.

The pencil-thin man said, "You the cocksucker who let the air out of my tire?"

"Can't get anything by your eagle eye—as long as it knocks on your car window two hours after the fact."

"I'm going to fucking report you to the PI board."

"Well, you know I'll get a copy of that complaint, and when I do I'll send it straight to your employer. Then you'll have to explain how you were unable to pursue Ansley Bell because, even though she was asleep at home the whole time you sat in front of her house padding your hours and expenses, when she tried to leave, a bad man let the air out of your tire while you were jacking off to Big Beautiful Women."

"What the fuck is your problem, pal?"

"Why are you talking like that? What are you trying to do?"

"I'm trying to ascertain why you're muscling in on my subject."

"Ascertain?"

"It means find out."

"Ah. Now I understand."

"I oughta get out of this car and kick your ass."

"Yeah, you ought to. But you can't. For one, physically, and I'm sorry about that. I really am. And two, you'd lose your job. So listen. You're going to see a light turn on in Ansley Bell's apartment any minute. Then I'm going up to talk to her. Yep, there's the light. And during that talk I'll tell her that a skinny-ass fuck with a skinny-ass mustache will knock on her door at nine o'clock tomorrow morning. You're not going to talk to her before then, so you might as well go home and get some sleep."

"Fuck you."

"Guess you used up your big words. Sweet dreams." I rapped the top of his car good-bye and walked toward Ansley's duplex.

There were two doorbell buttons, one labeled WILLIAMS and the other labeled BELL. I hate puns—they're not the lowest form of humor because that would put them in the category of humor. This one, though, seemed unavoidable, so I did my best to get over it and pressed the doorbell. Ansley did not come to the door. A minute later, I pushed it again. The asshole in the Camry probably had a big smile on his face. I expected to hear a victory honk. I got out my phone, found Ansley's number in my pictures, and called. Two rings in, she answered.

"You running on me?" I said.

"No. Sorry, I forgot to tell you the doorbell doesn't work." Her inflection went up at the end of the statement, and I knew she didn't grow up here. "I had it disabled because med-school hours and Girl Scouts selling cookies don't mix. I'll be right down."

That explained why Ellegaard and skinny-ass struck out. The latter honked. Two bits and a haircut, no less. What a fucking hack. Fifteen seconds later, Ansley Bell came down and opened the door. I took off my mitten and gave skinny-ass the finger.

I walked into Ansley's apartment as if I were seeing it for the first time, complimenting her on the Wolf range and art deco chandelier. When I sat in the leather sectional, I realized why it felt familiar. Maggie Somerville had matching sectionals in her basement rec room. Robert Somerville never paid close attention. Maggie insisted on expensive furniture and clothing and everything else so she could skim the budget for Ansley Bell. How could Maggie be in love with Robert if she was in love with someone else?

Ansley asked if she could get me a drink. I declined. She disappeared into the kitchen then reappeared with a tumbler of red wine. She curled up in the corner of the sectional and cried hard like a child who'd just seen her dog hit by a car. Five minutes later, I wished I hadn't turned down that drink. She looked so alone in that corner. I wanted to put an arm around her. Instead, I went into the bathroom, did a little recon, and returned with a box of Kleenex. I gave her a few tissues and a cashmere throw that was draped on the back of the sectional.

"Thank you," she said.

"Edina PD and another private detective have been trying to contact you all day, but were stymied by your broken doorbell and you not answering your phone." I looked for a reaction—I only saw grief. "The reason that the police want to talk to you is because you're the most frequently called contact in Maggie Somerville's phone. I don't know what the private detective wants, but I don't like him. And if I were you, I'd do your best to avoid him. He's going to knock on your door at 9:00 A.M. tomorrow. Don't answer it."

Ansley Bell curled herself into the fetal position and leaned into the corner of the sectional as if it were her great love. Then a river of pain rushed out of her. It was too much for another human being to see. I walked over and sat next to her. She shifted her weight from the corner to my shoulder. I put an arm around her, held her tight, and said nothing.

After ten minutes or maybe an hour, her breathing steadied into something near aerobic. "Why do the police want to talk to me about Maggie?"

"They want to know why she called you so often. They want to know the nature of your relationship."

"How did she die?"

"As far as we can tell, peacefully. It seems she was drugged and then smothered in her sleep."

"Oh, God . . ." said Ansley. She pushed her face into my shoulder. Her tangle of dark curls smelled like rosemary and mint, and I couldn't help wondering if she ever found herself attracted to men. "Why would anyone want to hurt her? She was the most lovely human being I've ever known."

"Honestly, we have no idea why. Or who. When you're feeling up to it, I was hoping you could shed some light on that. You'll have to talk to the police tomorrow. They'll want to know why no one else who knew Maggie knows who you are. You'll have to answer some uncomfortable questions. About your personal life. About your love life." She grew quiet and still. She sat up, and I retracted my arm. She took a new tissue and dried her eyes. "My advice is, be honest. Tell the police everything you know. Even if it seems small." She nodded. "Her ex-husband is planning the funeral. He seems like a nice enough guy. And he's progressive. If you want to be involved in any way, I bet he'd be open to it."

"What are you talking about?"

"Robert Somerville won't care if his ex-wife was sleeping with a woman."

Ansley Bell's fog of sorrow lifted just enough for me to see a gleam in her wet eyes. "Maggie Somerville was not my lover," she said. "Maggie Somerville was my mother."

I kept my eyes fixed on Ansley's—they looked straight at me and avoided nothing. "Maybe I will take that drink," I said. "Stay put. I'll see what you have."

I grabbed her empty tumbler and went into the kitchen and found wine, a few stray bottles of beer in the fridge, and a bottle of Grey Goose in the freezer. I grabbed a Summit Oatmeal Stout, refilled Ansley's tumbler with Old Vine Zin, brought both back into the living room. She started talking before I sat down.

"Maggie had me when she was fifteen. She grew up Catholic and knew it would be hell when her parents found out she was pregnant. She couldn't hide it when she was throwing up all the time so she told them, and they sent her to live with an aunt in California where I could be born without disgracing anyone in Minnesota."

"Maggie just left Minnesota?"

"She was a competitive figure skater so they told everyone she was going away to train for a shot at the 1992 Olympics. The Web hadn't been invented yet. No one expected posts on Instagram. No one questioned it."

"I'm guessing the father wasn't the boy next door."

"Maggie told me her family didn't even know any black people. She only knew one—my father—but her family didn't know he existed. But Maggie was in love with him and wanted to protect him, so she told them the father was a kid in school named Josh Edwards."

"I'm sure Josh Edwards loved that."

"Actually, he did. Josh was gay and kids were starting to figure it out. It was not a happy time for him. He was my mom's best friend—they were the only people who knew each other's secrets. If my mom's secret somehow got out, Josh would've gladly assumed responsibility to appear heterosexual."

"But her secret didn't get out?"

"No, it didn't. She came back a year later with a story about getting injured on the rink. The lie worked and that was that. She had a normal high school life and no one in Minnesota knew I existed except for her parents, her aunt, and Josh. And of those people, only Josh knew who my real father was."

"Maggie's aunt knew you're biracial."

"Actually, she didn't. Maggie told her obstetrician in Los Angeles that if her family back in Minnesota found out she had had a black baby, it would make things extra difficult for her. So the doctor protected her by not letting my aunt in the delivery room. I was born then whisked away and taken to a couple that had arranged a private adoption."

"Did your father know about you?"

Ansley sipped her wine then placed her tumbler on the coffee table. "Maggie didn't tell him she was pregnant. He moved away while she was in California and never learned a thing."

"But you and Maggie found each other."

"Yes," said Ansley. "We did. Actually, I found Maggie."

"Was it an open adoption?"

"No. My adoptive parents had a safe. One day, when they had both left for work, I called my dad and told him I needed to bring my passport to school for International Day. It was total bullshit—there's no such thing as International Day—but he didn't question it. He wasn't about to turn around and come back home, so he gave me the combination to the safe. I looked for and found my adoption papers inside. Maggie's name was on them, but it was her maiden name, Sundt. Then I went online and searched for Margaret Sundts born fifteen to twenty-five years before me. I found the only one in the entire country in an Edina High School yearbook." Ansley Bell took a sip of wine and stared at nothing. "After that it was easy to find her on Facebook as

Maggie Somerville, still living in Edina, married with two kids."

Ansley Bell took another sip of wine and shut her eyes. She looked exhausted from telling a story she'd never told before. Or maybe it was just from grief.

"It took me a while to get up the nerve, but eventually I called Maggie and said I wanted to meet her." Ansley opened her eyes. "She was apprehensive but agreed to the meeting. The first time I saw Maggie was surreal—a white woman with blue eyes and blonde hair—but her eyes were shaped like my eyes. And we have identical mouths with big, full sets of teeth in narrow faces. It felt so good to see myself in someone else. You know, all of a sudden, I was sure I didn't come from another planet.

"Maybe it wouldn't have meant so much if I'd had a better relationship with my adoptive parents. But from the moment we met, we both knew . . . knew we'd be in each other's lives . . . I was going to say forever. But . . . it won't be forever now."

I asked if the fireplace worked. She nodded. Kindling and logs and a box of long matches lay on a brass rack near the hearth. I got on my hands and knees, opened the flue, lit a couple sticks of kindling, added a few more, let the flames build, then lay a birch log, bark-down, across the grate. The wood must have been sitting there over a year—the fire grew to a roar within minutes. I silently thanked the pops and hisses for filling the awkward silence and returned to the sectional.

"Maggie paid my tuition at Carleton. Northfield is close—I saw her on weekends. I got into the University of Minnesota Medical School, and I've lived here the past four years. She's paid my tuition and for this apartment and everything in it."

"So why now, after all this time, does no one know you exist?"

Ansley took another sip of wine. "Because of my biological father."

"Who's Somali."

"How did you know?"

"It's a look, and you got it."

"I suppose I do," she said.

"So what about your father?"

"My father's name is Omar Bihi. He grew up in a prominent Somali clan that opposed the then-government, which was run by the Supreme Revolutionary Council. In the mid-1980s, its president almost died in a car accident. While he was in the hospital, there was a power struggle. The Red Berets tortured a lot of dissenters, and my father's family fled to the United States. The Catholic and Lutheran social services invited them to visit Minnesota, anticipating civil war would break out in Somalia, which it did a few years later. They hoped refugees would come to the Twin Cities."

"How did Maggie and your father meet?"

"Catholic youth organizations reached out to immigrant families."

"Competing against the Lutherans."

"Probably," she smiled, "it is Minnesota." The fire whipped and hissed. Ansley removed the throw from her shoulders and said, "Maggie became my father's goodwill ambassador, helped him with homework, meeting American kids and all that. My father's family lived in north Minneapolis. It was a black neighborhood and hip-hop was taking off. But when the Africans wanted to participate in the African-American culture, the African-Americans wanted nothing to do with them."

"Like, 'Go back to where you came from'?"

"Basically, yes."

"So my father was a total outcast. Except with my mother. They spent a lot of time together and fell in love. It was under the guise of Catholic charity, so no one paid much attention. That's how I got conceived.

"But then my mother's parents shipped her off to California, and Omar and his family returned to Somalia to participate in the president's overthrow and the civil war that followed. Maggie said Omar was one of the sweetest boys she had ever known, and that I was conceived out of a gentle and innocent love. She told me several times to make sure I understood it, especially since Omar rose to power as a warlord and became one of the most ruthless tribal leaders in the region.

"By the time I'd met Maggie in 2008, she was afraid that maybe Omar had reestablished ties with Minnesota and would somehow find out he had a daughter and would have me kidnapped. I don't know how real a possibility that is, but it's scary enough to keep me far from the Somali community. I have zero interaction with them. And I do everything I can to scream I'm not one of them, whether it's wearing a Dave's Bar-B-Que T-shirt or short shorts or a Jack Daniel's hat."

"So you and Maggie kept your relationship a secret."

She nodded and told me a little more, and then Ansley Bell talked herself to sleep. Sometime after midnight, I grabbed a couple of pillows and a duvet from her bedroom and tucked her in on the leather sectional.

When I got in my car, the temperature on the dash read -17. But synthetic oil and a six-month-old battery makes an old Volvo new again, and it started right up.

My phone had died in the pocket of my parka so I

plugged it in while waiting for the engine to warm up. When it came back to life, I saw three texts from Ellegaard.

9:17 *Where are you? Lyle's, remember?*

9:34 *I missed tucking my kids in tonight so I could sit in Lyle's exchanging information with myself. Shap, this is a problem.*

9:49 *Leaving. Perkins on 50th tomorrow at 8:00 A.M. No excuses.*

11

Perkins Restaurant & Bakery is a business that lacks such confidence it just comes straight out and says what it is, for fear that you'll mix it up with Perkins Tool & Die or Perkins Tropical Fish. It's distinguished by Formica tables in a woodgrain finish, vinyl booths, and loud carpet designed more to hide stains than please the eye. The servers' uniforms don't have a natural fiber in them. Insurance agents and telecommuters conduct meetings at its tables, drawing charts and graphs on paper place mats bejeweled with coffee-mug rings. The whole place is a testament to the innovation of Man.

I arrived early, but Ellegaard sat waiting in a booth, drinking tea. I slid in opposite him, turned over my coffee cup, and waited for something hot and brown to wake me up.

"Thanks for showing up," said Ellegaard.

"You still mad about last night? Because you know me. If I wasn't there, I had a good reason."

"Let's hear it."

I hadn't seen Ellegaard get pissy before. I didn't care for it and decided to knock him back on his heels. "I saw Andrew Fine and your boss talking in McGinnis's unmarked Edina SUV yesterday. I don't know what they talked about, but it looked pretty fucking chummy."

Ellegaard set down his tea. "Shut up, Shap."

"They had a clandestine meeting in a parking lot when they thought no one was paying attention. But someone was." I showed Ellegaard a photo on my phone. "What the fuck, Ellie. What's going on here?"

Ellegaard looked like I'd sucker-punched him in the stomach. "I don't know," he said.

"Do you know McGinnis has been raising money for Eleanor Nordahl's gubernatorial campaign?" Ellie's dumbfounded expression answered the question for me. "He's been talking to Edina money, including Robert Somerville. Word is that Eleanor promised to appoint him as the Commissioner of Minnesota Department of Public Safety if she wins. Don't you think that's something he should have told us, Ellie? That he's met with Robert Somerville? That he's making out with Andrew Fine in parking lots?"

Ellegaard's six-foot-three frame shrunk a few inches. "What are you implying, Shap? That McGinnis is coaching Andrew Fine and Robert Somerville on how to respond to our investigation in exchange for political contributions?"

"There he is." I looked up and saw McGinnis approaching our booth. He wore khakis, a navy crewneck sweater over a white oxford, and that damn red scarf. Red, white, and blue. I guessed those would be his colors from now on, a subliminal or not-so-subliminal branding for his political ambitions. He caught the eye of a passing waitress. "I'll take some coffee, Carly, when you have a chance."

"Be right there, Chief," said Carly with a smile.

"So Nils," said McGinnis, sliding into the booth on Ellegaard's side. "What have you found out so far?"

"More questions than answers."

"That's what happens when you dig. That's good."

"Is it?" I said. "Why didn't you tell us you'd met with Robert Somerville at his office?"

"It's separate business," said McGinnis, "it has nothing to do with our investigation."

"Maybe, but that's an odd omission."

Ellegaard fidgeted. The Boy Scout didn't like seeing his troop leader addressed with such disrespect. "Hey, come on," he said. "We're all on the same team here."

I locked eyes with McGinnis. "Did you warn Andrew Fine about me working on the investigation?"

"Shap," said Ellegaard. "Enough."

The waitress came over, filled McGinnis's cup with coffee and topped off mine. She threw another smile McGinnis's way—he managed to return it. She winked and left.

"No," said McGinnis. "I haven't told Andrew Fine anything."

"But you've spoken with him since the murder."

I set my phone on the table and unlocked the screen. Ellegaard looked like he'd run from the booth if McGinnis didn't have him pinned in.

McGinnis hesitated for a moment—he sensed he was

trapped. "I met with Andrew Fine yesterday. I told him I had to return the donations he's made to Eleanor Nordahl's PAC. She's running for governor—I'm fund-raising for her. When Fine asked why, I explained that he's a person of interest in our investigation of Maggie Somerville's murder. He was incredulous, to say the least. But I explained that past allegations against him, his romantic relationship with Maggie, and his lack of an alibi put us in a difficult spot. We have no choice but to consider him as a possible suspect."

"Where did you have that meeting?"

McGinnis looked annoyed but answered, "In a car outside the Global Midtown Market. I chose the location out of courtesy to Fine. If word gets out that we're looking hard at him, it will hurt his reputation in the community. I'm all for that if he's guilty, but if he's not, I don't see the value in damaging a man's reputation."

McGinnis had come clean. Ellegaard looked relieved.

But I wasn't finished. "I hear you're helping Eleanor Nordahl in exchange for an appointment as Minnesota's top cop."

"Yes. That's how these things work. You don't have to turn over a rock to figure that out."

"And now with Maggie's murder, your name's in the paper, your press conferences are on the ten o'clock news. It's awfully convenient when you needed a little press."

McGinnis darkened. His chin tilted downward and he glared at me through the tops of his eyes. "You think I killed her?"

"Did you?"

"Okay," said Ellegaard, "this is getting ridiculous. Let's just stop—"

"I get it, Shapiro. You're just doing your job. And I

respect that. But I had nothing, and I mean absolutely nothing, to do with Maggie's murder. I'm sorry I didn't disclose my existing relationships with Fine and Somerville, but that's where it ends."

Ellegaard exhaled something between frustration and sadness. He liked his procedure and chain of command neat and tidy. This was not that.

"I believe you, Chief. And not just because you're such a nice guy, but yesterday I had a friend in the Minneapolis PD run a search and your DNA is not in the system."

"Shap," said Ellegaard.

"And right now, I still believe our killer's DNA is in the system."

McGinnis took a sip of coffee then set it back down. "I had asked both Robert Somerville and Andrew Fine for contributions. But after Maggie Somerville's murder, I un-asked them. Not because I was worried it would hurt Eleanor Nordahl or myself, but because it's a conflict of interest for the investigation."

I knew it didn't take forty-five minutes to ask Andrew Fine to keep his money to himself, but that didn't make him guilty of murder. McGinnis was just a man trying to wring the last out of his career, to climb a little higher for a better view before sitting down for the rest of his life.

"Anything else you want to get off your chest, Shapiro?" said McGinnis.

"No, Chief. I'm good."

"All right. Then let's get back to business," he said. "I got some new information early this morning. Our mysterious Ansley Bell is turning out to be more important than we might have guessed."

"I know," I said. "Ansley Bell is Maggie Somerville's biological daughter."

"What?" said Ellegaard. "Why didn't you tell me that?"

"I was about to when the chief walked in."

"You should have called or texted."

"All right, Mom. Next time I will."

"Gentlemen," said Chief McGinnis, "not now. Shapiro, I assume you made contact with Ms. Bell."

"Yes."

"And?"

"And what?"

"What's your impression?"

"My impression is that she's devastated. She met her mother after she turned eighteen. The two became best friends but had to keep their relationship a secret." Ellegaard asked why. I told them how Maggie and Omar Bihi fell in love when they were fifteen and how Maggie went to California to have a baby, while Omar returned to Somalia and traded in his kind demeanor for a Kalashnikov.

"And you believe her?" said McGinnis.

"She's half Somali. You wouldn't doubt that if you saw her."

"I'm sure there are plenty of half Somalis in this world. From what you say, Ansley Bell did all right for herself claiming she was Maggie's daughter. Four years at Carleton. Four years at the university med school. A furnished apartment. If she somehow learned about Maggie's baby, there's quite an incentive there for her to say she's someone she's not."

I nodded then said, "There is a resemblance, but you're right. So here." I reached into my pocket and removed a sealed bag containing a wadded up piece of tissue paper. "Inside this tissue are a few eyebrow hairs I took from a tweezer in Ansley's bathroom. The roots should be intact so you can run the DNA and see if you get a match."

"Nice work," said Ellegaard.

"Very," said McGinnis. "And assuming for a moment it's really her, do you believe Omar Bihi doesn't know she exists? That they're not in contact in any way?"

"Yeah, I do believe that."

"Because if she believes in the cause—"

"What cause?" said Ellegaard.

"Al-Shabaab," said McGinnis. "Or Daesh. If she's on their side, or at least sympathetic to their mission, eliminating Maggie Somerville is a quick way to help."

"I don't follow," I said.

"Maggie Somerville named Ansley Bell as a beneficiary on her life insurance policy, along with her other two children. Ansley, alone, is about to receive one million dollars."

I knew Ansley's grief was real. I believed what she'd told me. But I also knew I was not immune to her charms. "I highly doubt Ansley Bell is in contact with her father, but what you're suggesting is a possibility we can't ignore. I'll dig deeper into it."

McGinnis's smile was smack-worthy. "Good."

Ellegaard said, "At least Ansley being one of Maggie's beneficiaries explains the private detective outside her house."

"What private detective?" said McGinnis.

"The one Shap was harassing yesterday. He obviously works for the life insurance company, doing their due diligence."

"I got an e-mail this morning from the life insurance company," said McGinnis. "They said they'd hold off on their investigation until they read our report."

"Are you serious?" I said.

"Read it for yourself."

McGinnis searched his BlackBerry. "Where is it? Oh, crap. They gave us new phones. Everything's different now. You'll figure it out faster than I will." McGinnis handed me his phone.

I read the e-mail from the insurance company. I saw another interesting e-mail, as well. "All right—I got it. Mind if I forward this to myself?"

"Go ahead," said McGinnis.

I did. Then handed the BlackBerry back to McGinnis.

Ellegaard said, "If that guy hanging outside Ansley's house doesn't work for the insurance company, then who is he?"

I had a bad feeling about that creep. "Maybe we should go ask him."

12

Ellegaard and I jumped into his unmarked Ford and drove north on Highway 100. The sun glared off the highway, which was wet with the antifreeze. MnDOT sprays it when subzero temps invite black ice. Rush hour was over. Traffic was light. A few minutes later, we exited onto 394 and headed toward downtown, the skyline sharp against the clear blue sky except for a white, billowy steam cloud that rose from the power company.

I texted Ansley. *It's Nils. If you're home don't answer the door. Be there in ten.*

We pulled in front of Ansley's duplex at 9:02. The dick stood on the front stoop, pushing the doorbell labeled BELL. Ellegaard stopped the car. I got out and approached the front door.

I saw skinny-ass out of the car and in daylight for the first time. He stood about six feet tall and weighed a buck fifty. His face had turned pink from the cold. His tiny brown eyes seemed too close together and he had a soft, fleshy mouth like a trout. He wore a navy blue, full-length, quilted down coat. That's what they'd sell you at REI by the airport if you just got off a plane and insisted on buying the absolute warmest jacket they had. I looked back at his Camry and inspected the fuel door. It was the non-locking kind. Only rental cars have those because their drivers can never find the release. This guy wasn't local and couldn't have advertised it better with neon.

"Welcome to our humble land. How are you liking Minneapolis?"

"What makes you think I'm from out of town?"

"Because either you are, or you're wearing your wife's coat."

"Fuck you and who's that fuck?" he pointed to Ellegaard, who had parked and was walking toward me.

"He's police, and he wants to see your ID."

"I just showed my ID to police yesterday. This town is bullshit. Everyone's harassing me."

"Yeah? Most people like Minneapolis. It's cultured. It's friendly. Ever hear of Minnesota Nice?"

"Ah, Christ. It's a fucking Frigidaire here. What's wrong with you people? Why don't you move someplace warm?"

"Sir," said Ellegaard, "can I see some identification?"

The guy patted his long coat. "Ah, goddammit, there's two hundred pockets in this thing."

"Is a gun in one of them?"

"No. Too much trouble to travel with." He found his wallet in an inside pocket. "Here you go."

Ellegaard took the wallet and opened it up. "You're a long way from Los Angeles, Mr. Kelly."

"No, shit. It was a ninety-degree difference when I stepped off the plane."

My phone dinged with a text from Ansley. *Working at the university hospital. Is everything okay?*

I looked up at the pink face with chattering teeth. "You want to grab a cup of coffee with us?"

"Yeah, I do. But I'm on the job."

"She's not home. I just got a text from her."

"Show it to me."

"I can't. It says where she is."

"Ah, fuck. I should've stayed in California."

"Come on," said Ellegaard. "We're buying."

I returned Ansley's text. *Yes. Are you up for talking again?*

Working a twelve today. Off at 8:00, does 9:00 work?

Yes. See you then. If you haven't eaten, we'll grab dinner.

In the Spyhouse coffee shop on Broadway, while drinking a soy latte with four pumps of hazelnut syrup, Brian Kelly told us he was a private detective out of Van Nuys, California. He mostly tracked down missing persons and suspected adulterers. Undocumented aliens and the porn industry were his biggest customers.

According to Kelly, two weeks ago a couple wandered into his strip-mall storefront on Oxnard Street. They had adopted a baby twenty-six years ago. She left home when she was seventeen and hadn't come back. She e-mailed to let them know she was okay, but wouldn't tell them any more than that. They had no idea where she was.

The couple got knocked off their feet during the Great

Recession, lost their jobs and home, and had to move in with one of their elderly parents in Long Beach. Now, almost a decade later, they're solvent and can finally afford to hire a private investigator to look into their daughter's whereabouts. They told Kelly the girl's name was Bella Snyder.

Kelly explained he had an FBI connection and, after a few calls, the FBI agent traced Bella Snyder's e-mails to an IP address at Ansley Bell's duplex. Armed with that information, her DMV records, and her high school graduation photo, Brian Kelly got on a plane without first looking at the weather forecast in Minneapolis.

I told Kelly I could help him, but he'd have to give us another day, to which he replied, "What the hell am I going to do for a whole day when it's this cold out?"

"I don't know," I said. "Maybe you'd enjoy the Mall of America. It's a classy place for a classy guy like yourself."

Ellegaard drove me back to the Perkins parking lot. We sat in his car a moment and then he said, "Do you think Brian Kelly is working for who he says he's working for?"

"As opposed to?"

"Omar Bihi." Ellegaard ran a hand across his smooth chin. "Maybe he found out about Maggie getting pregnant."

"Omar Bihi and his friends must all be on FBI, CIA, and NSA watch lists. For any of them to sneak around lily white Edina without attracting attention is nearly impossible."

"Well," said Ellegaard, "let's just talk it out. If Omar somehow learned about Maggie having his baby, maybe he'd be upset enough to kill her."

"Like an honor killing?"

"Yeah. For the sake of argument. And let's say Omar recruited a white kid here. Or even an African-American. Someone who wouldn't draw much attention if they were making a delivery or cleaning windows or scooping leaves out of the gutters. Someone who gained Maggie's trust and either got access to a key or knew where one was hidden. It's a possibility."

"I guess anything's possible," I said, and watched a pair of elderly women, wearing long wool coats in navy and butterscotch, step off the Perkins walk and into the parking lot. They locked elbows and began their journey with baby steps across the frozen asphalt. "That theory of Omar being involved in Maggie's death, is that yours or McGinnis's?"

"It's mine," said Ellegaard. "What are you getting at?"

"I'm getting at McGinnis using this situation to his political advantage. All he'd have to do is imply that Maggie's death is linked to Al-Shabaab. Nothing would be more effective to galvanize voters than pointing a finger at real terrorists who've done real recruiting in our own backyard. Rural Minnesotans would drop their usual objections to electing a Minneapolitan for governor. But to do that he'd have to tell Ansley's story, and that could put her in actual danger. Because who knows what nut job is out there—an Islamic extremist or wannabe Rambo dying to take out the daughter of one."

"What McGinnis does is out of my control," said Ellegaard. "But you and I have to investigate Omar as a possibility. Find out who's been working at Maggie's house. Talk to neighbors. Recheck phone records and financial statements—just to see if there's any chance Omar learned he has a daughter."

"Fair enough. But if McGinnis makes any noise about Ansley . . ." I finished the sentence with my eyes.

"Edina PD hasn't even questioned her yet, Shap. Something happen last night? What's going on between you two?"

"Nothing," I said. "I just don't want to be in the business of spoon-feeding twenty-six-year-old women to fuckheads who want to hurt them."

Ellegaard said nothing. I got out of his car. The cold felt clean and honest. At least something did.

13

I stepped off the elevator and onto the eighth floor of the Midtown Global Market building. Andrew Fine waited for me with tousled hair and a crooked smile. He held his tobacco-vaporizing lightsaber in one hand and extended the other toward me.

"Little Shap, welcome. Thought I'd give you a tour on the way to my office."

"I'd love to see it," I said, and shook his hand.

"Ninety percent of the floor is what you see right now." He presented the room with a flourish of his upturned hand. The entire space was covered in wall-to-wall carpeting impregnated with a shebang of color that seemed to be composed of available pigments rather than a coordinated palette. Cubicles filled most of the floor, each with their own phone and workstation and operator, most of whom were Somali.

"Business seems good."

"Can't complain," said Andrew. "Can't complain. Let's go this way."

He led me around the perimeter of the workstations. I overheard bits and pieces of sales pitches, all spoken in flawless English. "Was everyone here born in Minnesota?"

"Pretty much," said Andrew. "A few came over when they were babies or toddlers, but the majority were born here and they're all U.S. citizens."

I didn't see a face over twenty-five years old. Most of the women wore hijab, which covered their hair, but not their faces, a facet of Ansley Bell shining in each of them.

"They're selling everything. Extended warranties, magazine subscriptions, cruises, you name it. There's a full kitchen, which helps with dietary restrictions. The Islamic dietary traditions are very close to kosher laws. Do you keep kosher, Little Shap?"

"Never have. You don't, do you?"

"I do. Absolutely."

Bunny's didn't have a kosher kitchen. I saw Fine eating there twenty-four hours ago. And he knew I saw him there. He was just telling himself a story about keeping kosher, telling himself a story he believed with such passion he couldn't see the glaring holes in it.

"Really?" I said. "You're not reform anymore?"

"Conservative. Been going to Beth El for a while now. And I go to Israel once a year."

"You didn't seem all that interested when we were kids."

"Everyone grows up. And after 9/11, we can't sit back, you know? Militant Islam's spreading everywhere—

especially in Europe—and we all know what a dangerous combination hate and Europe is.

"That's why I hire as many Muslims as I can. We can talk about democracy and capitalism until we're blue in the face, but if we provide opportunity and let them share in the American dream, well, there's no stronger olive branch than that. It's pretty tough to hate when you can take care of your family and send your kids to good schools, which leads to even more opportunity. Sometimes I think we should have taken a tenth of the money we spent in Iraq and Afghanistan and dropped it in cash and merchandise. We probably would have had more success, and success that could sustain itself."

We reached the corner of the big room and took a left. The floor opened up to our right. "Here's the prayer room. Since we're working three eight-hour shifts, it gets used five times a day. You'll notice it's on the east side of the building."

"This is a good thing you're doing here, Andrew."

"I hope so. Don't kid yourself—it's not a charity venture. I hire good people—they're smart and work hard. They make a good wage, and I make a good profit."

We turned down a short, wide corridor. In it, a desk with a receptionist. A young Somali woman with a cheerleader's smile and cover-girl eyes under a hijab of red and gold.

"Khandra, this is an old friend of my brother, Steve. Nils Shapiro, this is my assistant, Khandra Aden."

"Nice to meet you, Mr. Shapiro," said Khandra with a polished grace, like a spokesmodel or beauty-pageant contestant. She stood to shake my hand. She was tall, maybe five ten, and curvaceous under the most delicate jaw and long neck.

"Nice to meet you, Khandra. And you can call me Shap."

"Little Shap!" laughed Andrew. He put an arm on my shoulder and led me toward his office. "Hold my calls for a bit, Khandra. Thanks." We entered Fine's office and he shut the door. "Have a seat," he said, pointing to a chair made of black-and-white cowhide. "Notice the carpet. Same in here as it is out there. It sends a subtle but powerful message. We're all in it together. Know what I'm saying?"

I knew what he was saying, and it had little to do with what he was doing. But I played along. "Yeah," I said. "It does send a powerful message."

"Motivation is everything, right? I mean we're all, to some degree, a bundle of unrealized potential. But the closer we get to reaching that potential, the more worthwhile life becomes. For everyone."

"I didn't realize you're an industrial psychologist."

"School of hard knocks, man. No better way to learn." Andrew sat behind his desk, rocked back in his chair, and sighed.

"So, what did you want to talk to me about?"

"Right to business. I like that, Little Shap." He twisted something on his lightsaber and took a hit of vapor, held it a few seconds, then exhaled it. "I know you're working on the Maggie Somerville murder."

"You do?"

"Minneapolis is the biggest small town in the country."

"That it is."

"And I'm sure you know I was kind of dating Maggie."

"Kind of?"

"Who's that comedian who had that great fucking line? The one that goes like, 'I don't have a girlfriend, but I know a girl who'd be really mad if she heard me say that.' "

"Mitch Hedberg."

"That's his name?"

"Yeah."

"Man, I gotta go see that guy sometime."

"Sorry to tell you. He's dead."

"Really? That sucks." Fine took another hit off his lightsaber. "Drugs?"

"Yep."

"Could've been me."

Fine got lost in himself and disappeared. I guess he went into the place narcissists go, the place that allows them to hear someone died and somehow make it about themselves.

"So," I said, "Maggie thought you guys were dating, but you thought something else?"

"You're single, right?"

"I am."

"You know when two people start dating and one person is ready to lock it down before the other person?"

"That's what happens most of the time."

"Yeah, well, three dates and Maggie was ready to get married."

"Not you, though?"

"Not anyone who's sane. And even if I wasn't, legally, I still am married. Separated six years, but we haven't finalized the divorce."

"Why's that?"

"It ain't love, that's for sure."

"Money?"

"She wants too much. It's fucked up. We only communicate through lawyers. Lynn Diamond. Do you know her?"

"I know who she is."

"But even if I wasn't still legally married, I never fel
for Maggie the way she fell for me."

"But you stayed in the relationship."

"More or less, yeah. Sweet woman. And physically, we
had something crazy. But long-term, I didn't see it."

"Did you tell her that?"

"No. That would have ended it. And it was one of
those things that I thought might end up going somewhere. Like, I was open-minded about it. Didn't think it
would last, but you never know."

"So are you worried about the investigation? Is that
why you wanted to see me?"

"I'm not worried about anything serious. I didn't kill
her, and I have no idea who did. Frankly, it's weird anyone would want to kill Maggie. She was kind of like a
lamb, you know."

"Then what's your concern?"

He took another hit of vapor and blew it toward the
ceiling. "How much can the cops poke into my private
life?"

"I'm not a lawyer, Andrew. I'm a private detective."

"I know, but you know cops. You know how these
things go. And I trust you to be honest with me. I'm paying you for your time, by the way. So feel free to lay it all
out there."

I bit my lower lip to look like I was giving his question serious thought, but I was stalling to figure out how
to handle the moment. Robert Somerville was easy. We
connected—we could've been friends in real life—so I
just exploited that by telling him to distrust Edina PD
and imply he could trust me instead. But Andrew Fine
was different. We weren't friends, would never be friends,

although he probably didn't reciprocate the animosity I felt toward him because that would have required him to give me some thought.

"Are you afraid of what the police will find?"

"I'm not afraid, but I'm not crazy about it either. I got a reputation in the business community and at Beth El. I also got a weakness for beautiful women. The police go poking around, they'll hear some unflattering stories about me. And if they find who killed Maggie, but the defense's strategy is to point a finger at me, some not-cool shit's going to hit the fan."

"Hookers?"

"No. Never. Well . . ." He took another hit off the lightsaber. "Yeah, but not for a while. I got a few women who are legit employees here and at other businesses. But I'm also involved with them socially. I shouldn't do it, I know, but fuck, you know what? I love the power in the relationship."

"Of the employer-employee relationship?"

"I know it's wrong, but there's something old-world about it. Everything's defined on one level and muddy on another level. Makes things interesting."

"That's what power's all about."

"Little Shap the philosopher. I like it."

"Here's the thing, Andrew. The police aren't your biggest concern. They'll look into your background. It's nothing personal, it's just because you're the boyfriend. Or at least from Maggie's point of view, you were her boyfriend. They'll talk to Maggie's friends, see what she said about you. They'll talk to her family, see if they know anything. It's all about determining the state of your relationship. Did you guys fight? Stuff like that. And again, it's not personal. They'll do the same with

Robert Somerville. He's the ex-husband. Statistically chances are one of you two killed her. So that's where they start."

"The low-hanging fruit."

"Exactly. Do you know anyone over at Edina PD?"

"Just the cops at the bottom of the hill on 50th who write me a ticket or two each year."

No mention of Chief McGinnis. There it was again, the lie that was so easy for me to discover. Talk about low-hanging fruit. "Well, my advice is to cooperate with them. You didn't kill Maggie, so you have nothing to worry about. If some less-than-pleasant details come out about your personal life, then they do, but that won't hurt you in the long run. But if you actively try to prevent those unpleasant details from coming out, it'll look like you're trying to cover up something. And the cops will assume it's murder. Then you will have a big problem."

"Thanks, Little Shap. Good advice. I appreciate it." He took another hit off his lightsaber then exhaled a cloud of vapor into the air. "You coming to the party Thursday night?"

"Yeah. If I'm still invited."

"Of course."

"Kind of had to invite me when you invited the nurses."

"Yeah, I guess I did. You, uh, talk to either of them?"

"Nah. Figured you might have your eye on one of 'em."

"Kind of like that blonde."

"I kind of like the brunette."

"That one's got some curves."

"I fell for her eyes."

"Yeah, right you did." He looked at his watch. "Whoa, hey. I got to run. I'll see you Thursday night."

I handed him my card. "Call me if you have any more

questions." I had one foot out the door when I stopped and turned back to him. "You mentioned you have this business and others. What are they?"

"I back a couple of restaurants and I own a commercial real-estate venture."

"Buildings?"

"An office park in West Bloomington."

"Hyland Lakes?"

"That's the one."

"Stevey's your property manager then. I just ran into him the other day."

"Yeah. I'm not there much, so it's nice having family run the place."

"I bet," I said. "See you Thursday."

I called Ellegaard from the car. "The Hyland Lakes office park on 494 and 100—the one that's about five buildings with a duck pond in the middle—compare their vacuum-bag dust with the dust found in Maggie Somerville's house."

"What's the connection?"

"Andrew Fine owns the whole thing. That's a lot of square footage with a lot of carpet that needs a lot of vacuuming."

"On it," said Ellegaard.

I pulled out of the parking lot and onto Lake Street. I'd driven a couple of blocks west when I noticed a gray Buick three cars back. A mile later, it was still there. I took a left on East Calhoun Parkway. So did the Buick.

14

Fifteen minutes later, I turned onto Bruce Place, stopped and watched my rearview mirror. The Buick passed without turning. I continued, parked in front of Beth Lindquist's house and got out of the Volvo. The Lindquists' garage door was open. Perry stacked paper bags of leaves against the back wall. He wore khakis and an old pea-coat and a pair of worn black Weejuns—the left one was missing its tassel.

"Need a hand?" I said as I walked up the driveway.

"No, I'm just about done. But thanks. It's Nils, right?"

"Yes. Nice to see you again, Perry."

"I tell you, the weather's getting stranger every year. Leaves weren't done dropping until mid-November, but they stop picking up November first. Can't burn 'em anymore, so we got to store 'em until they start picking up again in the spring. Now we're in a deep freeze, so I need to make room in the garage for the cars. And apparently, it's all because I don't drive a Prius."

I chuckled at his joke. It's part of the job. Just like on a first date. "You come home for lunch every day?"

"Every day I'm in town."

"That's a good deal."

"Sure is. Saves money. Get to see Beth. Helps make up for the times I was away."

"Yeah, I wouldn't mind being away this time of year."

"I'd rather spend January here than in Afghanistan. None too warm there either, and here you don't have to wear Kevlar every time you leave the house."

"I didn't know you're military."

"Was for twenty years. But the last ten I've worked as a private contractor for DBC Systems."

"Oh, I've seen that place. Off 77th?"

"That's us. I work on the IT side, finding what the bad guys thought they'd hid on their hard drives. I thought business would have wound down by now but it's booming more than ever. I take no pleasure in that." He placed both hands into the open top of a leaf bag and pressed down. The dry leaves inside crackled as they compressed. He removed his hands and folded the top of the bag then rolled it down. "Are you here to see Beth again?"

"Yeah. Just got a quick question."

"Come on in."

"Thank you." I followed Perry into the house from the garage. We found Beth in the kitchen, removing a tea bag from a canister the label maker had labeled TEA. Unlike yesterday, she was dressed. A wool skirt over stockings and a heavy wool sweater.

"Look who I found," said Perry.

Beth turned around—she seemed disappointed to see me. "Oh, hello," she said. "More questions?"

"Just one. Is now a good time?"

"Sure," she said.

"Have you've seen any workers at Maggie Somerville's lately?"

"What kind of workers?"

"Landscapers. Window washers. Gutter cleaners. Maybe Maggie was having work done inside."

"Well, there's her maid, Marsha Brady."

"Marsha Brady?"

"I know. That's her real name. We laughed so much over that. Whenever Maggie couldn't find something because the maid had put it in the wrong place, we'd say, 'Marsha, Marsha, Marsha!' "

"Funny to them," said Perry. "After you hear it a few thousand times, it's not so funny anymore. Sandwich, Nils? I'm making roast beef today."

"No, I'm good. Thanks, Perry."

"Suit yourself." He turned, but stopped. "Nils, you don't live in the neighborhood, do you?"

"Kind of. I'm just on the Minneapolis side."

"Too bad. We could have used your 'no' vote on the big sidewalk issue."

"You don't like sidewalks?"

"They'd make our lawns smaller. I like 'em the way they are." He wandered back into the kitchen.

"So Beth, is there anyone else you can think of? People working in Maggie's yard?"

"Maggie did her own yard."

"Even that huge backyard?"

"She was determined. She did have people come to clean the gutters and the windows once a year. She didn't have any work done inside since she and Robert split up. Oh, except for some painting. Robert liked colorful walls. Maggie liked neutral, so she had a few rooms repainted."

"Did you see any East Africans working at Maggie's?"

"You mean Somalis?"

"Yes."

"No. I only see them in Uptown or at the university or working at Target. I think they're Somalis anyway. You know, the women with the head scarves."

"That's them."

"They have beautiful features," said Beth. "Such pretty faces."

"But none working at Maggie's?"

"No. I know the painter. I've used him for years. A young woman cleans the gutters and washes the windows. She's an artist and pays the bills with odd jobs. I grew up with her mother. Sweet girl, but she has a lot of piercings and tattoos. Not the mother, the girl. I don't know why kids do that—it's not attractive."

"And that's it? No one who might have stuck out in some way?"

"No. I would remember. Perry and I kind of kept a lookout after Robert left. It's a safe neighborhood, but still, Maggie being a single woman and all . . ." The tears came. Beth sat and let her head hang as her shoulders shook.

"I'm sorry, Beth. I appreciate your taking the time."

She didn't look up, and I left.

Even inside the car, the cold bit hard so I pulled up my hood. I turned right on 50th and then left on Maple Road. It wasn't the most direct route to get to Robert Somerville's, but Maple Road had no cross streets. If the gray Buick wanted to tail me, it had no option for turning off. I saw it in my rearview a couple hundred feet back.

I took a left on Townes Road and snaked my way up to Sunnyside. At the stop sign at Grimes, Robert Somerville stopped on the other side, facing me in his electric RAV4. He had no way of recognizing me with my hood up, so when he turned right onto Sunnyside, I followed him. He didn't go far. A few turns and a few blocks later, he parked in the U.S. Bank parking lot near 50th and Halifax, got out of his car, and entered the bank.

I'm not a big fan of disguises. Sometimes they work. Sometimes they don't. And when they don't, it's embarrassing. Tough to say a casual hello when you're wearing a fake beard. But a baseball hat can do wonders. So can a pair of sunglasses. And a thick parka can hide your natural posture. Sunglasses draw more attention than no sunglasses when you're in a bank, but I grabbed a navy baseball cap from my backseat that I kept for just such an occasion. I dug my earphones out of the center console, plugged them into my phone, got out of the car, and started toward the bank, hoping it was busy inside.

It wasn't. I entered and saw no line for the tellers. No one filling out deposit slips. Just Robert Somerville sitting with a loan officer in the private banking area. And a guard. I opened the Ear Spy app on my phone. Anyone watching would think I was listening to music, but I was listening to the bank's amplified ambience, including Robert Somerville's conversation with the loan officer. I walked up to a teller and played the idiot.

"Hi," I said. "How do I apply for a car loan?"

"Let me get you a form," said the teller. She was young and pale and round-faced. "You can fill the form out over there, and then someone will be with you after that."

"Thank you," I said. "North Dakota?"

"Yes! How did you know?"

"Just heard a little something in your voice. Thanks for the form."

"You're welcome!"

Truth was, I guessed she was from North Dakota because she seemed too goddamn happy to be working in a bank. I took the form to the counter that held deposit and withdrawal slips, which they still had in case anyone wanted to pretend they were banking in 1978. I kept the earbuds in my ears, faced Robert Somerville's back, and pretended to fill out my form.

". . . come on, Jerry. I've been doing business with this bank for fifteen years."

"I'm sorry, Robert. The bank just needs to see a return on your bison business before we can lend any more money."

"I can't get that return until spring. The animals' metabolisms have slowed because of the cold, which means less manure, and what manure there is we can't get out of the fields when the snow's this deep. If I can't get the new barn built . . ."

I lost the conversation when two men entered, bellowing away about the importance of keeping up your golf swing during winter. Robert Somerville stood and shook the loan officer's hand. I turned and walked toward the exit.

I left my car in the bank parking lot, crossed 50th, and walked east toward France Avenue, passing the movie theater and a clothing boutique and a cosmetics bar, whatever the hell that is. I turned right at Sur La Table after catching a bad case of Le Creuset envy from the window display, then continued half a block south to the Edina Grill, an American bistro featuring local favorites like wild-rice soup and Fulton beer. I found a spot at the bar and ordered a soda with bitters, to honor Ellegaard, and a bison burger, to mock Robert Somerville.

Thirty seconds later, a dark-skinned black man wearing rimless sunglasses, a blue suit, white shirt, and silver tie sat next to me.

"How you doing today?" he said.

"Not too bad. How about yourself?"

"I've been warmer, I'll tell you that much. Happy to be inside the Edina Grill."

He pronounced *Eh-deena*. Common mistake for an out-of-stater. I said, "Good day for lobster bisque. That and a cup of coffee will bring you back to life."

"Thanks for the suggestion," he said, "I appreciate it."

"If you don't mind another suggestion, next time you're walking around in weather like this, leave the five-hundred-dollar leather-soled shoes at home."

"You don't like my shoes?"

"I like your shoes. It's just the sidewalks and streets are full of salt—they'll eat those shoes alive."

"How do you know I've been walking around? Maybe I parked out front."

"If you'd done that, those Transitions lenses you're wearing would be warm enough to transition back to clear. But when they get cold, it takes 'em forever to turn back."

He took off his glasses and looked at the lenses. "Damn, I thought it was dark in here." He put his glasses back on and studied the menu for a few seconds, then flipped it over. "I don't see the soups."

"Check under FBI Special Agent specials."

He laughed. The game had ended before it started.

"Special Agent Delvin Peterson." He extended his right hand.

I shook it. "Nils Shapiro, private investigator. And just so you know, Delvin, the town you're in is pronounced *Ee-dinah*, not *Eh-deena*. They should have taught you that before you left D.C."

"I'll be sure to mention it in my Yelp review of the Hoover Building."

"And another thing, Special Agent Peterson, I do not put out on a first date."

"Then I'm not buying you lunch."

"If you want to start our relationship that way, be my guest."

"You've been keeping some interesting company the last few days, Nils Shapiro."

"Hey, why didn't you guys grab me off the street and throw me into the back of a Town Car and talk tough to me. That's on my bucket list."

"Smartphones and YouTube, baby. Those two things wrecked all our fun. Now we have to behave all civilized and pretend we want to be pals with every private detective who's fucking up our investigation."

"That last part, that's the kind of talk I was hoping to hear. Keep going."

"We've been working around the clock to keep U.S. citizens from going overseas to fight for jihadists."

"As you should."

"Problem is, you're nosing around one of our CIs. The more noise you make, the less confidential the informant will be."

"I don't know what you're talking about."

"I know you don't. That's the confidential part."

The bartender approached Delvin. "You know what you'd like, sir?"

"Lobster bisque and a cup of coffee, please."

"Coming right up." The bartender took Delvin's menu and walked to the other end of the bar and punched the order into the register.

"I was kidding about the lobster bisque," I said. "It's shit."

Delvin chuckled again. "You should work for us. We could use some laughs."

"I don't like big organizations."

"Why not? A chance for advancement. Good benefits."

"Travel to beautiful places like Minnesota in January. The thing with big organizations, the people inside them seem to care more about the organization rather than the ideals on which it was founded."

"Someone's thought this through."

"I got a lot of free time on my hands."

"We'd like you to have even more."

"What specifically do you want me to do? Or not do?"

"I can't tell you exactly, other than stop working the case you're on."

"Do you know who I'm working for?"

"Edina PD."

"They told you?"

"We're the FBI. No one needs to tell us anything."

"Golly, Special Agent Delvin. I have a feeling you're BFFs with someone who listens in on other people's phone calls." Agent Delvin Peterson's glasses had warmed enough to lose their tint. I could see the impatience in his eyes. I said, "Listen. I'm working on a local murder. You're working on national security. Both noble endeavors and we both want each other to succeed. So your big organization has to be more forthcoming with me, tell me what part of your investigation I'm fucking up, then I'll accommodate you in any way I can."

Our food came at the same time. Agent Peterson sipped a spoonful of lobster bisque. "This is delicious," he said. "I knew you wouldn't steer me wrong."

The bartender put my check in a glass and said, "No rush. Take your time."

Agent Peterson said, "I got this." He grabbed the check. Our date had just begun.

15

The FBI building in Minneapolis isn't in Minneapolis. It's in Brooklyn Center, a northern suburb that bears no resemblance to Brooklyn. The building looks like it was constructed yesterday, a five-story box sided in faux brick. The grounds consist of a simple, flat lawn studded with young, skinny trees, staked so they don't blow over, their trunks taped so rabbits don't eat their thin bark. Plenty of windows overlook freeways 94, 100, and 694 twisting into one another like an asphalt pretzel.

I parked the Volvo, got out, and walked toward the heavy black gate. Agent Peterson and another agent got out of a nearby car to greet me.

Peterson spoke first. "Nils, this is Special Agent Don Olson." FBI Agent Don Olson stood a little shy of six feet, had dull, pasty skin, lackluster brown hair, gray eyes, thin lips bordering a tiny mouth, and no chin whatsoever—a face so forgettable it was impossible to forget.

"I recognize Agent Olson," I said, "from the Duluth case a couple of years ago."

"I thought you might," said Olson. "That's why I hung back during our surveillance."

He hung back like a trophy wife on a plastic surgeon. But I saw no upside in saying it out loud.

They led me inside and past the security desk. The whole place felt more corporate than federal law enforcement. We got in the elevator and rode up to the fifth floor, where the view of the ugly freeways was spectacular.

We sat in a conference room and were joined by a woman who introduced herself as Special Agent in Charge Colleen Milton. She was about my height, had shoulder-length brown hair, a wiry body, and a drawn face. Another fucking runner. She probably ran more marathons a year than she has functioning toenails. We sat down at a conference table made of fake woodgrain. No one offered me a hot beverage, and I was none too happy about it.

"We understand you're investigating Andrew Fine," said Colleen Milton.

"He's a person of interest in an ongoing murder investigation. But you know that already."

"We'd like you to back off him," said Peterson.

"Even if he killed Maggie Somerville?"

"There's no statute of limitations on murder," said Milton. "If he's guilty, Edina PD can arrest him in six months or a year. But not now. Fine's given us complete access to his call center, which employs a significant number of Somali immigrants."

"Actually, almost all of them were born here," I said. "So they're Americans—not Somali immigrants."

"They're of Somali descent," said Milton. "We're monitoring the activity of eleven of Fine's employees—it's vital that we continue that operation. But if you're snooping around the call center or if Fine gets arrested, our operation is blown."

"Since I'm sitting here alone, I assume you've had this conversation with Edina PD."

"We have," said Agent No Chin.

"I wonder why they didn't share that with me."

"We asked them not to," said Milton. "We thought it'd be better if you heard it directly from us."

"Does all of Edina PD know or just McGinnis?"

"We told McGinnis. We don't know what he's communicated within his department."

"Huh. So that's it? Stay away from the call center and don't get Andrew Fine arrested?"

"That's it," said Milton. "Think you can do that?"

"I have one question."

"What is it?"

"Are you going to reimburse me for my gas and time to come out here? Because Delvin could have told me that at the Edina Grill."

"Charge it to Edina PD," said Milton. "We're not reimbursing you for anything. Any other questions?"

"Yeah. Is the coffeemaker broken, or am I not cleared to drink coffee?"

"Good-bye, Mr. Shapiro."

I drove back down Highway 100, exited on 50th, and went straight to the Edina police station. It had an architectural exterior of limestone and copper, but the inside felt as bland and as corporate as the FBI building. I asked for Ellegaard at the front desk. He came out and we took a walk over to the city-hall side of the building. We found an empty conference room usually reserved for the power brokers of the Edina Soccer Association and the Fourth of July Parade Committee.

I told Ellegaard about my meeting with the FBI.

"McGinnis hasn't said anything to me about backing off Fine," said Ellegaard.

"It would make sense that McGinnis brought me in to take the heat for tailing Fine. But to do that, he would have had to know Fine would be a suspect and cooperating with the FBI. McGinnis asked for a PI to join the investigation an hour after Maggie Somerville's body was discovered. He couldn't have known all that then."

"Why not?" said Ellegaard. "Maybe he has known Fine was cooperating with the FBI for a while."

"Maybe. The surveillance operation going on at Fine's call center is probably more than FBI. It's got to be the whole Joint Terrorism Task Force. That includes NSA, CIA, DEA, ATF, State Patrol, and Minneapolis police. But because Fine is an Edina resident, and, in theory, sticking his neck out, McGinnis may be involved, too."

"The thing I don't get," said Ellegaard, "is why McGinnis withheld that from me."

"Because if the call-center operation nets any recruiters or, even better, terrorists, McGinnis would have Edina's share of the spotlight to himself." I stood and walked over to the windows overlooking Perkins and, farther to the left, the Edina Country Club. There was a skating rink on the tennis courts and cross-country ski tracks crisscrossing the golf course. "I thought the FBI was going to tell me I was interfering with their surveillance of Ansley Bell. Or maybe something about Robert Somerville's threatening letter to Bush. Backing off of Andrew Fine was the last thing I expected."

"You going to Fine's party Thursday night?"

"He invited me. It'd be kind of rude not to, don't you think?"

"I think I'll follow you. Make sure your new friends in Brooklyn Center aren't trying to tag along."

"I've never seen you like this, Ellie."

"Like what?"

"Coloring outside the lines."

"Yeah, I don't know, Shap. Maybe I'm outgrowing my little suburban police department."

16

At 9:00 P.M., I texted Ansley Bell from in front of her place. A minute later, she met me at the downstairs door. She had just stepped out of the shower and into a pair of ripped jeans and a pale yellow corduroy blouse. She'd left the top three buttons unfastened—her brown skin lay molten in the vee of her neckline. I followed her up the stairs. She smelled like orange blossoms.

Ansley said she was exhausted from her long day at the hospital and had neither the energy nor the desire to brave the cold. We ordered Thai off a well-worn take-out menu. Then she asked if I'd get a fire going. I felt grateful for a simple and achievable task.

I wadded up a few sheets of old newspaper, placed them on the grate, and wondered why a woman would smell like orange blossoms at nine P.M. when she intended to stay in for the night. Did Ansley Bell consider this some sort of date? I built a fort of kindling over the newspaper and considered alternative explanations. Maybe she was just a person who liked to wear a scent at home because she wasn't allowed to at the hospital. Maybe it wasn't a scent at all—maybe it was her fabric softener. Maybe it wasn't even orange blossoms. She dabbed on a bit of citronella because she's afraid of mosquitos. In January. When it's twenty below zero. Or maybe my first instinct was right. As far as I knew, I was the first and only person Ansley Bell had confided in, the only person to know that Maggie Somerville was her mother. It would make sense if that made me more attractive than I would have been otherwise. Who else could she share herself with? Her whole self? No one.

For the first time since I'd been divorced, I felt nervous about being alone with a woman. Compartmentalizing business and personal had never been a problem, but it had never been tested, either. Assertive twentysomethings had been tested, and so far, I had declined them all. Not because I think I'm too mature for them, but because I can't stomach someone wanting to build a life. After living thirty-eight years, I've concluded life is something to be salvaged, not built.

"I'm going to pour myself a glass of wine," she said. "Can I get you anything? A beer?"

"Yes, please. Whatever you have."

She smiled and pivoted on one stocking-toed foot. Who purposely smells like orange blossoms if they're not even going to wear shoes?

I built an airy grid of small birch logs over the burning kindling. When Ansley returned, a small blaze flickered light throughout the room. She handed me a Stella Artois.

"Do you want a glass?"

"How little you must think of me to even ask that question."

She laughed. I took the beer and rose from the hearth, my eyes passing her ripped jeans with their little windows to the softness beneath. When I stood upright, she hugged me. I held her and said nothing. She had at least two inches on me—probably three—I felt her stoop to bury her head into my shoulder. It was a junior high slow dance with neither chaperones nor corners of comrades awaiting our return. After a long minute, she said, "Sorry."

"Don't be."

"It was not an easy day."

"I bet."

"Come on, let's sit."

I found my same spot from the night before. Ansley took the corner of the sectional rather than the far end.

"The funeral is on Thursday," I said. "I think you should be there."

She nodded.

"Has anyone from an insurance company contacted you?"

"No. Why?"

"Maggie named you as one of the beneficiaries of her life insurance policy. You have some money coming your way."

"She shouldn't have done that. She has young kids."

"Maggie took care of them, too. Each of you is getting a million dollars."

Ansley looked almost mad. "What?"

"I found out about it this morning."

"I don't want the money. I want my mother back."

"I wish you had that choice." Ansley Bell smiled the saddest smile. "Also, the private detective who's been wanting to talk to you isn't from the insurance company. Your parents hired him to find you."

"Dammit," she said.

"I can get rid of the PI if you want, but your parents know you're here. The only way to avoid them is to take off."

"That's impossible," said Ansley. "I have my second round of boards soon. I guess I'll just have to deal with them. I'm sure they'll be happy to hear Maggie's dead."

"I doubt that."

"They were always paranoid that I'd leave and not come back."

Apparently, they should have been. "Maybe 'fearful' is a better word."

"It probably is, yeah."

We talked some more and then the food came. I opened my wallet but Ansley said, "No. I'm a millionaire now. Remember?"

"At least take a twenty."

"Hold on to it. You can get the next one." *So there'd be a next one?* She set the food on the coffee table then went into the kitchen. I got up and put another log on the fire then poked at it with the poker to feel a sense of accomplishment. Ansley returned with a tray of plates, napkins, silverware, a bottle of chardonnay, two wine glasses, and a bottle of Sierra Nevada.

I returned from the fire and sat next to her. She said, "The fire's beautiful. Thank you."

"Good wood."

She smiled and refilled her wine glass. "Wine or beer with your red curry?"

"What year is the wine?"

"A very good year, Mr. Shapiro. So good that grapes grew. What else do you want to know?"

"Is that the original bottle or did you refill it with a box of wine from the back of the fridge?"

She almost laughed as she handed me a glass of chardonnay so full I had to handle it like nitroglycerin to avoid spilling. She raised her glass, "To meeting new people and telling old secrets."

"Hear, hear," I said. We touched glasses. Wine sloshed over the edges then we drank and assaulted the paper boxes of spring rolls, curry, pad thai, and brown rice.

"Tell me a secret, Mr. Shapiro."

"The only secrets I keep are work related. And nothing big, just white lies and half-truths. As far as my personal life goes, I'm an open book."

"No one's an open book."

"Try me. Ask me anything you want."

"Don't tempt me."

"Jesus, this is spicy. I hate to go all Minnesotan on you, but wow."

"Sorry," she said. "I asked for two out of four on the spice meter and it's different every time. Guess the spicy chef is working tonight."

"I like it. I just wasn't ready for it."

She said. "You're not married, are you?"

"No."

"I bet you don't have a girlfriend, either."

"So there's a spicy chef and a not-spicy chef?"

"No, no, no, Nils. Answer the question. Do you have a girlfriend?"

"I do not."

"You want to know what I thought when we talked last night?"

"I don't want to burden you with carrying another secret, so you'd better tell me." I lifted my wine glass—it was nearly empty. That's the problem with drinking whiskey—it makes wine go down like water. The conversation, the spicy chef, Ansley Bell's caramel eyes dancing in the firelight, and my wine was gone. She refilled my glass before I could set it back down.

"I thought that Nils Shapiro is an inside-out human being. How rare a thing that is. It must cause him so much pain."

"That's a lot to think the first time you meet someone. Especially after they just told you your mother passed away."

"You're unprotected because you're not bonded with someone else. That's the way it is for inside-out people. They need someone else for stability, just like an oxygen atom needs another oxygen atom. They're more stable when they're in a pair."

"Where'd you learn about this inside-out personality type? I didn't see that quiz on my Facebook feed."

She placed her left hand on my right knee. "Maggie was an inside-out person. It was hard for her to be on her own."

"I think maybe you've misread me."

"Oh, sweetie. Your pain is front and center."

I put my fork down and took another sip of wine. If I were the open book I said I was, I would have told Ansley Bell she was substituting me for Maggie or falling for me because she could be honest with me, or both, or maybe those two were the same thing. Either way, Maggie Somerville's death had emotionally field gutted Ansley, and I was there to fill the cavity. Just there. Nothing more. Nothing special.

But I did not tell her that.

I kissed her. Slow and soft and silent, like a scout parachuting down behind enemy lines. I pulled back. Ansley Bell's eyes were shut and her head didn't move. She said, "Solve any mysteries?"

"No, but you paid for dinner so I figured I owed you that much."

"That a boy." She laughed something soft and sad.

I wanted to apologize but had made that mistake enough times to know it was a bad idea. And I wasn't all that sorry. Neither was she. The kiss was unprofessional, but these things happen. If they didn't, if I never bent the rules, I'd work for one of the big security companies or legal firms or insurance companies. Someplace with a steady paycheck and benefits and a Secret Santa party come December.

She said, "I don't want to be alone tonight."

I shoved a forkful of curry and rice into my mouth so I didn't have to respond. Maggie Somerville died peacefully thanks to wine and Rohypnol. That led Ellegaard to think maybe a woman killed her. Ansley Bell was educated in pharmacology and was about to receive a life insurance benefit of a million dollars.

I said, "I didn't bring a toothbrush."

Ansley Bell put a hand on my shoulder and looked me directly in the eye. "Any other logistical problems?"

After dinner, we went into the bedroom and lay on her bed fully clothed, propped onto our sides to face each other. She said, "Where do you come from, Mr. Shapiro?"

"How far back would you like me to go?"

"Far. As far as you know. Blood lineage fascinates me."

"Okay. I'll give you the highlights, or lowlights, depending on how you look at it." She took my hand—I kept talking. "My great grandfather, Chaim Shapiro, emigrated from Germany to the United States and settled in St. Paul, Minnesota, where he ran a liquor store until the Volstead Act took it away. He accepted a low-level office job with his older brother, who ran a print shop. The job and Chaim ended a few years later when he stepped into an open elevator shaft and fell five stories to his death. No one knows if he stepped into the elevator shaft deliberately, or if it was an accident."

"So far, kind of sad."

"Chaim's son, my grandfather, Victor Shapiro, was fourteen years old when Chaim died. He moved to Michigan's Upper Peninsula and joined a cousin running Canadian whiskey across Lake Superior, where it was then trucked in hollowed-out logs to the Twin Cities, Detroit, and Chicago. Victor dabbled in Chicago's gangland, served time in jail, then returned to the small town of Marenisco on the western side of the U.P., where he, at age forty, married for the first time."

Ansley said, "You have a jailbird in your blood. I like that."

"My grandparents owned a little cabin and pond out of town. My grandfather let a lumberjack live in the cabin, a Swedish immigrant named Nils Bjornson. When he wasn't clearing forest, Nils hunted deer and trapped beaver and fished. My grandfather spent a lot of time with Nils and they formed a close friendship based on their mutual love of guns, whiskey, and the burlesque houses in nearby Hurley, Wisconsin.

"Those interests made my grandfather a natural for politics. He was elected first as mayor of Marenisco, then to the Gogebic County Board of Supervisors, and then to the Michigan State Senate. His criminal past never seemed to be an issue. My grandfather was so busy politicking that by the time my father turned ten—"

"What was his name?"

"Harry. Short for Harold. Anyway, by the time Harry turned ten, Nils Bjornson was the person who had taught him to fish and hunt and navigate the forests along the south shore of Lake Superior."

"So your father became the first Jewish lumberjack?"

"He might have, but one winter day, when he was eleven, he stood on an ice shelf while fishing the Black River."

Ansley said, "What's an ice shelf?"

"When a river freezes along the edge but not in the middle, the frozen part is called an ice shelf."

"Got it. Okay. Keep going."

"Ice shelves are fickle bastards, and the one my father stood on collapsed and he fell into the icy river."

"I know he lived," said Ansley, "because he was only eleven. He couldn't have conceived you yet."

"You doctors are hard to tell stories to."

She smiled and said, "So what happened?"

"Well, my father's ice shelf collapsed in Nils Bjornson's favorite section of the Black River. Nils probably showed him the spot, which explains the extraordinary good fortune that Nils Bjornson himself was sitting high in a deer stand a hundred feet away with a Browning bolt-action rifle and a flask of rye, one eye out for deer and the other admiring how well my father had learned to fish. The worm has to drift naturally with the current. If the line drags, the fish won't bite. Nils was full of pride watching my father's draggles drift when Harry tumbled into the water.

"Nils climbed out of the deer stand and caught up with my father, but not until the river had carried Harry downstream and he had gone over a small falls and banged off the granite rock below and then rolled unconscious, facedown, into a shallow pool. He would have died within minutes if Nils Bjornson hadn't lifted him from that pool, carried him ashore, and started a fire with twigs and branches and the box of wax-covered matches that any good steward of the North Woods carries.

"As the fire grew, Nils stripped off my father's wet clothes and wrapped him in a wool army blanket he kept in the stand. My father thawed and regained consciousness and never stepped onto an ice shelf again.

"Twelve years later, on the very day my parents got married, Nils Bjornson died of a massive stroke. I was born within a year and named after the man who saved my father's life. The end."

"I like that story," said Ansley. "I like that story a lot."

Then Ansley told me more about Maggie. Just last week they'd been talking about when Ansley should meet her younger siblings. They decided it would be when Ansley returned from her residency. No sense meeting them then disappearing out of their lives right away. Now, she didn't know when she would meet them.

Ansley cried. I held her as she fell asleep with her head on my chest. I lay awake and listened to the sounds you hear the first night in a new place—the refrigerator's hum, the radiators' moans and clangs, footsteps in the unit below, and the hardwood floor's pops and creaks in the dry heat. I stared at Ansley's ceiling knowing sleep wouldn't come. Nothing physical happened between us. Not because of my quality of character or sense of propriety or even common decency, but more likely because of my cowardice. I was afraid of the aftermath, afraid I'd distance myself from her for no other reason than she wasn't Micaela. I couldn't bear to do that to Ansley Bell. Maybe with a little time I'd fall in love with Ansley, then Micaela couldn't touch her.

17

When I looked out Ansley's living room window at 5:00 A.M., Brian Kelly was already parked out front, his rented Camry pumping a cloud of exhaust into the sub-zero air. I exited the back way, through the alley and down to the cross street. I had parked the Volvo a block away in case he or anyone else showed up. The steel hunk of Swedish engineering started right up. I drove right past Brian Kelly. He either didn't see me or didn't recognize me or didn't care. I rounded the corner, pulled over and texted Ansley a warning—if she wanted to avoid him she should leave the back way, as well.

The shitbox felt cold and dead and lonely. I crawled under my down comforter and slept a couple of hours until the sun rose. I got up and drank two cups of whatever the dark blue Nespresso capsule makes and could think of nothing but Ansley Bell. I started the shower but stopped it. I wasn't ready to wash off the orange blossoms.

Ellegaard called at 8:00 on the nose.

"You up?"

"I am. Caffeinated and everything."

"You did it, Shap."

"Uh-oh."

"Not uh-oh. This is good. The carpet fibers in the gray dust at Maggie Somerville's house match the carpet fibers at Andrew Fine's office park."

"Really."

"I'm going to get warrants to search Andrew Fine's house, the office park, and the call center."

"Have you told McGinnis?"

"Not yet."

"What about the FBI?"

"Let's meet for breakfast," he said. "We need to talk this over."

My phone beeped. I looked at the screen. "Call you right back. I got Robert Somerville on the other line."

"Make it quick."

I accepted Somerville's call. "Hello?"

"Hi, Nils. It's Robert Somerville. I hope I'm not calling too early."

"Not at all. What can I do for you?"

"The police took Maggie's computer the day she was killed to look at e-mails and Web history and whatever else they could find. So I don't know what's on there, but I was going through Maggie's personal things for the funeral tomorrow and I found some letters."

"What kind of letters?"

"Love letters."

"Did you read them?"

"A couple. Then I stopped because I felt I was violating Maggie's privacy. I know that sounds ridiculous. She's dead. But I thought it might be better if you read them."

"How old are they?"

"Not very," said Robert. "There are references to things that happened only a few months ago. But they go back awhile. I'm not sure."

"Have you told the police?"

"No. I thought about what you said. Even if the letters aren't important, the police might use them to placate the press. And that could embarrass my kids. So I'm calling you instead."

"How many are there?"

"A couple dozen, at least. You want to come take a look at them?"

"I do, thanks. And don't touch them anymore. We'll have to turn them over to the police eventually and they'll dust them for prints."

"Got it. The kids are out with their grandparents until this afternoon. Think you can drop by before then?"

"I'll be there before lunch."

I clicked back over to Ellegaard. "The Lowry at 8:30?"

"Sounds good."

"And E, I want to invite Gabriella. We could use her input on this."

"Can we still trust her?"

"Absolutely."

We met at the Lowry in Uptown, away from Edina's pricked-up ears and the red-scarfed Chief McGinnis. Ellegaard sat across from me, and Gabriella to my right, in a booth of tufted black vinyl near a wall made of cherrywood horizontal planks.

Inspector Gabriella Núñez wore black wool pants and a gray herringbone wool blazer over a baby blue crewneck sweater. Her brown face had a soft smile in a hard jaw. You both would and would not want to meet her in a dark alley. Either way you'd lose, but depending on what she thought of you, it might be worth taking a few on the chin.

Gabriella had round black eyes under accent-mark eyebrows. She'd braided her straight black hair and pinned it behind her head. Seventeen years had passed since we'd been cadets together at the Minneapolis Police Academy, and of the three of us, she had, by far, aged the best. Other than a few lines around her eyes and mouth, she could have passed for twenty-five.

She'd also surpassed Ellegaard and me at the job. I'd heard a hundred different people, all of them cops, lawyers, or politicians, say Gabriella would be the Minneapolis Chief of Police before she turned fifty. I believed it would happen if Los Angeles, New York, or Chicago didn't make her chief first.

Ellegaard fidgeted, drank two cups of tea, and told the waitress he'd have the same eggs and toast I ordered even though he'd already eaten breakfast at home. A tall blonde with a soft, round face and muffin top spilling over her jeans said our food would be up in a few and left us to it.

"Two breakfasts," I said to Ellegaard. "You're a six-foot-three hobbit."

"I eat when I'm nervous."

"You should be nervous," said Gabriella. "You two are dick-deep in shark-infested waters."

"Hey, watch the language around Ellegaard. They don't talk like that in Edina. You're going to embarrass him."

"Dick-deep water for Ellegaard is chest-deep water for you. You're the one who should be embarrassed."

"Hey, I'm embarrassed just to be alive."

Gabriella Núñez smiled and Minneapolis jumped above zero for a heartbeat.

Ellegaard said, "How are we going to handle this Andrew Fine situation?"

I said, "Well, we can't put a tail on Fine without the FBI knowing. That's how I earned my little field trip to Brooklyn Center. So either you arrest Fine or we wait. But if we wait, we risk the chance of Fine finding out that we know about the carpet fibers. Then he becomes a flight risk."

"McGinnis still hasn't said a word to me about staying away from Fine."

"Of course he hasn't. He wants you to arrest Fine and get into it with the FBI."

"So your chief has his bases covered," said Gabriella. "Either the FBI hauls in a net full of terrorists and he associates himself with the bust, or he clashes with the FBI over the Somerville case and plays the local hero standing up to the big bad federal government."

Someone other than the blonde brought out our food. Everybody's a fucking specialist.

Gabriella said, "You boys up for a drive to Brooklyn Center?"

I said, "What do you got in mind?"

"You can't trust McGinnis. You got to keep him a step behind you. And the way to do that is delegate to the Bureau."

"You just earned yourself a free breakfast."

"I don't know what you're talking about. Anything that came out of this little chat was your idea. I'm just a dumb girl with a pretty smile."

Ellegaard laughed for the first time since showing me the dust-covered body in the big bedroom in Edina. We finished our food and drank refills of coffee and tea and tipped the blond waitress too much because she hustled to get us on the road when we were ready to go.

Ellegaard and I said good-bye to Gabriella then pulled out of the Lowry parking lot. I called ahead and told Special Agent Delvin Peterson to clear the conference room. He told me to fuck off. Ellegaard called Edina CSU and asked them to keep their mouth shut about the carpet fibers from Fine's office park matching the dust in Maggie Somerville's house. We drove north on Hennepin and merged onto 94, which took us straight to the FBI building.

Agents Delvin Peterson and No Chin Olson sat across from Ellegaard and me in the conference room. We didn't say a word until Special Agent in Charge Colleen Milton entered with a perturbed look on her face.

"I left halfway through an acupuncture session, so this better be fucking good," she said as she sat down at the head of the table.

I said, "Did they take the needles out? I'm just asking because of the look on your face."

"Can we get to it, please?" said Milton.

Ellegaard said, "We have physical evidence linking Andrew Fine to our murder victim in Edina. The evidence is strong and, normally by now, we'd have warrants to search his home and places of business. But you told us to back off, and so we have."

"So what's the problem?" said Milton.

"The problem," said Ellegaard, "is we're afraid he'll get wind of our discovery and run. And since we can't tail him, you'll have to."

"I can't spare the manpower to tail a guy who's no going anywhere."

"Fine has the means to take off and not get found."

Agent Delvin Peterson took off his glasses and rubbed his eyes. "You really think Andrew Fine killed someone while cooperating with us on a national security op?"

"We do," said Ellegaard.

I said, "It's nice to have friends in high places when you do bad things."

No Chin glared at me. "You're pushing it, Shapiro."

"The only thing I'm pushing is Andrew Fine is now your responsibility. If he runs, it's on you. If he kills someone else, it's on you."

"And if there's a terrorist attack because you're fucking with our operation," said Agent No Chin, "it's on you."

"We're not fucking with your operation. That's why we're here."

"What are you, again," said Milton, "a private investigator? A stakeout guy with a long lens who spends his time hunting adulterers? Why are we even talking to you?"

"What's with the disrespect? Agent Peterson offered me a job yesterday."

"I did not!" said Peterson.

"This is Mickey Mouse bullshit," said Milton. "And don't have time for it."

"Then we'll leave. But unless you step aside so we can proceed with our investigation, Andrew Fine is your responsibility. Anything happens, it's going to blow back on the FBI."

"Get the fuck out of here," said Milton. "And stay away from Andrew Fine."

I stood and started toward the door. Then stopped. "Oh, by the way . . ." I set a few business cards on the table, ". . . in case any of you are having spousal trouble, I got a long lens."

18

I sat across from Robert Somerville at his kitchen table made of reclaimed wood, half excited to read Maggie's love letters and half afraid of getting a splinter. Robert handed a box to me, cardboard but printed up to look like it was made of an old map. I reached into my front pocket and removed a pair of latex gloves. I'd convinced my dental hygienist to slip me a gross. They were deep purple, but they worked.

Each letter had been stored in the envelope it arrived in, slit open with a letter opener on the side. The envelopes were sealed with their own adhesive, the peel-and-stick kind. There was no saliva to test for DNA. Both the envelope and the letter had been written on a computer and printed on plain white office paper, no return address, no handwriting anywhere. And the envelopes had been postmarked from various post offices around the Twin Towns.

Twenty-seven love letters. The writer had been careful not to identify himself. No moments or references to places or people, just professing his love for Maggie Somerville. Real love. Unselfish love. I read sentences like, *You deserve happiness and love more than any person I know.* And, *Your generosity of spirit makes this world a better place.* And, *Your beauty, inside and out, makes me happier to be a man than anything else on this earth.* And all signed, *I will love you until the end of time.*

I was sure Andrew Fine didn't write them based on their content and lack of grammatical errors.

"These are remarkably not-creepy," I said. "Any idea who could have written them?"

"None. Like I said, I only read a few, and they just made me feel like a shitty husband. Are you going to turn them over to the police?"

"I don't know," I said. "They can dust the letters for fingerprints, but chances are the prints won't be in the system. These are hardly the rantings of a criminal mind. They can analyze the ink, but that will only narrow it down to a few hundred thousand printers in town. Are you comfortable with me taking them?"

"Of course."

I looked at the dates on the postmarks. The earliest was two years ago and the most recent a week before Maggie Somerville was murdered. Then I packed the letters back into their decorative box. "How are the kids holding up?"

"They're not," said Robert. "They're having a terrible time. They loved their mom an awful lot."

"I'm sorry," I said. "Listen, I was wondering if you're okay with me being at the funeral tomorrow."

"Sure, if you think it'll help with your investigation. My only request is that you stay away from the kids."

"Understood. I will be there strictly as an observer."

"Fair enough," he said. "Hey, I talked to the insurance company today. They said Maggie had named the kids as co-beneficiaries on her life insurance. A million each, which I was surprised to hear."

"Maybe that'll cover a couple years of college by the time they get there."

"Maybe. Then the agent let it slip that there's another beneficiary, but wouldn't tell me who. Do you know anything about that?"

"I do, but I can't tell you right now. Hopefully soon."

"I guess it's none of my business," said Robert. "I just thought it was strange and maybe the police should know about it."

"They do," I said.

My phone dinged. I looked at the text. *Could use you at the hospital. That detective showed up.*

Be there soon.

"I have to run. Thanks for the letters. Do I have your permission to turn them over to the police if I decide that's what's best?"

"Yes. I just wanted you to see them first."

"I appreciate that." I started out then stopped. "You know what? Do you mind just writing a note saying I have permission to have them? I know it's kind of weird, but I want to make sure everything's on the up-and-up in case the letters lead us to a suspect. You just never know with defense attorneys."

"Yeah, no problem," said Robert.

I handed him a pen. He found a piece of paper and

wrote the note. I folded it and clipped the pen onto the paper. "Thanks, Robert. I'll be thinking about you and your family tomorrow."

"I appreciate that, Nils."

I stepped out of Robert Somerville's house, and a brisk wind slapped me in the face. The mucus in my nose froze and my cheeks stung. I drove back home to grab a cashmere scarf that Micaela had given me for Christmas. It probably cost more than my house. I had yet to wear it. But a thirty-below windchill felt like a special enough occasion.

On my way to the university, I stopped at the Edina Police Station to give Ellegaard the letters. I had no intention of keeping them from the police, but letting Robert Somerville think I did kept me in his trust. Ellegaard said he'd give them to CSU, though it was unlikely they'd find anything of value. We sat in his office, a small windowless box lit by fluorescents in a suspended ceiling.

"We have Fine's fingerprints on record, so if they turn up on the letters we can compare them. And I have Robert Somerville's right here." I handed Ellegaard the pen, which I'd put in a ziplock bag back at the shitbox. "This way we don't have to ask our dear friends at the FBI for them."

"You think Somerville would turn over letters he wrote to his ex-wife?"

"Maybe. He might have thought someone else knows about them. Maybe Maggie told a friend, and if the friend told us . . . I don't know. It's possible."

"I suppose it is," said Ellegaard.

"I got to go, but—"

McGinnis stepped into Ellegaard's office and shut the door. "Good. You're here, Shapiro." He was wearing the red scarf again. I'd had the decency to clump my scarf in the corner with my jacket and mittens. He spoke without raising his voice. "I just got off the phone with Colleen Milton at the FBI. She told me about your visit. What I want to know is, why didn't you come to me with the Andrew Fine issue?"

Ellegaard and I looked at each other, not sure who should answer. Then Ellegaard spoke. "We assumed you didn't want to talk about Fine since you never told us the FBI wanted us to back off him."

"I didn't share that information with you because I didn't want to color your investigation. I wanted you to proceed without preconceptions and deal with the issue when it came up." Then his calm, quiet voice grew louder. "And it sure as hell would have come up if you'd told me the carpet fibers from Fine's office park matched the carpet fibers on Maggie Somerville's body! What the hell were you two thinking?!"

I turned toward McGinnis. "I can tell you what I was thinking. I was thinking your political ambitions have interfered with your judgment on this case."

"And I'm thinking I've about had it with you, Shapiro."

"There's a communication problem here, Chief," said Ellegaard. "And a trust problem. Forget about Nils. You haven't been forthright with me, and I'm trying to identify a suspect in the biggest murder case Edina has seen in decades."

"Detective Ellegaard, you deliberately withheld information from me and you instructed CSU to do the same. You're in no position to talk about communication problems. Or trust."

"Well," I said. "Nothing would make me happier than hearing more platitudes from under the red scarf, but I'm late for an appointment."

"Shapiro, invoice us for four days. You're no longer working for Edina PD."

"Chief," said Ellegaard.

"There's a chain of command, here. Without it, this investigation is chaos. You have broken that chain of command before today, Shapiro. You broke it again when you went to Brooklyn Center and you broke it yet again in this office. You are no longer working for Edina PD. Nor will you again."

"Whatever you say, Chief. But you're going to find I'm much less of a pain in the ass when I'm working for you than when I'm working for me. And you'd better not fuck up, because I'm going to be the first person to shine a big old spotlight on it when you do."

"Get out of my sight," said McGinnis.

"Have a beautiful day, Chief."

I gathered my jacket, scarf, and mittens and walked out of Ellegaard's office.

19

I had been fired before. When your job is to dig up ugly truths, it happens. The all-of-a-sudden happy spouse is cheating. The missing daughter is dead. The tax shelter is a scam, and the money is in Moscow and unrecoverable. But getting fired off the Somerville murder was the first time it hurt. The case had reconnected me with Ellegaard and Stevey Fine. Even Micaela popped back into my life an extra time because she read about the case. People I loved came from different points in my life like spokes from a rim, my investigation of Maggie Somerville's death the hub. And without the hub, it felt like the wheel would collapse.

I pulled out of the Edina PD parking lot and onto 50th Street. I was too late to help Ansley deal with Brian Kelly at the hospital. I called her. No answer. I drove to Bunny's, unbundled, sat at the bar, and ordered a burger. I couldn't help but scan the place for Emerald Eyes, but my favorite nurse wasn't there. I ate my burger and tried Ansley again. No answer. I rebundled for the cold and left.

You practically need a Ph.D. to find a parking spot at the University of Minnesota. After driving around for fifteen minutes, I discovered a ramp with vacancies four blocks from the hospital. I parked the Volvo on the ramp's roof, grabbed my hat, mittens, and scarf from the backseat, pulled up the hood on my snorkel parka, and walked against a stiff wind out of the north.

I texted Ansley when I got to the hospital. I waited for a reply. It didn't come. I approached the receptionist at the hospital's information desk who looked more like a bouncer. Black, two-eighty, shaved head. Guess that's the way it is with hospitals now. You're on the list or you're out on your ass.

"Hi," I said. "I'm here to see Ansley Bell. She's a medical student."

"Is she expecting you?"

"She is."

"Name?"

"Nils Shapiro."

"It'll be a moment. Take a seat."

I sat in the waiting area and stared at the elevators. The doors opened and people stepped off, but none of them were Ansley. Fifteen minutes later, a chubby-cheeked young man in a lab coat approached. He had dark hair on top of his head, but the sides were shaved. Maybe he thought it made his head look thinner. It did not. He had a stethoscope around his neck and fidgeted with it the way a newlywed does with a wedding ring. "Are you Nils?"

"I am."

"I'm Ansley's friend, David. She left."

"I thought she was working a 9:00 to 9:00."

"She was scheduled to, but she had a family emergency. She told me to tell you if you showed up."

"Why wouldn't she have just called or texted?"

David shrugged and what little neck he had disappeared into his lab coat.

"Did she leave with anyone?"

"Yeah. A skinny guy with a weird mustache wearing a long down quilted coat."

"Did she say when she'd be back?"

"Nope. Sorry."

"Thanks."

I walked away and tried calling again. No answer. I texted. No return. If Ansley didn't want to leave the hospital with Brian Kelly, she didn't have to. She either wanted to go or somehow felt compelled to go. I looked at my phone. My text had been delivered but still no response.

Ansley asked me to come to the hospital. But instead I stopped at home and then the Edina police station and got myself fired off the case. I was out of work, Ansley wasn't where she was supposed to be, and the receptionist wouldn't validate my parking. That cold wind out of the north was the least of my problems.

20

I took University Avenue back to Northeast and parked in front of Ansley's duplex. Brian Kelly's rental car wasn't out front. Ansley's Subaru wasn't in the garage. I let myself in the back door and climbed the staircase and tried the door into the kitchen. It was unlocked. Maybe Brian Kelly had finally grown impatient enough to do what I had done, pick an easy-to-pick lock and snoop around. Only he forgot to lock up as he went.

The kitchen, dining room, and living room looked neat and undisturbed. So did the bedroom and bathroom. The front door was still locked. I felt her bathroom towel—bone dry. But that didn't mean much when the humidity was zero. She could have used it an hour ago.

I walked back through the living room and dining

room and into the kitchen and was reaching for the back
door when I saw it on the side of the refrigerator. A sheet
of paper with the heading USMSLE Study Group Schedule. If Brian Kelly had seen that, even he could figure out
where Ansley Bell spent her days. I walked back into the
living room and sat in the leather sectional. It seemed my
only option was to drive back to campus and wait for
Ansley to return to the hospital. Chances were, she was
having coffee with Brian Kelly and listening to whatever
message he was hired to deliver.

But why didn't she text me where she was going? Especially when she asked me to come down to campus
because *that detective showed up*. I got up and left the
way I came, then drove back to the university and parked
in the same crap ramp, then walked the same cold four
blocks into the same biting wind out of the north. I approached the same bouncer/receptionist, and before I
could say anything, he said, "She ain't back yet."

"What about David, that kid who came down and
talked to me earlier?"

"Have a seat."

Fifteen minutes later, David approached. "Hey, Nils.
Ansley's not back yet."

"I know. Can you tell me where she parks so I can see
if her car is still there?"

"All the med students park in the hospital ramp. Second floor on the wall facing the river. I have a white Toyota 4Runner with Colorado plates. If her car is in the
ramp, it should be around there somewhere."

"Thanks."

I walked across the street to the hospital ramp and
climbed the stairs to the second level. I would have
parked there myself if three and half years of parking
tickets on this campus hadn't scared the shit out of me.

The concrete floor was splotched with dried salt and the black icebergs that form in wheel wells then fall out to make the ugliest place even uglier. On the west side of the ramp, I saw Dave's white 4Runner. Ansley's Subaru occupied a space five spots away. I felt the hood. It was cold. I returned to the medical school to hear the bouncer behind the receptionist's desk say, "She still ain't here." I took a seat in the waiting area.

My phone rang. It was Ellegaard.

"I'm sorry about what happened with McGinnis. Come over to the house for dinner tonight. We'll talk after."

"I can't," I said. "Ansley Bell disappeared."

"You're not on the case anymore, Shap."

"This isn't about the case."

"Aw, jeez, Shap. What'd you do?"

"Not what you're thinking, Ellie. Or maybe what you're thinking. I like her, and I'm concerned about her safety right now. So, thanks for the invite, but I can't make dinner."

"E-mail me your invoice tomorrow. I'll walk it over to accounting and get you paid right away."

"I appreciate it. Thanks, buddy."

"The Lowry at 8:00 for breakfast. Okay?"

"Yeah, but I have a funeral later tomorrow morning."

"Shap, you realize McGinnis fired you today, don't you?"

"Maybe I'm working for someone else."

"Who?"

"You know I can't say who. See you at breakfast, buddy."

I hung up and was about to put the phone in my pocket when I opened the Find Friends app and there, on the map, was a blinking dot that said Ansley Bell. I zoomed in. She was in the Loring Pasta Bar, a restaurant in Dinkytown.

I bundled up, told the receptionist/bouncer to have a nice evening, walked back outside and over to Coffman Union, where I took a footbridge over Washington Avenue and into the quad. I walked past the old buildings with columns where the university started in the 1800s. I cut in front of Northrop Auditorium then passed the bookstore and a new building I'd never seen before. Half a block later, I stood outside the Loring Pasta Bar and checked my phone. Ansley Bell was still in there, or at least her phone was. I stepped inside.

The Loring Pasta Bar is an open space of exposed brick three stories high and filled with street lamps and framed photographs and plants entwined with year-round Christmas lights. Any place with year-round Christmas lights is a place I want to be. I usually see them in dive bars, strung along cheap sheet paneling where they cast their twinkly glow on the tap handle of Pabst Blue Ribbon beer, where Pabst is drank for what it is instead of ironically, like in some other bars.

The Loring Pasta Bar, though, is far from a dive. An early dinner crowd half-filled the place. Students crowded the bar for happy hour. That's where I saw Brian Kelly sucking on a mug of something foamy and light colored while chatting up some coeds, who seemed far from interested. An iron staircase led up to a balcony of romantic tables for two. I glanced up and it appeared empty, so, like a sniper, I climbed up to the highest vantage point to scout my target.

Ansley Bell sat with a man at a round table in the middle of the restaurant, under a potted tree wrapped in white lights. The man was in his late twenties and appeared tall and thin and had the general all-American good looks of an Olympic volleyball player. I walked to the middle of the balcony and stood nearly straight above them. A waiter brought their dinner, and I sat down to think.

Either the man below me was Ansley Bell's brother, the biological child of her adoptive parents maybe, or a cousin or a family friend. Or, more likely, Brian Kelly lied about who he was working for and the man below was his real client. I considered the possibility that dumb Brian Kelly had outsmarted me. Never trust a private investigator.

I walked back downstairs, pulled a waiter aside and told him I'd like to send the skinny creep at the bar a double Macallan straight up. For an extra twenty, the waiter agreed to include a note and tell Kelly it came from a leggy blonde. I wrote it on a cocktail napkin.

Saw your handsome face at the bar! Had to get to the library. Call me sometime!

Then I Googled the number to a porn-addiction hotline, wrote it on the note, and put a heart over the "i" in "sometime" to give it that special touch.

I took one more look at Ansley Bell from across the restaurant. She was too far away to make out her expression. But whoever volleyball boy was, he didn't take away her appetite. I texted her. *Heard you had a family emergency. Hope all is okay. Just left the hospital. Let me know if you still want to get together tonight.*

A few seconds later, Ansley picked up her phone from the table, read the text, then put the phone in her purse and reached a hand across the table toward volleyball boy. I walked out of the Loring Pasta Bar and trekked back to the parking ramp.

I pulled out of the ramp and drove down to the East River Parkway. I continued south, past the University of St. Thomas and St. Kate's, and crossed over the Mississippi River at the Ford Parkway Bridge, not far from Minnehaha Falls, which, in winter, trickles over giant ice formations. The falls are fed by the same creek that runs behind Maggie Somerville's house. I drove west on Minnehaha Parkway, the frozen creek snaking back and forth under me, past lakes Nokomis and Hiawatha, along an urban green space with separate paths for walking and biking. And even though it was ten degrees below zero and nothing was green, Minneapolitans walked their dogs, both human and canine breath crystalizing in the arctic air. Runners ran, their faces shielded behind balaklavas. And cyclists—crazy fucking cyclists—pedaled their fat-tire bikes into the Novocaine wind.

I considered calling Ellie and accepting that dinner invitation, but I wasn't much up for company. I passed under 35W and Nicollet Avenue. Here the creek had little footbridges over it, each lit by an old-fashioned street lamp. It was goddamn romantic. I hit 50th Street and five minutes later pulled into my garage.

I got halfway between the garage and house when I saw a hole in my rear door where the window used to be. Shattered glass bejeweled the stoop. I started back to the car to get my gun, but stopped when I saw a shovel lying near the rear gate. Whoever went into my house had come out, and they'd used the shovel to flatten their tracks.

I crunched across the stoop, opened the shitbox's back door, and stepped into my tiny mudroom. Hats and gloves and scarves covered the floor, the canvas boxes they'd been stored in dumped in the corner. The jackets that had been hung on hooks also lay on the floor, their pockets pulled out and their sleeves inside out.

My breath fogged in front of my face. I wanted a board to replace the window and give my little furnace a respite from trying to heat the entire state of Minnesota. Then the smell hit me. It took a moment to realize what it was. Red wine. Big and heavy with pronounced tones of desperation and vengeance and a delicate undertone of heartache.

21

I stepped into the kitchen. The refrigerator lay facedown, coil-side up. The dust in the coils reminded me of the dust on Maggie Somerville's dead body, and for a moment I wondered if we got it wrong assuming it was vacuum cleaner dirt. Then I remembered the carpet fibers from Andrew Fine's building matching those at the crime scene.

The kitchen cabinets were all open. Pots and pans and food littered the floor. The sugar and flour canisters lay empty, their whiteness dumped over the countertops. Either someone thought I had something worth looking for, or a bear tore through my house.

Three wine bottles lay broken on the counters. Red

wine seeped into the grout of the tile countertop. The wine had already started to turn—the air was pungent.

The intruder violated the living room, bedroom, and bathroom, as well. Furniture lay turned over with drawers pulled out and contents strewn all over the place. The TV lay screen-down—its back cover had been taken off. Cushions and my mattress suffered knife wounds, and their insides spilled all over the place. The little laundry-chute door in the bathroom had been ripped off. My shampoo had been dumped out of the bottle and onto the floor—not in the tub, not in the sink, not even in the toilet-—onto the floor.

I didn't know if I should clean or call the police or light a match.

Someone had been looking for something, but I had nothing of value except a bottle of Irish that I found intact on the kitchen counter. I took it into the living room, grabbed a couple of mangled cushions, arranged them into a sad excuse for a chair, and sat with the bottle.

I checked my phone. 6:14. No calls. No texts. The day had been a complete fuckery. Yelled at by the FBI, fired by McGinnis, I found Ansley Bell with a volleyball player, and someone turned my house inside out. I was sitting in messes both literal and figurative, and the warm buzz of whiskey wasn't helping. My phone rang. Micaela's face peeked out at me from the screen with her blue eyes, fair skin, and smattering of freckles, all framed by a tangle of strawberry blonde.

"Hey."

"Hey, Nils. What's going on?"

"You don't want to know."

"Tell me."

I told her.

"Jesus, Nils. That's awful. Are you okay?"

"I'm fine."

"What were they looking for?"

"I have no idea."

"I'll be right there," she said. "And I'm calling my cleaning crew from the office. They'll get your place pulled together in a few hours."

"No," I said.

"Why not?"

"I have to call the police. The place can't be picked up until they've come and gone. I need their report for my insurance claim. But thank you."

"We'll talk about it over dinner. I'm taking you out and that's that."

"A guy does need to eat."

"Be there in an hour."

I hung up with Micaela and called Gabriella Núñez and told her what had happened. She said she'd meet me at the house in twenty with a couple of uniforms and CSU. They arrived in fifteen and went to work. I explained to Gabriella I was gone most of the day, but the place was fine when I was last home around 11:30 A.M. The uniforms went out to knock on doors in case a neighbor saw something.

Gabriella and I righted a couple of chairs near the kitchen table and sat.

"What do you think they were looking for, Shap?"

"I honestly don't know. I have nothing of value. To anyone."

"Any idea who it could have been?"

"A junkie looking for drugs?"

"Too systematic of a search for that."

"Look at me, Gabriella. I'm not fucking kidding. There

was no reason for anyone to break in here unless they knew I have a gun and thought they could steal it."

"Is your gun in the house?"

"No. It's in the car."

"Jesus Christ, Shap. You can't leave it in the car."

"It's not sitting on the dash. It's well-hidden."

"Don't tell me that. I don't want to know that."

"Someone out there thinks I have something that I don't. The problem is, I have no idea what that something could be or who that someone is."

"Could it have anything to do with your Somerville case?"

"It's not mine anymore. I got fired off it today."

"Who'd you piss off?"

"The Edina Chief of Police and the FBI."

"Meeting didn't go so well this morning, huh?"

"We got a bit snippy with each other."

"Do you have anything they're looking for?"

"I've told you—no."

"I'm calling Ellie. He needs to know about this."

"Please do."

Micaela texted that she was waiting outside.

"I got to go, Gabriella."

"Keep your phone on. We'll board up your back door and lock up when we're finished."

"Thanks." I checked my phone one more time for texts and e-mails. Nothing from Ansley Bell. It was 7:40, and our 9:00 get-together, as far as I was concerned, was off.

Micaela Stahl drove a Range Rover that had the word "autobiography" in the model name, and made no apology for it. I opened the passenger door, stepped onto the running board, and climbed into the seat. Needing a stepladder to get into your ex-wife's $200,000 car so she can take you to dinner doesn't do much for a man's ego. But I was grateful to see her and gave her a kiss on the cheek.

She wore a gray Arc'teryx puffer coat and white knit hat that capped her long frizzy hair like the nub of a badminton birdie. "I'm so sorry," she said, and put a cashmere glove on my hand.

"Thanks." I buckled myself in, and she slipped the gear selector into drive. There's nothing more beautiful than a woman's face lit by a car's instrument panel. I caught a gleam off her lips, and her face sparkled with a million baby diamonds. Makeup. When Micaela wore makeup, I was in for a hell of a night.

She looked over and smiled. "I made a reservation at Bar La Grassa. Good?"

"It's kind of dark in there."

She laughed her throaty, hoarse little laugh and said, "Most people like that."

"Not me. I do most of my communicating with facial expressions. You know that. Otherwise I tend to chatter away like a schoolgirl."

"I'll talk to the manager. See if they can goose the dimmer a bit."

"That's not fair to all the unattractive people who go there because it's so dark."

The hoarse little laugh again. "Maybe we should go somewhere else."

"No, no," I said. "We'll go to Bar La Grassa. But if you can't read my facial expressions, you'll just have to come straight out and ask what I'm feeling."

Micaela turned right on Excelsior Boulevard. I stole another glimpse of her in the dash light and worshiped the faint smile on her face. She was on the precipice of adventure, a leader of and, simultaneously, coconspirator in misbehavior.

I said, "Fuck Bar La Grassa."

As if she were ten and I'd just asked if she wanted a pony, she said, "Okay."

"We'll cook."

"We can do that."

At the bottom of the hill, she turned left into the Calhoun Commons parking lot. We shopped Whole Foods and MGM and, half an hour later, stepped out of an elevator and directly into her penthouse condominium overlooking Lake Harriet with two bags of groceries, a bottle of wine, and a bottle of Bushmills 1608. We dumped our coats on a bench in the foyer. She wore a cashmere V-neck in soft green and old blue jeans and toe socks with all ten toes a different color. We carried the groceries into her open living space and set them on the kitchen counter.

Her kitchen was white—the cabinets, marble countertops, and subway-tile backsplash. Micaela lit half a dozen candles and dimmed the lights—the white surfaces glowed and danced as if they, too, were on fire. We started with whiskey, neat in lowballs and Johnny Cash *American III* on her invisible sound system. I said, "I'll take the prison job." Johnny sang "I Won't Back Down" while I peeled carrots, parsnips, turnips, and beets. Micaela trimmed and halved the brussels sprouts, cut the potatoes, and chopped the parsley, green onion, and dill. I tossed the vegetables in a roasting pan with olive oil, rosemary, salt and pepper, then threw them in the oven. Micaela opened a plastic clamshell of arugula and dumped it into a bowl. She seasoned the greens, pan roasted slivered almonds, and diced a red onion while I unwrapped the salmon, sprinkled it with salt and pepper, then drizzled it with olive oil and lemon. Johnny sang "Field of Diamonds," and we poured our second lowballs of whiskey.

Micaela rinsed the cutting board in the sink. I stepped behind her and put my hands on her hips. She turned off the faucet and put her hands over mine. I buried my face in her hair. She took her left hand off mine and swept her hair in front of her shoulder, and I found the back of her neck with a whisper. Then she grabbed my left hand and brought it up to her breast and I felt her excitement through her sweater. She looked at the timer on the oven and said, "Come on."

We walked to her bedroom as if we were late to catch a bus. When we entered, she flopped back onto the bed and put her arms over her head. I kissed her stomach and pushed up her sweater, which she lifted over her head and threw to the floor. I reached behind her bra, and she said, "It's in front."

"You know I can't do those."

"I do." She laughed her hoarse laugh and somehow removed her bra and jeans and underwear at the same time, and I made a note to put that skill in the pro column the next time I made a pro and con list headed "Micaela." She unbuttoned my jeans and slipped them off. I pulled off my sweater and T-shirt while she removed my boxers.

Then she lay back again. "Hold on," I said. "I have to remove my socks or I'll look like a tourist." She laughed and thirty seconds later I was inside her, and, like every time before, I felt a tidal wave of something—gratitude, happiness, sadness, I couldn't tell what—but I had to knock it down before it prevented me from continuing. I recovered and moved slowly. Then she pushed me off of her and climbed on top of me, took me into her, and ground herself down onto my hips in perfect time. I had to close my eyes because she was too beautiful and seeing her made me want to come, but I held it off by thinking of us in a cold room with two cold lawyers who handed us pens then slid us copies of documents to sign. Then I opened my eyes, and she said, "I'm going to come. Nils, I'm coming." Then I breathed in all of Micaela's beauty and came with her.

We dressed and returned to the kitchen without saying a word. I covered the salmon in the chopped herbs and put it in the oven, then uncorked something yellow and oaky. Twenty minutes later we sat in the living space at a table for two, eating salmon and roasted vegetables and arugula while overlooking Lake Harriet.

I said, "I got fired off the Edina case today."

She thought a moment, then said, "I'm sorry." She looked out the window. I noticed the leather chair in the living room hobnobbing with fine furniture. I thought of its twin in the shitbox, now slashed open, its down and foam spilled all over the floor. Life, even for chairs, is not fair.

"We found crucial evidence pointing to a suspect," I said, "but the person in question is cooperating with an FBI investigation, so the FBI told me to back off. I didn't handle it as well as I might have."

"Well," she said, "if you had to back off your suspect, kind of doesn't matter if you got fired. You would've had to stop the investigation anyway."

"Maybe if I'd been more politic, I could have seen it through."

"So see it through. What can they do to you now?" She took my hand and gave it a squeeze. "More wine?"

"I got it." I went to the kitchen. She was right. She was always right. Micaela gave me a freedom I wouldn't give myself. Problem was, I didn't always know how to handle it. She knew how to handle freedom. That's why she had her own elevator and a view of the lake. I got the wine bottle and brought it back to the table.

As I poured, she said, "You're sleeping here tonight."

"Okay."

"Your house will be put back together in the morning."

"I'm paying you for that."

"Fairies don't take currency."

"I'm pretty sure you don't have wings. I've looked. Everywhere."

"I'm not the fairy. The fairies are cleaning."

For dessert we ate squares of dark chocolate we broke off the world's most expensive candy bar. We cleaned the kitchen and returned to the bedroom for another round, but took our time. And though I'd never been right before, I had a feeling it'd be our last naked assault on that bed or any other bed.

At 3:30 I woke to pee and checked my phone.

Ansley—8:36 P.M. *So sorry. Yes. Still on for tonight.*
Ansley—8:52 P.M. *Are you there?*
Ansley—9:25 P.M. *I screwed up. Sorry. Much to tell you. Pick me up for the funeral at 11:00?*

I went back to sleep and woke just before 7:00. Micaela had already gone to work.

22

I took an Uber from Micaela's to the Lowry to meet Ellegaard for breakfast. From the backseat, I answered Ansley's text. *No worries about last night. Pick you up at 11:00.* At least one of those sentences was true. Ansley Bell, if nothing else, was my ticket to Maggie Somerville's funeral. Staying on the case wouldn't pay my rent. It wouldn't pay my health insurance. But it would get me through the day.

"We're really supposed to get it tonight," said the Uber driver. She had tattoos on her neck, piercings in both eyebrows, and gauges in her ears big enough to fit a dime through.

"I haven't heard."

"Another foot at least. Maybe more."

"You're kidding."

"Nope. Saw it on the news last night. And after the snow, it's going to get warm."

"Well, no one is going to complain about warm."

"That's for sure," she said, pulling into the Lowry parking lot.

I got out of the car and entered the Lowry, where Ellegaard waited for me. He wore jeans and duck boots and a Minnesota Wild baseball hat. He hadn't shaved and didn't appear to have showered.

"You get fired, too?" I said.

"I took some vacation."

The hostess sat us in a booth looking out on Hennepin Avenue. The same blonde from the day before swooped by with greetings and menus and coffee. When she left, Ellegaard said, "We've got to flush out Fine."

"We?"

"I need your help, Shap. I'll figure out a way to pay you."

"You're not paying me, Ellie. What's going on with you?"

"Nothing's going on with me. I'm on vacation. I can do whatever I want. And I want to flush out Andrew Fine."

"And if we flush him out," I said, "who's going to arrest him?"

"I don't know. But I bet Fine doesn't realize to what extent the FBI is protecting him, so maybe he'll do something so stupid they'll have to let us arrest him."

"All right. So how do we flush him?"

"You're going to his party tonight, right?"

"I can, yeah."

"Pull him aside and tell him your buddy at Edina PD told you that the carpet fibers in Maggie Somerville's dust match the carpet fibers from his office park. See if that lights a fire under him."

I looked out the window at the cars driving down Hennepin Avenue, their sides coated white with road salt because it was too cold to wash them. "And if Fine runs? How are we going to track him with the FBI on our backs?"

Ellegaard's jacket was crumpled next to him in the booth. He reached into one of its pockets then held his hand, palm up, in front of me. In it I saw what looked like a computer chip in a matchbook-size plastic bag. The chip was no bigger than a Cheerio. "Plant this in something he'll take with him. His keys. His wallet. Whatever you think he can't live without."

"Is that property of Edina PD?"

"The sales rep gave me one for personal use when I bought a dozen for the department. There's a piece of paper on the back. If you peel it off, it'll expose an adhesive that'll stick to almost anything. Don't stick it to yourself. That would be an embarrassing trip to the doctor. For both of us."

I took the micro tracking device and put it in my pocket. "I'm going to the funeral with Ansley Bell. If I see Fine there, I'll tell him I need to talk to him tonight. I'll say it in my most ominous voice."

"You don't have an ominous voice."

"I know," I said. "It's a real problem."

23

I pulled in front of Ansley's duplex at 11:00. A few minutes later, she came down and got in the Volvo wearing a navy wool overcoat with semi-opaque black tights.

"You clean up well," she said. She leaned over and kissed me. She'd replaced the orange blossoms with something spicy. "Do you want to talk about yesterday?"

"We're on our way to your mother's funeral. It can wait."

"I'd prefer we do it now if that's okay."

"Of course."

"There's something I haven't told you about me. Because we've basically just met and, to me, it's not that big of a deal, but I guess it is kind of a big deal to most people. And now I'm embarrassed about it so I'll just say it—I'm married."

I didn't say anything. I just kept my eyes on the road and drove.

"It turns out that private detective wasn't working for my parents. He was working for my husband. His name is Hunter Priem. He's a couple years older than me and lives in Rancho Palos Verdes in a house that overlooks the Pacific Ocean. You can see whales migrating up and down the coast while you're eating a bowl of cereal in the kitchen. It's quite beautiful. Hunter's a trust-fund kid. And despite having had everything handed to him, he's a kind and decent human being.

"My parents weren't great parents. Having a child was something on a checklist for them—they didn't know what they were getting into and, when it got hard, they both retreated to their comfort zone, which was work. They aren't bad people. I just wasn't their priority. And when you're a kid, you know that. If your parents aren't your people, you start looking for your people.

"I was at a party in the Hollywood Hills when I was seventeen and met Hunter, who went to USC. He fell in love with me on the spot."

"Imagine that," I said. I smiled and put a hand on Ansley's hand, which was gloved in soft leather. Probably a gift from Maggie Somerville. Or maybe from Hunter Priem—sounded like he could afford them, too.

"In a weird way, Hunter was in the same boat I was in. He'd been isolated. Me by my parents and him by his family and wealth. Hunter is sensitive and introverted. There's something poetic about him. But his parents and siblings are Tea Party billionaires, friends with the Koch brothers and those types of people. Hunter wants nothing to do with them.

"Then he met me and swept me off my feet. When I turned eighteen, we flew to Hawaii and got married. I didn't know it at the time, but it was our way of saying 'fuck you' to the world. If the world wasn't going to give us a place to belong, we'd create our own. I had a semester of high school left. I'd seen pregnant girls in high school and thought, *Boy, that is weird for them and everyone else*. Then, I was the girl in physics with a huge rock on my finger and I was creating the weirdness. Hunter would drive me every day from Rancho Palos Verdes to Notre Dame High School in Sherman Oaks. It took almost two hours. Then he'd go to classes at USC and then pick me up after school and we'd drive all the way back. But it was just us, an eighteen- and twenty-year-old against the world."

I turned onto the 35W entrance ramp off of University Avenue and wondered why I hadn't taken 94. An old habit of forgoing the easy way, I supposed. "So what happened?"

"It's more like what didn't happen," said Ansley. "Hunter was and still is genuinely a good person. He's tall and handsome and rich. And he was deeply in love with me. But what happened was that I never fell in love with him. I fell in love with my life with him, but not him."

"I'd think that might not matter, considering you weren't happy at home."

"That's what I thought, too. Everything was so much better with Hunter. But the dishonesty of not being in love with him took its toll on me. I started to have fantasies that something bad would happen to Hunter and then I'd be living that life all by myself, independent of my parents, independent of Hunter. I'd be free to do what I wanted and meet my true love. And the guilt of having those fantasies started eating away at me. That's when I decided to contact my birth mother."

The freeway was wide-open. Gray clouds had gathered in the west. The Volvo's dash registered a balmy twenty-one degrees.

"Hunter was studying archeology at USC. He went to Mexico for a dig and was gone a couple of weeks. So without telling him, I flew to Minneapolis and met Maggie. Within a few days she became my mother and my best friend. I knew I couldn't go back. So I wrote Hunter a letter and told him the truth. I wasn't in love with him and the guilt was killing me and I had to go away and not to bother looking for me. I knew he would look for me, of course, so I used his credit card to buy an airline ticket from Los Angeles to Paris. A friend of Maggie's was also going to Paris, and she mailed the letter back to Hunter. I legally changed my name and started my new life. Every year or so, one of Maggie's friends would travel to Japan or Moscow or Vietnam, and I'd give them a letter to mail telling Hunter I was okay and had found a new life overseas and he should move on."

"And Hunter's been searching for you ever since?"

"On and off. Eventually, he moved on with his life. He has a girlfriend now and wants a divorce. He was about to get the divorce in absentia, but then received a tip that I'm here."

"From who?"

"He doesn't know. It was anonymous."

"When did he get the tip?"

"Last week sometime."

Ansley's husband being tipped-off to her whereabouts the week before Maggie Somerville's murder was too big of a coincidence to be a coincidence. I said, "Who mailed those letters from around the world for you?"

"Once it was her friend Peggy. Once it was her friend Natalie. Once it was her friend Beth. I can't remember them all."

"Beth Lindquist?"

"Yes. She and Maggie were close. Beth and her husband mailed the letter from Vietnam."

"Did Beth know about you?"

"No."

"Are you sure?"

"I asked Maggie who knew about me. She said no one. She didn't want her and Robert's kids to find out. She thought they might feel displaced. Like I told you before, she planned to tell them after my residency."

"Is it possible Beth could have opened the letter and resealed it before she sent it?"

"Sure. I guess anything's possible."

The freeway bent south with a ninety-degree turn that had no business being in a freeway, the concrete barrier riddled with collision scars to prove it.

"Are you in contact with Hunter now? Can you ask him if the seal was ever broken?"

I kept my eyes on the road but could feel Ansley's cold glare.

"Did you really just ask me that?"

"What?"

"You know I saw Hunter yesterday."

"You didn't say that. You said the PI was working for Hunter."

"Oh, Nils, you're so full of shit. I know you came to the hospital. Twice. You were looking for me. You found me once before—I'm sure you found me yesterday."

I looked at her. She smiled. "I kind of rigged your phone to make you easier to find."

"Of course you did. So I'm sure you saw me with

Hunter yesterday. And the reason I didn't respond to your texts or calls is I wanted my time with Hunter to be about him. If I interrupted it to respond to you, it would have muddied the conversation. Do you know what I'm saying?"

"I believe I do."

"He's headed back to LA today. He doesn't know anything about Maggie. All he knows is I'm in medical school. He brought divorce papers. I signed them. He and that creepy private detective are out of my life forever."

I transitioned off 35W and onto 62 West, where we drove straight at the wall of gray in the sky. "Looks like we're getting more snow," I said.

"Nice night for a fire."

"Wish I could. I have plans."

There was a long silence filled only by the buzzing of my snow tires on the clean highway.

"What's her name?" said Ansley.

"Andrew Fine."

"Maggie's boyfriend?"

"Yes. He invited me to a party. I accepted for obvious reasons."

"It's not so obvious to me. Do you mean because you're investigating Maggie's murder and he's a suspect?"

"Yes. That's exactly what I mean."

We cloverleafed onto Highway 100 South and I stayed in the right lane to exit on 70th.

"And you can't bring a date to this party?" she said.

"It's not a good idea."

"Because whoever you're working for will get mad at you for mixing business with pleasure?"

"Whoever I'm working for fired me." The moment it

came out of my mouth, I regretted saying it. But it was
out, and I had to deal with it.

Ansley adjusted her seat belt and turned sideways in
her seat, drew her knees up, and faced me. "But you're
still going to the party."

"I'm still on the case."

"Working for?"

"I'm just on it."

"Then let me hire you."

"It's too late for that."

"Why?"

"Because I'm in too deep now. There are things I can't
tell you. Not because it's you. But because other law-
enforcement agencies are involved."

She said nothing for a while. I exited on 70th and
turned left under the highway.

"I know what's going on," she said.

I said nothing and turned left onto the drive of Christ
Presbyterian. The church is made of red brick with white
columns. A steeple towers above it, and dormers cut the
roofline. Arched stained glass windows line the sanctuary. The place looks like it belongs more in Colonial
Williamsburg than in Minnesota.

"You're not going to tell me but I know," she said.

"You couldn't possibly know. Again. Nothing personal."

"So you say. We'll see."

I parked the Volvo toward the back of the lot so I
could scan the cars for Andrew Fine's Porsche while
walking to the building. You'd think a big white Porsche
would be easy to find, but the lot was crowded with
Range Rovers and Escalades and Lincoln Navigators.
Some believers burn incense as part of their ritual devot-

ing themselves to God. The members of Christ Presbyterian burn fossil fuels.

We got out of the car and, when we met in front of it, Ansley towered six inches above me. I said, "The underside of your chin is beautiful."

"Shut up," she said. We started walking. "You're not balding. That's good."

"You're so shallow."

"You started it." We walked a few more steps, then she said, "So are you here for me or are you working?"

"To be honest, a bit of both."

"Thank you for your honesty." I squeezed her hand. She squeezed mine.

"Did you know Maggie went to this church?"

"She never talked about it."

"I don't get the sense she was conservative."

"She wasn't."

"Status-minded?"

"A little, yeah. She joined the Edina Country Club."

"Did she ever invite you for lunch there? Maybe a dip in the pool?"

Ansley looked down at the asphalt parking lot and said, "No. She didn't."

I spotted Fine's Porsche between a Chevy Suburban and Mercedes G550. "Ansley, listen. If I have to leave the funeral, I'll cover the cost of your Uber."

"What are you talking about? Why would you have to leave?"

"It's a possibility. Just in case, okay?"

She looked at me from somewhere far away, and I placed my hand on the small of her back. We entered the church, and I helped Ansley with her coat and hung it on a hanger. The rack was full—I had to pry a space open to hang it up. We looked into the sanctuary. It was crowded like Easter morning.

"Wow," said Ansley.

"You okay sitting in the balcony?"

"I guess."

"Good. It's where they make the Jews and blacks sit anyway."

She swatted the side of my head and we headed for the staircase.

24

The sanctuary of Christ Presbyterian Church has white walls and red floors made either of carpet or stained cherry, depending on the area. A couple thousand people were in attendance, maybe a few hundred legit mourners and the rest rubberneckers or press. Ansley and I sat in the first row of the balcony, which was sparsely populated, nearly all of the funeral-goers wanting to be on the same level as the casketed body of the woman whose picture they saw on the local news.

Ansley looked down at her grandparents and uncles and aunts and siblings. She pulled a tissue from her purse and wiped her eyes. "I should be down there with them. They should know me."

"You should be with them, and they should know you. Do you want that to happen today?"

She shook her head. "Not today," she said, "but soon. Very soon."

The service began. While Ansley mourned the death of her mother and best friend, I identified heads below. Robert Somerville and his two children sat in the front row with four septuagenarians, most likely Robert and Maggie's parents. Younger adults sat in the same group, probably Maggie and Robert's siblings. Chief McGinnis was there, sans scarf, with a woman I assumed to be his wife and, most likely, the scarf giver. Beth Lindquist sat toward the front, head tilted down. Her husband, Perry, had his arm around her and held her tight. I saw him turn his head to whisper something in her ear—his face was red—he wiped away a tear on her shoulder. I doubted he cried for Maggie but rather for his wife's pain in losing her friend. There was a man who'd found the love of his life.

Ellegaard sat with a few other detectives, representing the Edina police department and, if they were doing their jobs, keeping their eyes open.

When you're five foot nine on a good day, it's almost impossible to accumulate the ten thousand hours necessary to become an expert at identifying people by the tops of their heads. So when I saw a head of dark curls, a dozen rows back from the front, I couldn't place it. I knew it. I just couldn't recall from where. I shut my eyes and tried to see that head in other places, but nothing came. I waited for the man to turn around and show his face, but the head didn't turn. I moved on, hoping the face would come to me. I knew it would. Maybe not during the funeral or even that day, but the next day or the day after that, the way a forgotten song name comes a day or so after I hear it, when I'm showering or shoveling the driveway or in half-sleep.

I scanned the pews for blond heads and spotted Andrew Fine toward the front, but on the very end of a side section. He was effectively sitting in the wings, next to the choir, and watching the funeral in profile. He appeared to have come alone. He wore a black suit and black tie with a white shirt and his hair seemed more orderly than usual.

The pastor spoke in platitudes. Hymns were sung. We stood and sat. Stood and sat. Then Maggie's eleven-year-old daughter went up on the dais and read a poem about her mother. The weeping in the pews made it difficult to hear the girl's small voice. Ansley dug another clump of tissue from her purse. I put an arm around her and held her and then, in my periphery, saw someone get up and walk toward the exit.

It was Andrew Fine.

I reached into my jacket pocket, grabbed a couple of twenty-dollar bills, and put them in Ansley's purse. She looked at me. "I'm sorry," I whispered. "I'll call you." She was too bereft for my departure to sting. Keeping her relationship with Maggie a secret had isolated her, and my leaving left her in a place she knew too well.

I got up, exited the balcony, and descended the stairs. When I neared the lobby, I stopped on the staircase. If Andrew Fine had hung up a coat, I would run right into him. I listened and heard nothing. I bent down to look at the coatrack—no one was there. I continued down the stairs, into the lobby, and approached the glass doors facing the parking lot where I saw Andrew Fine walk toward his car, hands in his pockets. I went back toward the stairs and exited a door on the other side of the lobby. I stepped onto a shoveled walk that hugged the building for thirty feet then turned right toward the parking lot. If I followed the walk, I would have headed straight toward Andrew Fine where he most likely would have seen me. Instead, I climbed a four-foot snowbank and skidded down the other side to a field of snow. I ran through virgin white powder into a wooded area that paralleled the parking lot. Snow wedged into my shoes and up my pant legs. The cold stung and my back ached as I hunched in hope of avoiding Fine seeing me.

I heard his Porsche start and looked over. There were too many SUVs in the lot for me to see if he'd pulled out yet. I took a chance and ran toward the lot. When I reached the pavement, I sprinted to the Volvo, got in, started it, and pulled out into the lane. I saw the back of Andrew Fine's Porsche turning right onto 70th. I hung back, hoping his eye was on the westbound traffic. When he made his turn, I stepped on the gas. A hundred yards later, I reached the end of the church drive and followed Andrew onto 70th, where I caught the back end of his Porsche accelerating up the entrance ramp onto Highway 100 North. If he was headed home, he would've stayed on 70th, but it appeared he was going to the call center.

He exited onto Excelsior Boulevard, as I expected, but stopped at the Jiffy Car Wash. It was the drive-through kind of car wash where you stay in your car. Nothing unusual about getting a car washed, especially with the weather warming. There was a line of half a dozen cars. I parked on Kipling Avenue where I had a clear view of both the cars waiting and the cars exiting. I reached under the passenger seat to grab the Nikon with the telephoto lens.

Andrew Fine sat patiently in line. He didn't seem to be on the phone. He didn't seem to be doing much of anything except taking an occasional hit of tobacco vapor off his lightsaber. Nor did he seem upset. He drummed his fingers on the steering wheel and checked himself out in the mirror and messed up his hair. It was all ho-hum waiting-in-line-for-a-car-wash behavior. Nothing unusual whatsoever.

But when Andrew Fine exited the car wash something had changed. He went in alone. He came out with a passenger. She looked different without the hijab, but I was certain it was his assistant, Khandra Aden. She wore her hair down and covered her eyes with sunglasses. On a cloudy day. She flipped up the collar of her shearling coat and sunk low in the Porsche's passenger seat.

I looked for the car that had entered in front of Fine's, which was most likely the car that dropped Khandra off in the car wash, but it was gone. Its driver and Fine must have coordinated getting in line. Or Khandra was already in there, waiting. Fine took a right onto Excelsior Boulevard. I pulled a U-turn and followed. I had assumed Fine showed up to Maggie's funeral because to not would have looked suspicious. And I had assumed Fine bolted the funeral because it had become too intense for him. Either sadness or guilt or both. But leaving Maggie's funeral and then picking up Khandra in a car wash implied Fine left for logistical reasons. How long could she hang out inside a car wash where the only other person was an attendant who took your token and handed you a damp rag to wipe down your dash? My guess was not long. She either was in the car in front of Fine's or one damn close to it, and she knew the attendant. Fine must have left because he received a text telling him to. Either that, or he'd always planned on leaving mid service.

Fine entered the ramp for Highway 100 South. I held

my position a few cars back. Then Ellegaard called. I answered.

"Ellie."

"Where are you?"

"Tailing Fine. Is the service over?"

"Yes. I thought about following him but saw you get up and figured it'd be too much if we both left."

"Can you do me a favor? Search Facebook for Khandra Aden in Minneapolis."

"Hold on. I got to pull over."

Fine stayed in the right lane on Highway 100. I was pretty sure where he was going so I dropped back another car.

"How do you spell her name?" I pictured the nameplate on her desk and spelled it for him. "What does she have to do with Fine?"

"Just see if there's anything on her page that would indicate how old she is."

"Hold on." Fine exited to Highway 62. It looked like he was taking Khandra to his house. "Okay," said Ellegaard, "looks like she's a junior at Washburn."

"Jesus Christ."

"What is it?"

"Fine's fucking a seventeen-year-old."

"You got to be kidding me."

"Call Gabriella. See if she can pull Khandra's records from Washburn. I want to know if she's in the work-study program."

"On it. Where's Fine now?"

"He's about to exit from 62 onto Tracy. He's headed home. Khandra Aden is with him."

"So what do we do?"

"Usual spot during the layoff?"

"See you there in thirty."

I stayed a block behind Fine, which was close enough to see him pull into his attached triple garage. I didn't believe Khandra was in any danger, so I kept driving, checking my rearview and side mirrors. No one was tailing me. I took side streets to the meeting spot, including driving half way around Lake Harriet, which is a one-way. Following the curve of the lake, I could identify eight cars behind me. When I turned off near the rose garden, none of those cars turned with me. I was confident I wasn't being followed.

Half an hour later, Ellegaard and I sat in Matt's Bar, home of the original Juicy Lucy, on 35th and Cedar. It was a long, narrow place. The bar ran along the right side and booths of brown vinyl ran along the left. Small tables occupied the space between the booths and bar. A cash machine told you how you'd be paying for your food and beverage. The walls were decorated with neon beer signs and framed accolades for the Juicy Lucy. And there was a big picture of President Obama from when he stopped by to try the famous cheese-on-the-inside cheeseburger. The place had become too famous for my taste, but year-round Christmas lights hung over the bar and there was a jukebox in front, and they saved it for me.

Ellie and I walked to the back and sat at adjacent sides of a small table so we could keep our eyes on the front door. Still wearing our suits, we looked like a couple of businessmen longing for our youth. They probably got a lot of suit-wearers in here doing just that. Responsible citizens pretending to keep it real. We each ordered a Juicy Lucy and soda with bitters from a kid who looked like he played a Flying V in a ZZ Top tribute band.

When the kid left, Ellegaard said, "Lay it out." It was

a game we played studying for our academy exams in that very bar fifteen years earlier.

"Andrew Fine doesn't have an alibi for the night of Maggie's murder," I said.

Ellegaard said, "Andrew Fine owns an office park. It's carpeted with the same fibers found in the vacuum cleaner–bag contents that covered Maggie Somerville's body and her house."

"Andrew Fine is a recovering substance abuser."

Ellegaard said, "Andrew Fine owns a call center that employs Somalis."

"Andrew Fine likes to sleep with his employees."

"Andrew Fine employs a seventeen-year-old girl as his assistant. Her name is Khandra Aden."

"Andrew Fine picked up Khandra Aden hidden from view inside a car wash. He then took her to his home."

I said, "Andrew Fine is a narcissist."

Ellegaard said, "Andrew Fine is untouchable because he's cooperating with the FBI in an antiterror investigation."

I said, "Andrew Fine was accused of rape in college. The case went to trial. He was acquitted."

Ellegaard said, "Maggie Somerville told her friend, Beth, that she and Andrew had a wild sex life."

"Robert Somerville thinks Maggie Somerville was in love with Andrew Fine."

"Andrew Fine is still legally married."

"Yes he is," I said. "Money is holding up the divorce."

"Andrew Fine invited you to a party tonight."

Ellegaard stared at me, hoping I'd provide another fact. But I was out. Neither of us said anything for a few minutes, then I said, "It's muddy."

"Yeah."

"Something doesn't track here. Something's not adding up."

We sat for another few minutes, then Billy Gibbon's stunt double brought our Juicy Lucys. We ate in silence, then Ellegaard looked at me and said, "Motive. Tell me Fine's motive."

"Money. If Maggie told people about the sex and it got back to his ex-wife, she could use it as leverage to hurt his standing in the divorce."

"But if that's true," said Ellegaard, wiping his chin, "then why would he sleep with a seventeen-year-old girl? That's much riskier behavior. If he gets caught, money isn't his biggest concern. Jail is."

I squeezed ketchup on my fries, then said, "Or not."

"Or not what?" said Ellegaard.

"If Andrew Fine's untouchable for murder, then he's definitely untouchable for statutory rape."

The front door opened. Agents Delvin Peterson and No Chin entered.

"Fuck," I said.

Ellegaard put down his burger. "Were you tailed?"

"Definitely not. I did the lake trick."

"I did the parking-ramp trick," said Ellegaard. "No way I was followed. They're tracking our cell phones."

"Technology's making life a lot less fun, you know that?"

"We're not doing anything wrong," said Ellegaard.

"Let's go say hello."

We left our table and walked toward the front of the bar where Peterson and No Chin had settled into a booth. I sat next to No Chin. Ellegaard sat next to Peterson. I sighed. "You guys must be close to breaking your case because now you're babysitting us."

No Chin spoke. "Well, we were a little disappointed you went to Maggie Somerville's funeral."

"I can't believe I'm looking at my tax dollars at work."

"We're not the enemy," said Peterson. "You know that. And you know there's a real enemy."

"Speaking of which, Shapiro," said No Chin, "who was your date for the funeral? Tall, high cheekbones. Al Shabaab recruits as well as Daesh—be careful with her."

"Don't tell me you practice racial profiling, Agent Delvin Peterson, my brother."

"Seriously, Shapiro. Who is she?"

I wasn't under oath, but all the same, lying to a federal agent can make your life hell. They have too many friends—the IRS, the ATF, the people who make the no-fly list. "Her name is Ansley Bell. She was born and raised in California. Now she's a fourth-year at the University of Minnesota Medical School."

"Why was she at the funeral?" said Peterson.

"She was my date."

"Really," said No Chin. "Fourth-year med students don't miss a day of rounds even if they have stage-four cancer. You're telling me this Ansley Bell took off a few hours to attend the funeral of a woman you didn't even know?"

They weren't stupid, these guys. And it was better if they thought I was on their side. Plus, when someone wants information, one way to get them off your back is give them too much. "Ansley Bell was adopted," I said. "Eight years ago she learned that her biological mother was Maggie Somerville. When I was consulting for Edina PD, we traced a frequently called phone number in Maggie's cell to Ansley. We thought maybe she was Maggie's secret lover. Turns out she's her secret daughter. Had her when she was fifteen. Maggie wanted the secret kept so she didn't have to explain to her tweens how her fifteen-year-old self got pregnant. Especially since the father is a Somali who was living in Minnesota before the first big wave of Somali immigrants. He went back to Somalia before the civil war and, to the best of Ansley's knowledge, still lives there."

"Do you know the Somali father's name?" said No Chin.

"Omar Bihi."

"Stay clear of Fine until we give you the okay," said Peterson. "Can we count on that?"

Ellegaard looked at me, then I said, "Yeah, you can count on it."

25

I drove back to the shitbox and went inside. Micaela's crew must have worked overnight and hit the stores as soon as they opened. Like elves with credit cards. They'd installed a new rear-door window. They'd bought new food and beverages and cleaned the kitchen to a gleam it had never known. Someone had even replaced my slashed furniture with far more tasteful pieces. The leather chair was gone. I found a note on its replacement:

> The piece that was here is being repaired. It will be delivered in two weeks.

They'd even had my sweaters dry-cleaned. I was

beginning to wonder if it was Micaela who'd broken in just for the excuse to clean me up.

I sent her a text. *Thank you*. She didn't respond.

I changed into jeans and a merino wool quarter-zip. I plugged in my phone, left it on the kitchen counter, and drove to Target where I paid cash for three pay-as-you-go phones. Then I drove down to the university. Ansley was surprised to see me when I had her paged to the lobby, and even more surprised when I asked for her phone and handed her a new one.

"Why?" she said.

"The FBI is using my phone to track my whereabouts. They saw me with you today, so now they'll be tracking you."

"Why would they be tracking me?"

"Well, for one thing, if they realize I've given them the slip, they'll track my last-known associates. Plus, the FBI will pay extra attention to anyone who is Somali."

"Seriously?"

"They have legitimate concerns. But those concerns aren't big enough to let someone get away with murder." She looked tired. Exhausted from sorrow. Exhausted from keeping so many secrets and having them all burst at once. "Keep your new phone on. I have the number. And I've e-mailed you a copy of your contacts."

I walked out of the hospital. Fat, quarter-sized snowflakes fell from gray sky. A veneer of fresh white covered the ground. The snowfall sucked the color out of the world. Only the brightest remained. A red city bus. A lime green Patagonia jacket. A yellow pedestrian-crossing sign. But even those had been dialed down to a dull version of their former vibrancy. It was Thursday, but the week was starting anew. Not because the calendar said so, but because the barometer did. Warm, wet air from the southwest.

I left the university and drove to Candy Alley. Couldn't give Ellegaard a present without having something for the girls. Then I stopped at the shitbox to drop off Ansley's iPhone. A little afternoon delight between devices. I charged it on the counter next to mine, then headed to Ellegaard's.

I stood on the stoop holding a pair of plastic bags and rang the doorbell. I heard running feet and a high-pitched scream, "It's him!" The door struggled to move, so I gave it a little nudge. When it finally swung open, I saw Maisy Ellegaard standing on the other side of the glass storm.

"What's going on, Shap?!" she said. Seven years old and already tall, Maisy was the only one of Ellegaard's daughters who looked like him. A towhead with blue eyes and paper white skin. But she had the outgoing personality of her mother, not her reserved father. I hadn't seen Maisy since she was four—the only possible way she could have remembered me was if someone had just shown her pictures or told me I was coming over. "Is that a present for me?"

"Are you going to invite me in, young lady, or should I just stand out here in the snow?"

"Oh, yeah! I forgot!" Maisy pushed open the storm door. I stepped inside.

"So is it a present or isn't it?"

"Maisy!" said her mother from the kitchen. "You're being rude."

"Nuh-uh! I'm just asking Shap a question."

"That's Mr. Shapiro to you," said an older child from the kitchen.

Maisy looked at me, her brow furled. I shook my head and whispered, "Call me Shap."

The smile burst back onto her face. "Come on, Shap!" She marched toward the kitchen. I followed.

Molly Ellegaard stood five-foot-two-inches tall with long, almost black hair and a heart-shaped face. Her dark eyes sparkled when she saw me. "Nils, where have you been?"

"I know," I said. "It's inexcusable." I gave her a hug.

"There's something in that bag, Mommy," said Maisy.

"You. Are. So. Rude," said a voice. I turned and saw Emma and Olivia Ellegaard, ages twelve and ten, their faces in their homework. Emma was the chastiser. She had dark hair and eyes like her mother with the same heart-shaped face. Olivia had the eyes and hair, but a more long and narrow face like her father.

"Can you say hello to Mr. Shapiro?" said Molly.

"I already did!" said Maisy.

"Not you, Maisy," said Olivia.

"Hello, Mr. Shapiro," said Emma. "Nice to see you again."

"Nice to see you, Emma. And you, Olivia."

"Hi," said Olivia with a smile.

"Maisy, tell 'em what my name is."

"It's Shap. That's what we're supposed to call him. He even said so himself." Emma rolled her eyes. Olivia laughed.

"I'm giving this bag to your mother. It's full of ancient candy. The kind cavemen used to eat. I'm talking Necco Wafers, Pop Rocks, Bottle Caps, Runts, Slo Pokes, Zotz. Never heard of those? Of course you haven't because cavemen ate them. I bought the whole mess at the museum of natural history." Emma wasn't buying it. Maisy was. Olivia teetered back and forth. "Your mother is the boss of this candy. So stay on her good side."

Ellegaard walked in from the dining room. "What do you say, girls?"

A flat, dull, in unison, "Thank you . . ."

Ellegaard led me down to the rec room. He'd finished half of his basement to make a five-hundred-square-foot space out of carpet, drywall, a sixty-inch TV, and a Wii. Beige carpet, white walls, and Ellegaard's head nearly touched the low ceiling. There was no furniture other than three beanbags.

He handed me his Edina PD–issued BlackBerry. "It's charged."

"Good. Report it missing tomorrow morning." He nodded. I handed him the pay-as-you-go phone. "I'm trying to do this without turning off the phones. Nothing looks more suspicious than a phone being turned off because they never are."

"I'll get in a lot of trouble for this," said Ellegaard.

"Might do you some good."

"I don't know about that. But I'm not letting anyone push me off my case."

"That a boy."

"Oh, one more thing. We got the test results back from the eyebrow hairs you found at Ansley Bell's."

"Yeah?"

"She's Maggie's daughter—no doubt about it."

We went upstairs. Molly had just given each girl a Zotz and told them not to bite into it, so, of course, all three did then screamed and spit into the sink. I said good-bye to their horror-stricken faces and gave Molly a hug.

"You're coming to dinner next week," said Molly. "And it's not up for discussion."

"Tell me what night and what to bring and I will be here."

I drove Ellegaard's BlackBerry north on Highway 100, then merged onto 94 West. The thermometer on the Volvo's dash read twenty-nine degrees. The snow fell heavy and accumulated on the frozen pavement. Half an hour later, I was in Rogers, Minnesota, where it would appear to anyone tracking Ellegaard that he was shopping at Cabela's, the outdoors superstore.

I dropped his phone into a creel in the fly-fishing department—unless someone had booked a trip to New Zealand or Patagonia, chances were slim anyone would be buying a creel that day. I returned to the Volvo, which, after sitting in the lot for only ten minutes, was dusted with snow. I grabbed the giant toothbrush from my trunk and cleared the Volvo's windows.

I needed gas, but would tip my hand if I used a credit card twenty-five miles away from my phone. So I stopped at a Holiday station, went inside, and handed the attendant a ten. With three new gallons of gas, I drove back to the shitbox, grabbed my phone along with Ansley's, and then headed back out. I filled up at the BP on 54th and France, paid with a credit card, then headed back to Rogers. It was shortly after 5:00 when I retrieved Ellegaard's BlackBerry from the creel in the fly-fishing department. Now, as far as the FBI knew, Ellegaard, Ansley, and I were all in Rogers, Minnesota. If anyone there were paying attention, our supposed location would raise a red flag. The FBI building in Brooklyn Center was only fifteen minutes away—I didn't have much time.

Ice fishermen and winter campers shopped before heading north for the weekend. I started in the ice-fishing department where two men in their midsixties looked at jigs. The tall one wore high-waisted jeans, a teal chamois shirt, and a camo baseball cap. The one who had a belly like a pregnant woman wore low-waisted jeans, a Minnesota Gophers sweatshirt, and a Minnesota Vikings winter hat with a purple ball on top.

"A Lindy jig and live minnow," said Tall. "That's the only way to go."

"Oh, I don't know, Paul. The Rapala Snap Rap—that's been working for me all winter."

"You fish it your way, Ed. I'll fish it mine. Loser buys the Grain Belt."

"Oh, yessiree. I like that there deal, eh."

I interrupted. "Where are you gentlemen headed this weekend?"

"Muskeg Bay," said Pregnant. "Ice is nice and thick. No global warming this winter."

"Because it doesn't exist," said Tall. "Got the lamestream media all confused, don't you know."

"Hey, young fella, don't be following us to our secret spot, now."

"Wish I could. You gentleman sound like a lot of fun. Plus, the dollar's so strong in Canada, you boys should get some Cubans for the icehouse. It won't be as fun when they become legal in the states."

"Hey, there's an idea," said Tall.

"Eh, I hate driving across the border," said Pregnant. "Takes up too much time."

"We'll see how they're bitin'," said Tall. "Where you headed?"

"Walker. Buddy's got an icehouse on Leech Lake. But not tonight. Taking a couple of days off next week."

"Okay. Sure," said Tall. "Good fishin' there."

"I hope so. Just picking up a few things now so I don't have to on the way up." I grabbed a package of jigs off the wall. "Well, tight lines up there, fellas. Hope you bring back a full cooler."

"We do, too," said Pregnant. They both laughed, although I'm not sure at what.

I hustled over to the camping department, ditched the jigs, and picked up a dry sack and package of bungee cords. I was headed toward the register when Micaela called.

"I'm making a turkey," she said.

"Why?"

"I just felt like it. Want to come over for dinner?"

"I do, but I can't stay much after."

"That's okay. Come over. I'll feed you and send you on your merry way."

I hung up, paid, exited the store, dropped the three phones into the dry sack and sealed it. I opened the bungees, threw out the package, and put the cords in my jacket pocket. The traffic on 94 crawled. Headlights and street lamps lit up the falling flakes. Red taillights decorated the freeway like Christmas.

Cabela's didn't display much outside during winter—not compared to the boats and canoes and deer stands in summer. But a few prefab icehouses sat out front, so I waited in one of those for Tall and Pregnant to exit the store. Fifteen minutes later, they did. I left the icehouse and followed.

I had no idea which vehicle was theirs, if it was a car, truck, SUV, or RV. One of them pushed a button on his key fob, and the lights of a Ford F-150 with a topper lit up. I got lucky—it happens once in a while. The pickup had a cargo shelf attached to the hitch. Tall and Pregnant threw their bags into the passenger cab, then Tall got into the driver's seat and Pregnant into the passenger seat. I sprinted toward the back of the truck hoping Tall would check his e-mail like every other asshole did when I was waiting for their parking spot. Maybe that's exactly what he did or maybe he was just getting his shit situated for the drive. Whatever he was doing, it gave me enough time to reach the back of the pickup and kneel behind the cargo shelf.

Two propane tanks were ratchet-strapped to the steel-mesh shelf. I sat my ass in the snow, pulled a handful of bungees out of my pocket, and hooked one end underneath the cargo shelf. That's when the truck started. I couldn't remember if a car was parked in front of it—if there was, Tall would have to back out of the parking space. My being in the way wouldn't stop him. I stretched the bungee, hooked the second hook underneath the steel mesh, and hoped Tall and Pregnant were fighting over whose iPod to listen to on the drive north. I slipped the dry sack, with the three phones inside, between the bungee and the steel-mesh shelf, then got into a squat. Maybe they were opening beef jerky or Salted Nut Rolls. Whatever they were doing, they gave me enough time to stretch two more bungees under the dry sack, securing it solidly underneath the shelf.

Pregnant and Tall wouldn't discover the phones until they removed the LP tanks, probably a few miles south of the Canadian border. I stood and walked straight back from the pickup. I made it all the way to the store before Tall put the truck in drive and headed for the parking lot exit.

26

I stopped at the liquor store and bought a bottle of Tyrconnell 10. It cost eighty bucks, but sending the phones on their trip north put me in the mood to celebrate.

Micaela made turkey, stuffing, mashed potatoes, and green beans. We ate at the little table overlooking Lake Harriet. The sodium lights on the lake's encircling parkway cast an orange hue through the falling snow. A pair of runners slogged across the unplowed path, their headlamps pushing two cones of white light in front of them. I caught Micaela's reflection in the window—she wasn't looking at the lake—she was looking at me. Her likeness doubled in the double-pane glass. My friend. My love. If I could only get both women into one image, one Micaela, I'd be okay.

She had grown more beautiful as she got older. In a few years, I'd have to blind myself just to carry on. But not beholding her would cure nothing. Loving Micaela exhausted me. What it was. What it wasn't. I wanted to fall in love with Ansley Bell, not because she was young and beautiful but because she might be the antidote for Micaela. I wanted to feel jealous when seeing Ansley with the guy who turned out to be her husband. But I wasn't. Not a bit. It should have at least stoked a fire of disappointment, but I felt nothing. I wished Ansley could hurt me. I wished anyone could other than Micaela. If I could feel anything in relation to another woman, I'd be cured. But I wasn't. Maybe I was having a bad week or maybe it was the Tyrconnell or the tryptophan or the combination of all three, but sitting at that table over-looking a snowy lake and the city behind it, I'd lost the strength to hold up my shield. I was collapsing under its weight. And she saw it.

"What's wrong, Nils?" she said.

I stared at her doubled reflection in the window as if she were a solar eclipse, as if it were the only safe way to do so.

"Tell me," she whispered.

I turned and looked at her but said nothing.

After a long silence, she said, "Do you want another whiskey?"

"Yes, but I can't. I'm working later."

"Anything new on the case?"

"Ellie and I are going to flush out our prime suspect. Something feels wrong about it, though. I just can't pinpoint what. I can't focus."

"Listen, I want to talk to you about something." She sat up straight. "I acquired a start-up that develops apps for surveillance. Webcams, motion detection, heat detection, metadata collection and analysis. I'd like to hire you as a technical consultant. It's good money, Nils. And benefits. And you'd work in an office with free coffee and a full kitchen. Paid vacation and sick days. You deserve a little stability. And you'd do a great job."

"Sounds interesting," I said.

"It'd be a win-win for both of us."

"Let me think about it."

"Please do. These cases are taking a toll on you."

"Yeah?"

"You're not yourself lately." She reached across the table and grabbed my hand.

"I don't understand what people mean when then say that. People are always themselves. They may not be the self they want to be at that moment, but they are themselves. Personality isn't a snapshot—it's a movie. A long fucking movie."

"Maybe," she said. "All I know is I haven't seen you like this before. Is it fair to say you're not your best self?"

I looked out the window again and found the runners at the south end of the lake. I rested my forehead on the cool glass.

"Nils, are you okay?"

I couldn't think anymore. I just let go. My voice came out tired and weak. "I hate that I love you." I pulled my head off the window and looked at her. She looked hurt but didn't say a word. I got up from the table and left.

27

Andrew Fine's estate was on Cheyenne Trail in Indian Hills, a subdivision in west Edina with street names like Navaho Trail, Dakota Trail, Iroquois Trail, and Blackfoot Pass. The trails and passes could have been dubbed "streets" and "avenues," but I suppose that would have diminished the illusion that Native Americans still wandered this land studded with six-thousand-square-foot homes, four-car garages, swimming pools, hot tubs, tennis courts, bass ponds, and, in winter, private skating rinks.

Fine's house was a monster of cedar shingles, arched windows, and a roof of at least a dozen peaks and half a dozen chimneys. The gables served no structural purpose, I'm sure, but existed to make a statement that rich people can have as many gables as they want, so, in conclusion, Andrew Fine was rich.

Shortly after 9:00, when I arrived, fifty or so cars were parked along Cheyenne Trail but none in the driveway of the four-car garage. Etiquette dictates that driveway spots are reserved for family and close friends, and, apparently, Andrew Fine had none. I parked my old Volvo right in the middle of that driveway then followed the flagstone walk to the front door. A sign said COME ON IN. So I did.

"Welcome," said a tall woman with short blond hair and big hoop earrings. She wore off-white wool pants and a red Scandinavian ski sweater with white snowflakes. "May I take your coat?"

"Yes. Thank you." I handed her my down sweater. She hung it in the front-hall closet and said, "The party's downstairs and out back. There's a full bar and a marijuana bar, if that's your thing. The hot tub is fired up. There's a bonfire and, further down in the yard, broomball on the pond."

"Won't I need my coat for broomball?"

"You will not because Andrew has red coats and blue coats so people know who's on their team."

"Just like Bunker Hill."

"Right on," she said, having no idea what I was referring to. She was in her early twenties, if that. You can't blame kids for not knowing their Revolutionary War battles—they're inundated with so much information now and anything they don't know they can learn in five seconds on their phone. "One more thing," she said, "I need to take your keys."

"Why?"

"Because there's booze and pot and Andrew wants you to enjoy it all, but if you're not in shape to drive, we'll have someone take you home."

"I'm sure Andrew's lawyer appreciates that." I handed her my keys.

The party was in full swing downstairs. The smell of marijuana wafted through the air to the steady four/four beat of Tom Petty's *Wildflowers*. Most everyone was outside, woven in a tapestry of smoke, drink, and heat lamps. The hot tub was full of bodies, steam rising off shoulders and heads. Down on the pond, broomball players slipped and skidded on the ice, lit by the reflection of city lights off the low cloud ceiling and falling snow.

The only people inside were a couple of guys immersed in a game of nine-ball on the pool table. Their game mattered—a serious endeavor among frivolous tomfoolery. It is what we all strive for—finding that thing on which to focus—the thing that makes time fly and lets us feel we earn the right to sleep at night. And those two found it on slate and felt with sticks and balls—lucky bastards.

A pretty woman with thick, long dark hair sat at a linen-covered table. Four glass jars, large ones—the kind you might see a brain floating in—sat on the table. Each was full of marijuana buds. Three people waited as she rolled a joint that looked like a tiny paper baseball bat.

I was looking for Andrew Fine when I heard, "It's super Shap, private eye!" I turned and saw Kallie, the blonde from Bunny's, stepping out of the bathroom in her bathing suit. "Quick, Sherlock Holmes! What's wrong with this picture?!"

"You have a cosmopolitan in your left hand and yet you're right-handed."

She made a buzzer noise. "Wrong, sir! It is January in Minnesota and I'm wearing a bikini!" She was flat-out drunk—the rack and pinion system that kept her eyes in alignment wasn't working properly. She walked over and put her arm around me. "But I am right-handed. How did you know?"

"Left-handed people grow up feeling they're outsiders. Most develop a sense of shame that, when they mature, morphs into a sense of humility. Since you have no humility, you therefore are most likely right-handed."

"Goddammit, you're right. Humility means being quiet, right? Because I am not that. I'm loud. I don't give a fuck. That's who I am. You know what, Shap? You're cute. I'd totally drop trou for ya." She took a big swig of her cosmopolitan then lost her train of thought. "What?" She looked at me with her misaligned eyes, then, "Oh, yeah! Me and Lauren Googled you. You've done some cool shit. It's sexy. But I know, Nils Shapiro, I know you're here for Lauren, not me. I saw the way you were looking at her at Bunny's and that's okay 'cause . . . don't tell her I said this . . . promise?" Another swig. "You have to promise."

"I promise."

"Lauren . . ." She looked around to make sure no one was near, as if she were a secret-teller in a play staged for children. "Lauren likes you. I mean like likes you. So go for it, dude. Ya might get lucky. Oh, fuck! Andrew's back! I gotta go!" She headed for the French doors leading to the patio.

"Kallie."

She stopped and turned back toward me. "What, Nils Shapiro, PI?"

"Where is Andrew back from? Where did he go?"

"He said he went to get me more cosmopolitan juice.

I like him. A lot. Can you believe how rich he is? Can you? I've never been to a house like this before. It's fucking amazing. He's going to give me a tour later. Do you think he likes a lot of girls? I bet he does but that's okay. One of us is going to snag him. I got just as good a chance as anyone." Then she whispered in the loudest whisper I've ever heard, "That's why I put on my bikini. Let him see the goods. 'Cause I'm a fucking blast in the sack." She winked, turned around, and opened the patio door. "Andrew! Over here!"

I waited a moment then followed. Emerald Eyes stood with her back against the bar as I walked out. "Look who's here," she said, "party's over."

Lauren wore a navy down vest over a muted pink turtleneck sweater, faded blue jeans, and white knee-high sheepskin boots made by Robert Somerville's company. She'd parted her straight dark hair on the side and her lips shone with something glossy but uncolored.

"Hi, Lauren." I walked toward her and noticed a pendant hanging outside her turtleneck, a trance-inducing medallion like those worn by the unattainable loves of my youth. I hugged her as if I knew her—I don't know why.

"You remember my name," she said.

"Yeah, yours I remember. What's her face's, no clue."

"Oh, I think you jest, Mr. Shapiro. Can I buy you a drink? The sun went down. You should be able to handle it."

I was on the job and already had a whiskey in me, so I ordered a Guinness. Everyone thinks you're drinking hard when you drink Guinness—no one believes it's a light beer.

The bartender went to work. Emerald Eyes said, "You going in the hot tub tonight?"

"I can't," I said. "It's my time of the month."

"Shove a tampon up there. You'll be fine."

"I just don't feel pretty. There's no way I'm getting in a bathing suit."

"Oh, you're pretty, sweetheart," she said. "You got pretty to spare."

"Shap. You made it." Andrew Fine walked behind the bar and grabbed a soda. "You bring your suit?"

"He won't go in," said Lauren. "He's on the rag."

Fine smiled. "You got a minute, buddy?" He took a hit of vapor off his lightsaber and exhaled it in two streams out his nostrils. Like a dragon.

"Of course," I said. "Lauren, my dear. I'll be back. Don't make yourself hard to find." I flirted with her for Fine's ears—the poor girl had become my cover. But I will admit she stirred something in me. I doubted it was something good. Maybe that was okay. Maybe that was long overdue.

"I like to hide in small spaces," Lauren said. "So I can't promise I'll be easy to find." And for that smart-ass remark she got a kiss on the cheek.

Fine led me away from the party and back upstairs into his home office. "Have a seat," he said. "I got to take a leak." He put his vaporizer on his desk. The desk was designed to look as if it were made out of old-time storage trunks. I don't know why someone went to all the trouble to design a desk that looked so stupid, but I was more troubled by Fine, who proved to be even more stupid by buying it.

He stepped into the bathroom and shut the door. I grabbed his vaporizer off the desk, unscrewed it, and took Ellegaard's tracking device out of my front pocket. I peeled away a spec of paper which exposed the adhesive and stuck it on the inside of the housing. I screwed it back together, then heard the toilet flush as I returned the vaporizer to Fine's desk. Fine came out of the bathroom and sat behind the faux trunk.

"I got a problem," he said. "I need your advice."

"Same thing we talked about last time?"

"I don't know. Maybe. That's what I need to talk to you about. The Edina cops have disappeared. No more follow-ups. No more asking about my alibi. Nothing."

"That's good, isn't it?"

"I think so—yeah. I had nothing to do with Maggie's death and hopefully they know that and are spending their time on whoever did kill her. But why did they back off if I haven't given them my alibi?"

"You told them you were alone the night Maggie was killed."

"Well, I wasn't."

"Why did you lie?"

"Because my alibi would get me in another kind of trouble."

"Worse than being accused of murder?"

"Yes," he said, "considering I'm not guilty of murder." I didn't respond and let the silence hang. He took another hit off his lightsaber then said, "I saw you at the funeral. In the lobby by the coatrack. Who was that woman you were with?"

"That was a friend of Maggie's."

"Why were you with her?"

"She didn't have anyone to go to the funeral with. I'd questioned her a couple of times about Maggie. She felt comfortable with me and asked if I'd go with her."

"Somali?"

"Half."

"You remember I told you I have trouble resisting the temptation of the employer-employee relationship?"

"I do."

"Can I trust you, Shap?" He stared at me with cold, dead eyes. "I mean really trust you?"

I could barely hear the party outside through the insulated walls and double-paned windows. These new houses are sealed so tight I felt like half a lemon in Tupperware. "I can't break the law for you, Andrew."

"But other than that, I can trust you?" I nodded. "You met my assistant, Khandra Aden."

"Yes."

"She's a high school student. Seventeen years old. On the work-study program. Goes to school between 8:00 and 10:00 every day then comes to work for me. The reason I didn't give the police an alibi for Maggie's murder is because I was with Khandra at the time. She spent the night." He glanced up at me for a reaction.

"Not for business reasons, I'm guessing."

"I'm sleeping with her, Shap."

"Why are you telling me this, Andrew? I just said I can't break the law for you. That's statutory rape and you know it."

"Because in the last few days, weird things have been happening."

"How does that change anything?"

"She's calling me all the time. Wants to know where I am. What I'm doing. When she can see me next."

"What's weird about that? She's probably in love with you."

"Yeah, maybe. But this is different. It feels more like she's keeping tabs on me. And she's smart. Really fucking smart. Plus she never talks about her friends or school or other seventeen-year-old shit. And the more I've been thinking about it, the more it seems like maybe she's not really a high school student. Maybe she's not really seventeen. I have not fucked an underage girl before her—I swear—well, except when I was seventeen, but that doesn't count—so I don't have a point of reference in recent memory. But I got to tell you, Shap, Khandra knows what she's doing in bed. I mean, that's why it's hard to quit her. She's good."

"Andrew, it's easy to find out if she is who she says she is. I mean, she works for you because of a work-study program at the high school. You can talk to them."

"Oh, I have. And they say she's a student. Her Social Security number and driver's license, it all checks out. But . . ." He sucked another cloud of vapor into his lungs and held it. Then it leaked out in wisps when he resumed. ". . . this is the part where I need your trust. Can't say a word to anyone."

"Again—"

"This part's legal."

"All right."

"I'm cooperating with the FBI. They're investigating Al-Shabaab and Daesh recruiting young Muslims in the Twin Cities. I employ a lot of young Muslims and, while working for me, they have access to phones and computers. I let the FBI tap the whole place, their conversations, their e-mails, their Web searches, their IMs to each other. Everything. And Khandra's been wanting to know so much about me lately. I'm getting the feeling she's FBI. I'm like an informant. They got to know if they can trust me, right?"

"Maybe," I said. "Does it matter if she's FBI? 'Cause if she is, she's probably twenty-three or twenty-four and just looks seventeen. Then you're in the clear and can use her as an alibi."

"No, I can't, because being with her doesn't clear me

of murdering Maggie. Khandra had a few martinis that night and passed out at 10:00."

"Andrew, I got to stop you. None of this makes sense."

"Why not?"

"How can she sleep over at your house if she's seventeen? Where are her parents?"

"I know, that's what I'm saying. She says they work nights. Or she tells them she's staying at a friend's. But she's slept over plenty of times. It's weird. That's why I think she's not who she says she is."

"I still don't understand. What's the problem if she's FBI? You're on their side. And if she is a Fed and was on the job and had too much to drink and passed out, she's not going to admit that."

Fine took another hit off the lightsaber and kept it in his hand. "What if she says she just fell asleep, that it had nothing to do with alcohol?"

"You're helping the FBI. They don't want to fuck that up."

"But listen. What about when they don't need me anymore? There's no statute of limitations on murder. She could turn on me. You know, tie up loose ends. Get me out of the picture."

"Why would they do that if you didn't kill Maggie?"

"I told you. To get rid of me when they don't need me anymore. Edina PD hasn't arrested anyone yet. Maybe they're waiting for me to be done with the FBI, then the FBI's going to feed me to 'em."

Andrew Fine's narcissism had spun him into a frenzy—there were just too many ways, in his mind, this was all about him. It was the perfect opportunity to flush him. All I had to do was plant the seed so Ellie and I could follow him to the one place that would prove his guilt.

And he'd gift-wrap it for us. But something felt wrong. Either Andrew Fine didn't kill Maggie Somerville or Andrew Fine had lost his mind. Or maybe both. Or maybe he was just crazy intuitive and Khandra was FBI.

Regardless, the time had come. I didn't expect Peterson and No Chin to tail my phone up north. I only hoped they'd think I was up there on a fishing trip with my pal Ellegaard and Ansley Bell. That's what freed me and Ellie to do what we'd planned. But the FBI wouldn't be fooled for long. Our window of opportunity was small.

Fine's cell phone rang. He looked at the screen. "Caller ID blocked. No thanks." He denied the call.

"So Andrew," I said, "a buddy of mine at Edina PD—"

His cell rang again. "Caller ID blocked again. Hold on. Let me see who it is."

Fine answered the phone. "Hello?" He looked at me and mouthed, "Khandra."

I whispered, "Let's hear what she has to say."

28

Fine put the phone on speaker and said, "Hey, K. Where you calling from? The connection sucks."

"A friend's house. My phone's dead." It was a bad connection, but in a strange way, like she was calling from the dark side of the moon, or from 1995.

"Everything all right?" said Fine.

"I'm bored. When's your stupid party going to be over?"

"Late, darlin'. You know that." Fine didn't take his eyes off me. "We'll get together tomorrow night."

"I bet there are a lot of drunk girls around there, Andrew. I don't like it."

"I'm talking to you. What don't you like?"

"That it doesn't sound like there's a party going on."

"That's because I'm upstairs at the moment."

"Alone?"

"Yes."

"Why am I on speaker?"

"I was in the hot tub. I'm changing."

"I don't believe you."

"Let it go, K. Hang out with your friends. We talked about this. So people don't get suspicious. You can get me in a lot of trouble."

"My friends are boring. And I don't want to get you in trouble," she said. "I just want to be with you. It's not fair you're having a party and I can't come."

"Man, I'm having a hard time hearing you."

"I can't help it. It's a crappy phone."

"Watch something on HBO Go or Netflix. That's why I gave you the passwords. I'll see you tomorrow night."

"My parents went to Iowa State for the weekend to visit my brother. Will you pick me up when your party is over?"

"Why didn't you tell me they were leaving for the weekend?"

"Because I didn't know. They were going to drive my brother down for second semester next weekend but his soccer coach asked him to come early for indoor workouts. This is so boring I can't even talk about it anymore. Just come get me after the party. Please?"

"It might not be until 3:00 A.M."

"I don't care. I want to sleep next to you. I want to wake up next to you."

Fine sucked in another lungful of vapor and held it.

"Andrew? Are you there?"

"I'll text you when I'm on my way."

"You have to text my friend's number. I told you my phone is dead."

"Why don't you charge it?"

"I dropped it in the toilet. She said I have to put it in rice but I don't know if that will help."

"What's the number?" She told him and Fine wrote it down. "Usual place?"

"I don't want to take a bus tonight. It's snowing."

"I can't pick you up at your building."

"I'll be at my friend's building a couple blocks away. I'll text you the address. No one will see."

"All right, K. I'll be there later."

"You don't sound excited."

"I am. I promise."

"I love you."

"I love you, too." Fine hung up the phone. He drummed his fingers on the steamer-trunk desk for a moment, then said, "What do you think?"

"About what?"

"Is she working undercover for the FBI?"

"If she is," I said, "she's doing a damn good job. She sounds seventeen to me. Listen, Andrew, do what you want. But if I were you I'd assume she's not FBI. My primary concern would be going to jail for statutory rape. What the hell are you thinking? You get busted and that *would* piss off the FBI. I don't understand why you'd take that risk."

"I quit drugs. I quit booze. But I'm not perfect."

"No one expects you to be. But if it's women you want, Kallie is downstairs and would love nothing more than if you asked her to spend the night."

"Who's Kallie?"

"The blonde from Bunny's."

"What are you talking about, Shap?"

"The other day. In Bunny's. I was sitting at the bar and you came over. The two nurses? You invited them to the party. It's why you invited me to this party."

"Oh, yeah, yeah, yeah," he said. "That's how I know that girl. Yeah . . ."

"She's under your spell."

"I'm not a sex addict, Shap. Well, maybe I kind of am. But who isn't, right? My problem is I'm . . . listen, this is going to sound weird but what the hell . . . I'm in love with Khandra. I fucking think about her all the time. I still hit on other women and flirt with them but it's just out of habit. Like I'm on autopilot with that shit. But I'm not into it. It feels like drinking and drugs did at the end, just a thing that made me feel shitty most of the time. That's why I got in the program. And now it's like that with other women because I'm in love with Khandra."

"Well, if you really love her, Andrew, behave until she turns eighteen. Then you can do whatever you want."

"Goddammit," said Andrew, not in anger but resignation.

"Andrew, I'm not officially working for you so I'm saying this only because we go back. But I'm hearing Edina PD might have a break in Maggie's case."

"What is it?"

"I don't know exactly. I have a buddy over there. I was talking to him earlier today and all he said to me was they couldn't find any forensic evidence in Maggie's house because the entire thing was covered in vacuum cleaner dirt. But it was covered in so much dirt, they figure it must have come from an apartment building or office building or hotel or something. So tomorrow they're going to start taking vacuum cleaner bags from a few key places they've identified and see if any of the dirt matches what they found in Maggie's house. You know, to see if it's made up of the same kind of carpet fibers and soil that could get tracked in from the grounds surrounding the building."

Andrew tilted back in his chair and looked at the ceiling. "About fucking time," he said. "I know they've backed off, but they're not going to stop suspecting me 'til they catch the fucker who killed her."

"Andrew, listen to me. They're going to check the fibers in the carpet at the call center. And they'll check the fibers in the carpet from your office park in Bloomington. If they find a match, you're fucked."

Fine ran his fingers through his tousled hair then scratched the back of his neck. He removed the top sheet from the pad on which he'd written the number to reach Khandra. He popped up from his seat, put his cell in his pocket, and grabbed his lightsaber vaporizer. "Come on, let's get back downstairs. People are going to think we popped up here for a quickie."

We went downstairs. Andrew stopped at the bar to chat with friends. I walked outside and down to the pond to watch some broomball and call Ellegaard. I told him about my conversation with Fine and that I'd planted the tracking device in his vaporizer.

"I'm picking up the signal," said Ellegaard. "If he leaves, I'll be on him."

"He said he'd pick up Khandra sometime before 3:00 A.M."

"Good thing I napped."

"Let me know when he moves. I'll be right behind you with the camera."

Lauren walked toward me. "Here's me making myself

easy to find." She'd put on a long stocking cap of tight horizontal stripes in a million colors. I told Ellegaard I had to go and hung up.

"I like a girl who can follow directions."

"Are you working tonight?"

"What makes you think that?"

"You appear very serious when you think no one's looking."

"Maybe you should be in my business."

"Thanks, but I like my own. Have you been to this house before?"

"No, this is my first time."

"Too bad."

"Why?"

"I want a tour."

"Ask Andrew. I'm sure he'll give you a tour."

"I want it from you."

Maybe she was drunk or maybe she just decided to go for it but Emerald Eyes stepped right up and kissed me. We kept kissing and part of me hoped Fine would see us to solidify my cover, but most of me felt like kissing her back so I did. After a minute or so we broke.

"Don't say anything," she said, and tasted her bottom lip. "You'll wreck it." She smiled, but only because she had good manners.

"I have to go," I said. She looked embarrassed and her eyes welled. "Not because of you—I just do because you're right—I am working. I promise." She looked down at the ground. "You want to grab dinner tomorrow night?" She lifted her head and nodded. "That was a good kiss."

"You're damn right it was." Then she started to cry, but more out of relief than sadness.

Her tears unraveled me. I kissed her and backed her

against an oak tree. I cupped a hand behind her head, pressed my hips into hers, and her breath found voice. "Don't go."

"What time is it?"

"Look at your phone like everyone else."

I did. It was 11:15. I said, "Let's go on that tour."

We walked up the yard and into the house. I didn't have to love Emerald Eyes. I just had to fuck her. Fuck her and fuck anybody else until I fucked Micaela out of my system.

We found a wing of guest bedrooms on the second floor and chose a small one with a full-sized bed. I shut and locked the door and kissed Emerald Eyes hard and put my hand up her sweater and ran it over her soft, fleshy breasts.

We made love on the floor. She came, and then I came, and then I got her off again with my hand. She turned her back to me in exhaustion or sadness or both. We laid there for a while and said nothing, then I got up and got dressed.

The moment I met Lauren in Bunny's, she impressed me with her dignity and humor. And she felt it—I had seen in her the qualities other men looked past because she was thirty pounds overweight or unable to hide her intolerance for their ignorance or ego. So she opened up. I figured she regretted that.

She spoke first, "At least we don't have to make the bed."

I laughed. "What do you mean 'at least'? What's wrong? Are we going to have an awkward dinner tomorrow night?"

I felt the tag on the outside of my T-shirt. I took it off, turned it right side out, and put it back on again.

She rolled toward me, her face wet and blackened with run mascara. "Are you serious?"

"Yeah, if you're regretting this—"

"No, not that. Are you serious that we're still on for dinner tomorrow night?"

"That was the plan, wasn't it?"

She nodded. "Yes. Thank you."

I knelt down to the floor and kissed her knowing full well I had failed, once again, to exorcise Micaela from my being.

29

Lauren and I went back downstairs separately but reconnected at the bar where she ordered a beer and I grabbed a bottle of water. She gave me a you're-no-fun look, and I said, "I really do have to work tonight."

"It's almost midnight," she said.

"It happens sometimes." We sat at a table under the covered patio. The big lazy flakes had given way to a harder snow. Six fresh inches had whitened the ground and rooftops and broomball players' hats. They ran with ease on the snow-covered ice, their screams and ball whacks muted by the fresh layer of insulation. I looked for Andrew Fine but didn't see him. My phone rang. It was Ellegaard. I said to Lauren, "I told you," and stepped away from the table.

"I'm parked on Gleason at the bottom of Indian Hills Pass," he said. "I borrowed a neighbor's Outback to handle the snow. Are you near Fine?"

"No," I said. "I can't see him. What's the tracking device telling you?"

"Says he's still home. You sure he takes that vaporizer with him everywhere?"

"It's his latest addiction. That and high school girls."

"Text me when you confirm his location. Just want to make sure everything's working right."

"Got it."

I told Lauren I'd be back in a few minutes and went to look for Fine. I found him upstairs in the living room talking to Kallie, who was still shit-faced and still wearing nothing but a bikini. They sat together in a chair and a half. Fine held his lightsaber in one hand and Kallie's thigh in the other.

"Shap!" he said. "You're still here, dude. I like it."

"Have either of you guys seen Lauren?"

"Ah . . ." said Kallie. "I knew it!" she slurred. "You two . . . love each other!"

"Haven't seen her, Shap."

"Thanks."

"If you find her let me know. I think Kallie here may need a ride home before she passes out."

"I'm not going to pass out," said Kallie. "I'm getting my second wind. Did you know Shap's a private eye? I'm going to hire him to find out if you have a girlfriend."

"I already told you I do," said Fine.

"Uh-huh. Likely excuse."

I headed back downstairs and stopped at the bottom to text Ellegaard that Fine was still at home and in possession of his vaporizer and it didn't look like he was going anywhere soon. I then sat down next to Lauren and told her Kallie needed a ride home and that I had to go.

"Work," she said.

"I promise." I kissed her good-bye, went back upstairs, retrieved my coat and keys and left. I was still the only one parked in the driveway. I took the giant toothbrush out of the trunk and swept the snow off the car. Ice froze to the windshield, and while scraping it away, I remembered I had already made dinner plans for tomorrow night with Stevey Fine. I had no choice about which one to cancel and decided to call Stevey in the morning. I wondered why he wasn't at the party.

I wound my way down and out of Indian Hills and found Ellegaard parked in his borrowed Subaru along the frontage road to Highway 62. I pulled a U-turn so our windows were a few feet apart. "Anybody follow you?"

"No one," he said.

"Coffee?"

"Yeah, maybe. But I don't want to leave this spot."

"I'll go get—"

"Hold on," said Ellegaard. "Fine's moving."

"One car or two?"

"Two. Just in case."

"Okay. Let's keep the line open."

I raised my window and drove up Gleason toward Valley View. Ellegaard started the Subaru but kept the lights off. Thirty seconds later he said, "Fine just came down. He's going left on Gleason."

"I'll turn around," I said.

"No, don't," said Ellegaard. "Keep going the way you're going—wind your way up toward Highway 100. If he's headed to the Hyland Lakes Office Park, you'll be closer. I'm going to follow but stay far behind with the tracker."

I took a right on Antrim Road and then a left on 70th. A minute later I was across the highway from Christ Presbyterian, where I'd attended Maggie Somerville's funeral that morning. I thought of Ansley, alone with her mother's death. I wanted to call her but couldn't hang up with Ellegaard.

I cruised up the highway entrance ramp and merged onto Highway 100 South. There were only a few cars on the highway. We were stuck behind a pair of side-by-side plows that pushed snow from the two rightmost lanes onto the shoulder. I said, "I got a couple of plows fucking up the freeway."

"Uh-oh," said Ellegaard.

"Is he coming up behind me?"

"No. He just went north on Highway 100."

"North? Then he's not going to the office park?"

"No, he's not."

"Fuck. I'll turn around." I exited on 77th, went under the highway and got on the ramp for Highway 100 North. "Maybe he's picking up Khandra early."

Ellegaard said, "Maybe he'll take her back to the office park so she can help him remove vacuum cleaner bags from the garbage bin. Or maybe he has a stash of them in the Midtown office. Tracker's working like a charm. I'm going to stay back."

"I'm a few minutes behind you." I hit the gas but felt the Volvo slide toward the center barrier. I eased off the pedal and kept it below fifty. Fine and Ellegaard had all-wheel drive. The Volvo did not.

"He passed Excelsior Boulevard," said Ellegaard. "Looks like he's passing Highway 7, too."

"Then he's not headed to the office."

"I'm going to get a little closer. No way he'll spot me with the snow coming down this hard." We said nothing for a couple of minutes, then Ellegaard said, "394 East."

"I'm behind you a mile or so."

"He's staying in the right lane."

"I have no idea where Khandra lives. I should have asked him."

I exited onto 394 East and headed for downtown Minneapolis. The skyline glowed soft and warm through the falling snow. Ellegaard said, "94 East."

A few minutes later, Ellegaard told me Fine transitioned onto 35W North, went over the Mississippi River bridge, and exited on Washington Avenue. "Looks like he's headed to the university," said Ellegaard. "West Bank."

The University of Minnesota's West Bank is part of the Cedar-Riverside area. Few students live there anymore. Now people refer to the area as Little Somalia. The Riverside Plaza high-rises tower above it all. The gray concrete structures feature bright multicolored panels to remind you they were built in the 1970s. The *Mary Tyler Moore Show*'s Mary Richards moved into the tallest of the structures late in the series. You can see it in the opening credits of the show.

"He's on Cedar now," said Ellegaard. "There are so few cars out here I have to hang back."

"I see the Subaru. I'm half a block behind you.

"Fine's pulling over near the Cedar Cultural Center. I'm stopping here."

"What's he doing in front of the cultural center? Khandra said she'd be at a friend's house. That's too public of a place."

"Maybe she's counting on no one being around. It's almost 2:00 in the morning."

"Maybe," I said. "I'm coming up behind you."

"Holy Mother of God!" shouted Ellegaard. I heard the gunshots from outside and then through the phone. "Stop, Shap! Stay back!"

I killed my lights, coasted in behind Ellegaard, and saw the last few muzzle flashes of the ambush. I counted six gunmen. They emptied their sawed-offs into Fine's Porsche, leaving a cloud of smoke, then they disappeared between the buildings.

"I'll call it in," said Ellegaard. "Goddammit."

"Just stay back. There's no life to save in that car."

30

Andrew Fine took so many shotgun blasts to the head and torso he had to be identified by a birthmark on his left calf.

The gunmen had approached through a vacant lot a few buildings from the Cedar Cultural Center. The lot sat between the Wienery, a restaurant featuring Polish sausages, and Samiya Store, a boutique that sold traditional Somali women's clothing. The gunman all wore size-fourteen moon boots. Their footprints disappeared into the McKnight Building, the tallest of the towers in the Cedar-Riverside complex. It housed thousands of Somalis. Not one of them, I was sure, would admit to seeing gunmen, who most likely had incinerated their moon boots and threw the ashes off the roof before police arrived on the scene.

At 3:45 A.M., Ellegaard and I found ourselves in our favorite FBI conference room in Brooklyn Center. Special Agent in Charge Colleen Milton sat at the head of the table and proceeded over the berating. Agents No Chin and Delvin Peterson sat on either side of her. They glared at us, no doubt pissed for being duped by a simple cell phone ruse, not to mention their yearlong operation was now floating in the shitter. Edina Police Chief McGinnis was there, too. He wore a tartan plaid scarf over a corduroy shirt, which confirmed that scarves were his affectation, a condemnation of his character that felt gratifying considering how much our relationship had deteriorated. Representing the Minneapolis PD—the killing happened there, after all—were Assistant Chief Rosalind Hardin, Deputy Chief Jacob Freeman, and Inspector Gabriella Núñez, who, I presume, was included because of her history with Ellie and me.

The only thing we all had in common was the desire to be in our beds. I'd stopped at Lunds on the way and bought two dozen freshly baked donuts—a transparent attempt at ingratiation that wasn't a total failure.

Special Agent in Charge Colleen Milton shut her eyes and took a few deep breaths as if it were an exercise she'd learned in anger-management camp. "Tell it from the beginning and tell it all."

Ellegaard and I looked at each other. He gave me a nod, and I told the entire story from the moment we left this room the last time. I told him about McGinnis firing me off the case and that Ellie and I had disobeyed the FBI's wishes by not backing off Fine. Our intent was to flush Fine into incriminating himself since we were sensitive to the ongoing FBI investigation. We hoped he would, in the middle of the night, try to retrieve vacuum cleaner bags from the Hyland Lakes Office Park, an act we would photograph so he could be arrested when the FBI's investigation was over. That's all we wanted. I admitted to giving our cell phones a ride up north to free ourselves of any encumbrances that might thwart the task at hand. There's no law against giving your phones a ride. And there's no law against accepting an invitation to the party of a longtime acquaintance, and him confiding in you because of your expertise.

"The ironic thing," I said, "is that Andrew Fine had convinced himself that Khandra Aden was working for the FBI, keeping an eye on him to make sure he was cooperating with you."

"You should have told us about Fine's relationship with Khandra," said Milton. "We could have determined she was working for Al-Shabaab."

"First you tell us to back off Fine. Now you're telling us we should have done your job for you? No wonder you fucking missed the boat on this one."

"Watch your mouth, Mr. Shapiro. I can make your life damn difficult."

"And it'll come right back at you, Special Agent in Charge Milton. I have a copy of an e-mail you sent to Chief McGinnis where you directed him to back off Andrew Fine, despite him being the prime suspect of a murder case."

McGinnis ground his teeth. "How did you get that e-mail?"

"You forwarded it to me. Sir."

"The hell I did."

"It's quite easy to prove," said Ellegaard. "Saying you didn't do it is only going to make you look worse."

"You're in enough trouble as it is, Detective."

"I've done nothing wrong, sir."

I said, "Maybe you should spend less time picking out scarves, Chief, and more time learning how to use your digital devices."

"Don't you fucking—"

"Shut up," said Milton. "That e-mail doesn't mean a goddamn thing. Asking you to hold off on Fine was a reasonable request."

"Maybe," I said. "But your carnival barking about the importance of your mission is just going to make you look that much more ridiculous because you botched that important mission. You did. Not me. Not Detective Ellegaard. Not Edina PD." McGinnis lifted his chin with my absolving him of any wrongdoing. "Fine drove all over town with Khandra Aden. Khandra Aden was working with Al-Shabaab. She slept at his house. In fact, she was with him the night Maggie Somerville was murdered—sound asleep, passed out after too many martinis. And if you were doing your job, Special Agent in Charge, you would have known that. You might have even been able to tell us whether or not Fine left the house that night, and then none of this would have happened."

"By the way," said Ellegaard, "does anyone know where Khandra Aden is now?"

Gabriella consulted a folder. "The call she made to Fine pinged a cell tower in New York."

"The sound quality was so shitty," I said. "Any chance it was relayed from another cell from out of the country?"

"I wasn't finished," said Gabriella. Her tone was kind. Ellie and I weren't in trouble with Minneapolis PD. "We know Khandra left the country. She flew United to Chicago yesterday then caught a Turkish Airlines flight to Mogadishu."

I said to Milton, "You didn't have her on the no-fly?"

"Fuck you," said Peterson.

I said to Gabriella, "Are you saying the call was relayed by two phones being held up to each other?"

"That's our guess," said Gabriella.

"Jesus Christ," I said. "Low-tech still wins the fucking day." The room went quiet for too long. "So just out of curiosity, did Fine's cooperation lead to anything or anyone?" Their silence answered my question. "So if you had just let us do our job, or maybe helped us, you would have found the one Al-Shabaab sympathizer in the whole goddamn building and she would have led you to at least half a dozen more."

"Goddamnit," said No Chin, looking at his phone. "Somebody just posted the ambush online."

"God save us," said McGinnis.

"Your suspect has paid for his crime," said Milton. "That had better make you happy." Milton stood and walked to the windows overlooking the tangle of freeways below. "The FBI is going to thoroughly investigate your recent activities, Shapiro and Ellegaard, and whether or not they impeded the work of federal law enforcement. My advice to you is don't leave the country."

I said, "You wouldn't fucking know it if we did."

"Get the hell out of here."

At 4:25 A.M., I texted Ansley. *My worknight has just concluded.*

Come over.

I need to sleep. I'll call when I wake up.

I'm working at the hospital from 6 A.M. to 8 P.M. See you after?

I have plans I can't change. Sunday?
Yes, please.

I got back to the shitbox just before 5:00 A.M. I lay under my down comforter and listened to the plows on 54th. Or at least on the Edina side of 54th. Someone from Minneapolis PD had already knocked on Stevey Fine's door and told him his big brother was dead. I pictured him hearing the news and was certain he'd be devastated. I envisioned Stevey Fine running a hand through his thick dark curls and dropping his head in sorrow.

I said "fuck" out loud and set my alarm for 8:00 A.M.

Stevey Fine's head was the one I'd seen from the Christ Presbyterian Church balcony at Maggie Somerville's funeral. Three hours of sleep would have to do.

31

At 8:15 I sat in my living room and drank coffee and ate a bowl of microwaved oatmeal. The monotone on the radio said it had snowed eleven inches at the airport—they always tell you the weather statistics at the airport even though no one lives there. The voice forecasted cloudy skies in the morning then another three to four inches starting late afternoon. The temperature would hover around thirty. Most schools were starting two hours late. Not a bad morning to go sledding or make a snowman or snow fort. Lucky kids on a Friday.

I wanted to call Ellegaard but decided to let him sleep. I thought of calling McGinnis but didn't want to talk to him before I spoke to Ellegaard. I'm sure their heads hit their pillows thinking the Maggie Somerville case was

closed. First murder in Edina in over a decade and
cleared off the books, or more likely book, in five days.
All without the hassle or expense of a trial. Maybe
Andrew Fine did kill Maggie Somerville, but last night,
when he drove north on Highway 100 instead of south
to the Hyland Lakes Office Park, I was almost certain he
was innocent of that crime. Andrew Fine suffered from
a fatal case of narcissism, but he wasn't obtuse. When I
told him I'd heard whispers of the Edina PD collecting
vacuum-bag samples to compare to the murder scene,
his only concern was Khandra Aden.

At the academy they taught us that when a woman is
killed, the investigator should focus on the husband or
boyfriend. The murder of a woman is most likely a crime
of passion, they said, especially when she hasn't been
robbed or raped. So that's where Ellie and I started, first
with Robert Somerville. He had no alibi for the night of
the killing. He did have financial trouble and, knowing
his children were the beneficiaries of his ex-wife's life
insurance policy, he had motive. But Robert Somerville
didn't seem to have it in him. Everything about him said
pacifist. His house, his clothing, his business. There are
two types of people. Those who will kill someone else
and those who will kill themselves to hurt the person
they can't bring themselves to kill. Robert Somerville
was the latter. He didn't even kill the sheep he used to
make sheepskin boots—he waited for them to die of
old age.

So we focused on Andrew Fine because most everything pointed to Andrew Fine. But most everything *isn't
everything*. The biggest detail being that Fine didn't love
Maggie Somerville. He never had. We rationalized that
away by theorizing that Andrew Fine killed Maggie to
keep her from talking about his sexual proclivities,

which would arm his ex-wife in their long-running divorce war. But that theory began to crumble hours before his death, when Fine's relationship with Khandra Aden revealed itself. And when Fine admitted to being in love with Khandra, I just couldn't see him caring enough about Maggie Somerville in any way that would motivate him to kill her. And the last misshapen piece of the puzzle: Andrew Fine was a creature in need of immediate gratification. He didn't have the patience or foresight to plot a murder like Maggie's—to conceive the logistics of such a plot, to accumulate the used vacuum bags over months or years, to have it all in place and then wait for the perfect opportunity coinciding with the right weather event.

But I continued down the wrong path of pursuing Andrew Fine because it was hard to let go of something that seemed so promising. Potential is a foul fucking temptation. It seems a noble and worthwhile pursuit. Its singularity promises great reward. But potential blinds and insulates you from the elements. Whether you're focused on a romantic partner or idea or job or murder suspect, your subject's potential feels warm and inviting. Letting go of potential is difficult because then you're out in the cold again. Then you're alone.

I opened my laptop, went to Facebook, and downloaded a picture. Then I read three e-mails from Micaela. She was worried because I hadn't responded to phone calls or texts. I replied that I'd lost my phone and would call her later. It was the kind of e-mail you'd get from your mom, and, for a moment, I thought I might understand the nature of Micaela's love for me. But the moment passed.

I put on my down sweater and boots then carried my laptop out to the garage. The Volvo proved itself again by conquering the icy, rutted alley. Three minutes later, I parked in front of Beth Lindquist's house.

She and Perry were home—they'd just returned from a walk up to Caribou for coffee. They were changing out of their boots and jackets in the small foyer when I knocked on the door. Beth seemed brighter than when I'd last spoken to her—maybe the funeral started her healing process.

"Nils, come in," she said. "Perry, you remember Nils."

"Of course I do. He's the guy who always refuses my sandwiches." Perry smiled and shook my hand. "Nice to see you again. If you want to take me up on my offer, we're eating at eleven A.M. sharp because Beth's running a twenty this afternoon. Needs time for digestion."

"No, I'm good. I just have one quick question for Beth."

"Would you like to sit down?" said Beth.

"No. This will only take a minute." I opened my laptop. "Do you know who this man is?" I turned the screen toward her.

She recognized him instantly. "Yes! That's Slim! Maggie's old boyfriend. You know, I said hello to him yesterday at the funeral. He's an awfully nice man. And I hate to admit it—I still don't know his real name."

"It's Stevey," I said. "Stevey Fine."

"Hey," said Perry, "he wouldn't by any chance be related to Andrew Fine, would he?"

"Yes. They're brothers."

"We saw on the news this morning that Andrew Fine got himself killed last night in Little Somalia. The Edina police said he was their lead suspect in Maggie's murder."

"That's true," I said.

"Then why are you still investigating?" said Perry. He glanced at Beth. The sadness had returned to her face and her thin neck seemed to shrink another size. Perry put his arm around her and kissed the side of her head.

"I'm not investigating. Just tying up a few loose ends. You have to be extra diligent when a case is closed without a conviction." The tension eased in Beth's eyes. "And don't tell anyone I said this, but I get paid by the day so I'm stretching it out a bit."

Beth laughed. What I said wasn't that funny—she just needed the release. Perry smiled, relieved that Beth's mood had lightened. "Nothing wrong with being enterprising."

"I can't believe Slim and Andrew Fine were brothers," said Beth. "It's strange Maggie went from one brother to another. Especially because Andrew was so awful and Slim—what's his name again?"

"Stevey."

"Right. Stevey was so good to Maggie. He really cared for her. Last year, Maggie went to Mexico with her kids for spring break. She was dating Stevey then. Well, while they were gone everyone in town was raking all the dead leaves and muck from winter out of their yards. Maggie refused to hire anyone to do it for her—something about the divorce made her want to do her own lawn, you know, to prove she was independent and okay on her own. And Stevey, he just adored Maggie. So when she was in Mexico he raked that whole yard by himself. Took him an entire weekend. Maggie came home to what must have been two dozen bags on the curb filled with yard debris. Oh, it's a shame, really."

"What's a shame?" I said.

"That Maggie didn't feel the same way about Stevey as he felt about her. They could have been so happy together, and Maggie deserved happiness and love more than any person I know."

The grandfather clock ticked in the dining room. Perry put his arm around his wife. I said, "Thanks, Beth. You've been very helpful."

I left the Lindquists and drove to Uptown where, at 9:55 A.M., I was one of several idiots standing in front of the Apple Store waiting for it to open. Half an hour later, I had a new iPhone that was bigger and lighter than my last one. I had four messages from Micaela, one from my brother, one from Ansley, and one from Stevey Fine. I listened to his first.

His voice was raw and deeper than usual. "Shap. I don't know if you heard, but Andrew was killed last night. I had to go down to the morgue. It was fucking brutal." He sobbed. "They blew his head off. There was nothing left of it." He cried more and then said, "Call me." The time of the call was 9:17 A.M.

I called Ellegaard at his home number and asked Molly to wake him. She said he was already up and building a snow castle in the backyard with the girls. A few minutes later he came to the phone.

"What are you doing up so early?" he said.

"I need to meet with you and McGinnis as soon as possible."

"Why? What's up?"

"I'll tell you when I see you."

"Can you tell me now? McGinnis is probably still asleep."

"Then have the station get ahold of him. It's urgent."

"I don't like the sound of this, Shap."

"Nor should you. Your office at 11:00."

"Eh boy."

"No fucking shit."

I called Stevey Fine from the car. He answered on the first ring, scratching out a weak, "Hello."

"Stevey, it's Shap. I am so deeply sorry."

"I want you to find out what happened."

"I know what happened."

"So why? Why did they do it? Fuck, Shap. They posted it on the Internet. What's going on?"

"We should talk. I can stop by this afternoon."

"My sister's supposed to land around 1:00. As soon as she's with my mom, I'm free."

"Want me to come over at 2:00?"

"Yeah. That'd be good. I'll see you then."

I got in the car and headed west on Lake Street. While I was waiting at a stoplight on the north side of Lake Calhoun, Ansley called.

"You got a new phone already," she said.

"They're a bad habit."

"Guess what I'm looking at."

"A spleen?"

"No, silly. A check for one million dollars. The insurance company said it'd take two weeks, but FedEx delivered it to me half an hour ago."

"I'd say congratulations but that doesn't seem appropriate."

"No," she said, "it doesn't. Listen, Nils. I'm having a hard time with all of this. I talked to my dean this morning, explained everything to him. He suggested I take a week off, get away."

"I think that's a good idea. Are you going to leave town?"

"I am. I'm going to go somewhere warm. The Caribbean or Hawaii. I'll call you when I get back."

"Okay, Ansley. I hope you find a little peace."

"Thanks, Nils. I hope so, too."

Ten minutes later I sat across from Ellegaard in his office. Chief McGinnis stood with his arms folded and said, "Why in the hell am I here this early after what happened last night?"

"Because, Chief," I said, "I don't think Andrew Fine killed Maggie Somerville."

"Oh, for shit's sake get the hell out of here, Shapiro. You don't even work for us anymore."

"I'm not happy about it either," said Ellegaard, "but let's hear him out."

McGinnis, as if he were a teenager being stopped by his parents on his way out of the house, glared at me and said, "What." So I laid it out. All my doubts concerning Fine and how they were confirmed just before he was ambushed.

"But what about the carpet fibers?" said McGinnis. "They're from his office park."

"Right," I said. "I'll explain that in a second. But for the moment, remove the carpet fibers from the equation. Consider everything else I just said about motive and aptitude and how that murder was plotted."

McGinnis thought about it and didn't say a word for a full minute. Then he looked at Ellegaard and saw they'd come to the same conclusion. McGinnis then said, "Shit."

"Good. You're with me. Now for the carpet fibers. We know we can't ignore that the carpet fibers from Andrew Fine's office park match the carpet fibers in the vacuum cleaner–bag contents found at the crime scene, so there has to be another explanation."

"There'd better be," said McGinnis. "And what about the anonymous letters? Do they figure in or not?"

"One thing at a time."

"We can't go down the wrong path again," said McGinnis. "Someone already tipped off the press Andrew

Fine was our prime suspect. If I have to undo that, I don't want to have to undo the next one."

I hesitated. Something didn't feel right. My doubt was starting to annoy me.

"Do you need more time, Shap?" said Ellegaard.

"I want to talk this out. See what you guys think." Neither said a word. They just waited for me to continue. "Before Maggie dated Andrew Fine, she dated a guy Beth Lindquist only knew as Slim. I asked Robert Somerville and Ansley Bell and a few of Maggie's other friends who this Slim was, but no one seemed to know. Apparently, for Maggie, she never discussed that relationship with anyone. From my experience, that means Slim was just a fling for Maggie. She was just fucking around with him and had no intention of the relationship materializing into anything real. The only reason Beth knew about Slim was because she lived in the neighborhood and saw the guy come over. According to Beth, Slim adored Maggie. He even raked her whole yard when Maggie was away on spring break.

"So I kept wondering about who this Slim might be. Thought maybe we should pull phone records going back to when Beth said he was around, but that's when our suspicion of Andrew Fine got white-hot so I forgot about it. Then yesterday morning at Maggie's funeral, I sat in the balcony and saw the back of a man's head on the ground floor. It looked familiar but I couldn't see the face and couldn't figure out who it was. Then it came to me when I got home at five in the morning. It was Stevey Fine."

"Andrew Fine's younger brother?" said Ellegaard.

"Yes. And I wondered why the hell Stevey was at Maggie Somerville's funeral. So this morning I showed a picture of Stevey to Beth Lindquist and asked if she knew who it was and she said—"

"Slim," said McGinnis.

"Yep. I don't know why Maggie called him Slim—I've known Stevey for decades—I've never heard him called that. And knowing that Andrew was such an asshole of an older brother, it made perfect sense that he'd swoop in on Stevey's ex-girlfriend."

"And you think Stevey Fine killed Maggie because she dumped him for his brother?"

"It's possible," I said. "Especially considering Stevey Fine manages Andrew Fine's office park. He walks on that carpet every day. He manages the maintenance crew. He knows when the garbage bin is full and what day the trash is emptied."

"Motive and opportunity," said Ellegaard.

"You suggesting we bring him in?" said McGinnis.

"No. I'm going to see him at 2:00. He called me this morning. He sounded devastated about Andrew. Andrew was such a prick to Stevey—I was surprised."

"A big brother's a big brother," said Ellegaard. "Even if he's a bad one."

McGinnis said, "Maybe part of him hated Andrew for dating Maggie, but the part of him that loved his older brother kept him from going after Andrew. So all the animosity he felt for Andrew and Maggie was focused on just Maggie. This is interesting, Nils. I'd like you back on the case. And I know you haven't stopped working on it, so your rehiring is retroactive. Consider you were never fired and invoice us accordingly. Do you think Stevey Fine's a flight risk?"

"No, I don't. Especially since I doubt Stevey Fine's our killer."

"What?" said Ellegaard. "Then why the hell did you drag us in here?"

"I wanted to see how easy it would be to frame him."

"Goddamnit, Shapiro," said McGinnis. "You're driving me out of my gourd."

"And it was easy. Just like it was easy to frame Andrew Fine. I'll know for sure when I meet with Stevey in a few hours," I said. "But it's highly unlikely he killed Maggie Somerville."

"Perfect," said McGinnis. "We're back to square one."

Ellegaard sighed. He looked tired and defeated. He leaned back in his chair and stared at the ceiling. "We've wasted the first week of a murder investigation. Now we're in serious trouble."

"No, we're not," I said. "Because I know who killed Maggie Somerville."

32

I met Stevey Fine at his loft in the North Loop. It was a one-bedroom that overlooked the Mississippi River. The walls were made of hundred-and-fifty-year-old brick. Timber posts, a foot square, met equally thick beams at heavy, black iron connectors. The floors were old, wooden, and undulating. They were coated with urethane and creaked underfoot. The kitchen was new and open to the living space. It had stainless-steel appliances and soapstone countertops and off-white cabinets with flat panel doors and iron pulls to match the beam and post connectors. The place was small and perfect and I decided right then the shitbox's days were numbered.

Stevey Fine's grief was real. His face was swollen, his eyes bloodshot, his nose stuffy. He hadn't showered or shaved and his curls sprung out of coil in places. I gave him a hug when I saw him. He offered me a scotch and, though the sun was hours from setting, I accepted it.

We sat in a couple of chairs that overlooked the river. The water was open except for a few ice shelves along the edge. The river ran dark and gray like the sky, a sharp contrast to the fresh white snow along its banks. We sat in silence for a few minutes, then Stevey said, "What was Andrew doing? Why did they kill him? Especially like that."

"Andrew was cooperating with the FBI in their investigation of terrorist recruitment in the Twin Cities. Because he employed so many Somalis, and gave those employees access to computers and phones, Andrew allowed the FBI to monitor all communication going in and out of the call center. There's a lot of questions to be answered still, but somehow, Andrew's assistant, Khandra Aden, either knew about the FBI investigation and Andrew's cooperation or suspected it. Her allegiance, it turns out, was with Al-Shabaab. I'm guessing she was instructed to initiate an affair with Andrew to get closer to him. No one knew about that affair because Andrew kept it secret."

"Because she was an employee?"

"That and she was seventeen."

"Jesus, Andrew."

"And once Khandra knew for sure about Andrew's involvement with the FBI, Al-Shabaab, or whoever it was, killed him. The brutal manner was a message to anyone else who might be thinking of working against them."

"Like the beheadings. That's why they posted it."

"Exactly. I'm sure it's no consolation, but the way they opened up on him with all those guns, your brother died a painless death. It was over before it started."

Stevey nodded. I was right. It was no consolation. "I guess I'm not really mourning Andrew's death," said Stevey. "He was such a prick to me. From the moment I was born, really. You saw it when we were kids. He did two nice things for me in thirty-eight years. He let me live here for free—I think it was his fuckpad when he was married—and he gave me the job managing the office park. And as generous as those things were, he held them over my head like the son-of-a-bitch he was. But what makes me so sad . . ." He shut his eyes and tears leaked down his face. He wiped them away with his sleeve. ". . . what's so sad is, well, one, my mom and sister have to live through this. And . . . and I had this fantasy that someday Andrew would come around and we'd be what brothers should be. So I guess more than anything, I'm mourning the loss of that chance."

"Yeah. That's a tough one to let go of."

"On the news they said Andrew was the lead suspect in Maggie Somerville's murder. Is that true? I mean Andrew was a dick, no doubt about it, but there's no way he murdered Maggie. I read about all the weird stuff in that case with the vacuum dirt and no forced entrance. To be blunt, Andrew didn't have the imagination."

"Stevey, did you know Maggie?"

"Yeah, I knew her."

"From when she dated Andrew?"

"She never dated Andrew. She thought she did, but Andrew was just sleeping with her."

"But that's how you knew her?"

"No," said Stevey. "No, I knew her because I saw her for a while before Andrew."

"Romantically?"

"For me, but not for Maggie. She thought of me the same way Andrew thought of her—a fuckbuddy. At best.

I took her to a party at his house one night. That's when she met Andrew. She was wowed by the house and grounds and . . ." He trailed off. "I saw her as this sweet, kind person. I guess there was something more ambitious going on. These sides people have to them, they're not mutually exclusive, you know? And Andrew knew how I felt about her. Didn't stop him though. But that was Andrew."

"Why did she call you Slim?"

"How do you know that?" Stevey looked at me for an answer but I didn't give him one. "Are you working right now? Jesus, Shap. Why didn't you tell me?"

"I'm just trying to wrap this up."

"Who are you working for? Maggie's family?"

"Edina PD."

Stevey ran his fingers through his mass of curls. "What? You think I killed her?"

A pair of mallards glided in tandem toward the river, their wings fixed as they descended then seemed to hover over the water before setting down. Every winter a handful of ducks refused to participate in the exodus south. Real Minnesotans, they didn't go for that snow-bird crap. Instead they found open water, big rivers, spring-fed creeks, and man-made ponds aerated to keep from freezing, fountains bubbling up at their center.

"No, Stevey, I don't think you killed Maggie. I'm just trying to figure out who did."

"Are you sure? I'm trusting you as a friend, Shap. Do I need a lawyer?"

I looked him straight in the eye and said, "You can trust me, Stevey. No fucking around. I promise."

Stevey looked at the river. Three more mallards, all green-heads, joined the original two. They'd found an eddy and let the current take them in circles. "Maggie thought it was cool I knew so many local musicians. We were at the Cabooze for a benefit to raise money for Slim Dunlap after his stroke. Everyone was there, and I introduced her to Bob Mould, Grant Hart, Curtiss A., Chan Poling, Chris Osgood, Paul Westerberg, Matt Wilson, Marc Perlman. And of course, the man of the hour, Slim Dunlap. Maggie was such a fan of the Replacements, she started calling me Slim. It didn't make any sense, but she thought it was fun and it made her happy so I didn't fight it."

"Were you in love with her?"

"I think so, yeah. I don't know. I only saw her for a couple of months and, to be honest, I have no idea if we were even officially dating. I'd see her once a week on nights she didn't have her kids, but they were with their dad three nights a week so who knows what she did on the nights she wasn't with me."

"Her friend, Beth, thinks quite highly of you."

"Yeah, Beth's a nice lady. She and Maggie were good friends. But there was something weird there."

"Tell me."

"One night Maggie and I were on the deck out back. We were grilling and drinking wine. Beth and her husband—is it Perry?"

"Yeah."

"They were working on their backyard. They didn't live on the same street, but they lived around the corner and you could see from one backyard to the other. So I whispered to Maggie something like, should we invite them over? 'Cause I knew they were good friends. Maggie gave me this reluctant nod and then asked Beth and Perry if they wanted to join us for some wine. Beth dropped her rake and practically ran right over. Really lit up when she got the invitation. Didn't even consult with

Perry. Perry followed with a smile that seemed more gracious than thankful. Like his wife wanted to come, him not so much, but he didn't want to be the party pooper.

"But Beth was all in, drinking wine and eating shrimp and having the time of her life. She talked on and on about her adventures with Maggie—how much fun they had when it was just the girls. Perry was pretty quiet but pleasant. After a couple hours went by, Maggie started cleaning up and dropping hints for them to leave. Perry got it right away. He carried a few things inside to be helpful and then told Beth they should get going. But Beth wasn't ready to go. She poured herself another glass of wine—and she'd had a few—and I saw a queasy look on Maggie's face.

"Then Maggie got all PDA with me. She never did that, even in private, but all of a sudden she was patting my ass and kissing me and draping her arms around my shoulders. Then Beth got the queasy look. And Perry's grace disappeared. He didn't get angry—he's too refined a guy for that—but you could see he was bothered. He finally had to drag Beth out of there, not literally, but pretty fucking close."

"Did Maggie ever talk about Beth when she wasn't around?"

"Once. I remember it because it was the longest conversation we ever had. Maggie and I had walked up to the Edina Grill and ate at the bar then hung around after and got pretty hammered. We walked back to her place and Maggie insisted we drink a lot of water so we wouldn't get too hungover. So we were drinking big glassfuls at the kitchen table, and her mail was on it— she hadn't opened it yet. She was sifting through and said something like, 'Oh, for fuck's sake, not another one.' When I asked her what she was talking about she said she'd been getting letters from a secret admirer. Remember, Maggie was drunk—I don't think she would have told me all this if she wasn't. I just happened to be sitting there so I'm the person she told. I asked her about the letters, and she said she'd been getting them for a while and they were actually sweet, but they were getting annoying. I asked Maggie if she had any idea who they could be from. She kind of swung her head in the direction of Beth and Perry's house. And I said really? She nodded. And then I said, 'They're from Perry?' And she got this incredulous look on her face and said, 'No. Not Perry. Beth.'

"I couldn't believe it. I asked Maggie if Beth had a crush on her. She said it was worse than a crush. Beth was in love with her. I said, 'Did anything ever happened between you two?' Maggie said not sexually. But Beth confessed her love to Maggie. Maggie told her that she appreciated Beth's friendship, but at forty years old, Maggie knew who she was and wasn't and who she wasn't was a lesbian."

"But Maggie stayed friends with Beth."

"Yeah, I asked her about that. She said they were neighbors and that wasn't going to change, so it would've been too weird if they didn't stay friends. And also, Maggie genuinely liked Beth, loved her even, as a friend. So they made it work. Beth wasn't sad or needy around her anymore. And she was always there in a helpful way—whether it was taking in Maggie's mail while she was on a trip or talking about Maggie's love life. Beth remained a true friend and only expressed her love for Maggie in those letters Beth thought were anonymous. She even pretended to be a man in them. But it didn't fool Maggie—she knew they were from Beth."

"Did they ever discuss the letters?"

"I don't think so. Maggie didn't want to say anything because, as she explained it, the letters were an abnormality that allowed everything else to be normal. Beth was fine as long as she had an outlet to express her love. I guess if you feel a true love like that, you just can't turn it off. You have to learn to live with it in its unrealized form, just like people have to learn to live with diabetes or herpes or whatever.

"After Maggie told me all that, I kind of admired Beth. She was in this position where she could have played the fool, but instead she played the knight in shining armor. Like, sometimes Maggie would smoke when she drank. But she always felt guilty about it so if you were with her she'd want you to smoke, too. A strength-in-numbers kind of thing. And Maggie told me that Beth, who's a pretty fucking serious marathon runner, like, way up there in her age class, would smoke with Maggie sometimes, even though she'd never touch a cigarette in any other circumstances. That's how much Beth loved Maggie."

"Ah," I said. "My fleet-footed creekmate behind Maggie's house."

"What?"

"Nothing." The mallards moved out of the eddy and drifted downstream. Maybe they'd decided to go south for the winter after all, floating instead of flying, all the way to New Orleans. "I heard you raked Maggie's lawn for her once when she was out of town."

"Who told you that?"

"Beth. She said it with admiration, not like you were trespassing on her turf."

"Yeah, Maggie was funny about her lawn. She loved to tell everyone how she did it herself. It was some sort of statement of being self-sufficient."

"But she didn't do it herself?"

"She kind of did, but she was in over her head. Sometimes her kids would help but they were so fucking overscheduled. Sports and guitar lessons and church youth groups and mountains of homework. So she'd try to do it all herself, and she would for the first couple waves of leaves. But those red oaks drop their leaves so late, weeks after the other leaves have fallen. So she had to rake all over again. It went right up to when the snow fell. So Perry and Beth would help. Even her ex-husband helped sometimes."

"Yeah, they appear to have had a pretty friendly divorce."

"Seemed to me like they did. From what I could tell, they split up because they grew apart. Other than their kids, they were interested in different things. I was in the garage once when Robert stopped by to pick something up for the kids. I didn't meet him, but Maggie was out front raking, and I overheard him say she should hire someone. She said she wouldn't. He said she was being stubborn and out of touch with reality and the whole family had the calluses to prove it. That was December a year ago, and she had a garage full of bagged leaves because they stop picking up around November first. But those damn red oaks drop long after that. So the leaves were just sitting there waiting until they started picking up in the spring again."

"Thanks for sharing all this with me, Stevey. Especially during such a terrible time." I stood. "I have to get going. When is Andrew's funeral?"

"Tomorrow afternoon. The chapel and cemetery on Xerxes."

"I'll see you there. And tell your mom and sister not to pay any attention to the news about Andrew being a suspect in Maggie's murder. That'll be all cleared up before Andrew's in the ground."

"Thanks, Nils. I appreciate it."

I put on my jacket and walked over to the front door and slipped into my Sorels. "Are these condos or apartments?"

"Condos. Are you interested? There's a few for sale in the building."

"Yeah," I said. "I am interested. I'll check it out."

33

I got back to the car and called Ellegaard. When he answered the phone he said, "We got a match."

"Exact?"

"Exact. The carpet is a hundred percent wool so it takes the dye differently every time. Anything on your end?"

I said, "A lot."

"Does it fit?"

"Oh, yeah. It fits. All of it. We'll need McGinnis's help—he'll have to be a real cop again. At least for a day. I'll meet you at the station in fifteen."

On the drive to the Edina police station, I called Lauren. She'd heard about Andrew Fine and assumed I'd cancel our date. I told her I was going on three hours of sleep and had a few more hours of work but hoped to make it. It might end early but, if she were still up for it, I'd love to meet her for dinner. She was and gave me her address. I said I'd pick her up at 8:00 unless she heard otherwise.

At 5:30, Ellegaard and I knocked on Beth Lindquist's door. Perry answered. He wore canary-colored wide-wale cords and a kelly green sweater.

"Mr. Shapiro. Twice in one day. I'm honored."

"Well, thank you. Perry, this is Detective Ellegaard from the Edina police department."

"Oh, sure," said Perry, "I remember Detective Elle-gaard. Please come in."

"Is Beth home?"

"No, sorry. She's out for her run. I told her to go be-fore the snow started but she's a creature of habit."

"Do you mind if we wait until she gets back?" said Ellegaard.

"Not at all. Come on into the living room and have a seat. She went out for a twenty but that was some time ago. She shouldn't be long." I sat on the couch. Ellegaard sat in the chair closest to the foyer. "I just got dressed for the big Edina game tonight. We're going up against Eden Prairie at Braemar. They're ranked one and we're ranked two. One of their wings and their center have already committed to play at the U. Should be a heck of a game. Make yourself comfortable, gentlemen. I was just about to help myself to a pre-game beer. Who'd like to join me?"

"No, thank you," said Ellegaard.

"I'm good but thanks, Perry."

He smiled. "Suit yourself. Be right back."

Perry went into the kitchen. Ellegaard adjusted the wire under his shirt. I heard Perry pry the top off his bottle of beer and then, "You sure I can't get you one?"

"Positive," I said. "The detective here doesn't drink, and I'm operating on a few hours sleep. But thanks again." I heard the cabinet door open and a glass being set down on the counter. A minute later, Perry joined us holding a glass of pilsner in one hand and a tobacco pipe in the other. He sat in the chair next to Ellegaard's.

"I'm not going to smoke the pipe. I smoke it in the duck blind and just like having it in my hand sometimes. Although I'll tell you, Beth does not care for it. When the door opens, don't think badly of me if I hide it before she walks in."

"We're all still boys at heart," I said.

Perry smiled. "That's true. Say, I hope you're here to tell us you tied up your loose ends and confirmed that Andrew Fine killed Maggie."

"I wish we were, Perry. But it hasn't worked out that way."

"Eh, that's too bad. My bride's been through an awful lot this week. Finding Maggie's killer would give her some relief."

"I know," said Ellegaard. "It'd be nice for Maggie's kids and family, too."

"Sorry," said Perry. "I was a bit selfish and insensitive." He looked at his watch. "She really should be back any minute."

The room was quiet except for the ticking of the grandfather clock in the dining room. Then Ellegaard said, "Nils mentioned you work at DBC Systems."

"That's right."

"We were out there last night. Your alarm went off."

"Really? I didn't hear anything about it."

"Apparently, the cleaning crew set it off. So not a big deal. But whenever an alarm goes off at one of the defense contractors in town, Edina PD takes it seriously."

"Well, I appreciate it, Detective. I really do."

I said, "Did you know that Andrew Fine owned the Hyland Lakes Office Park on Highway 100 and 494?"

"No, I didn't know that."

"His brother Stevey, the guy you know as Slim, manages it."

"Is that important?"

"It is. Because the carpet throughout all five buildings of that office park matches the carpet fibers we found scattered in the vacuum cleaner dirt in Maggie's house."

"Are you saying Slim killed Maggie?"

"It's hard to overlook the coincidence, don't you think?"

"It is. Have you questioned Slim? I suppose it's kind of tough right after his brother was killed."

"I've talked to him, but the police haven't. The thing that bugs me is that whoever killed Maggie did such a brilliant job of covering their tracks. I mean, I don't want to glorify such a horrible deed, but it was almost a perfect murder—eliminating any possibility of finding DNA evidence or footprints or fingerprints. . . . There wasn't even a forced entry that could give us clues. So it seems kind of simpleminded of the killer to use vacuum cleaner bags collected from his or her own building."

"In my line of work," said Perry, "everyone makes a mistake. They think they've taken all the precautions to wipe information off their laptops, but it lives in the recesses of their hard drives or in a server in some godforsaken place on this earth. It's almost impossible to hide information nowadays."

I looked at my phone. "Should we be worried about Beth? It must be slick out there."

"She hasn't had a fall yet," said Perry. "But if she's not back soon, I'll go look for her. I asked her to take her phone, but she doesn't like to."

"The strange thing is," said Ellegaard, "when that alarm went off at your company today, and we drove out to make sure everything was okay, I noticed that your building has the exact same carpet as Andrew Fine's office park."

Perry's genteel smile stayed put. "I'm not sure what you're implying, Detective."

"I can clear that up for you," I said. "Detective Ellegaard is implying—well, we're implying—you killed Maggie Somerville."

34

"Gentlemen," said Perry, "I don't know what went wrong with your investigation, but you've made an egregious mistake. Why would I kill Maggie?"

"You know, Perry," I said, "that's what's been so difficult in this case. Why would *anyone* kill Maggie? By all accounts she was a lovely, easygoing person. She wasn't sexually assaulted. Nothing was stolen from her. It wasn't a serial killer. Someone just wanted her dead. And when that happens, it's almost always the husband or boyfriend. So we looked hard at Robert Somerville and Andrew Fine. But Robert, that guy won't even kill the bacteria in his armpits—there's no way he'd kill Maggie. And Andrew, man, we had Andrew pegged for it. But what you couldn't have known is Andrew's an acquaintance of mine, so when he became a suspect, he consulted me about the investigation. I spent some time with him, got to know him better, and he opened up to me about his life. And the more I learned about Andrew Fine the more I realized he neither had the motive nor the capability of plotting and executing the crime. The guy was a great salesman, but he didn't have the attention span to pull off the logistics."

"That very well may be," said Perry, "but it doesn't mean I had anything to do with Maggie's death."

Ellegaard said, "We know Andrew Fine's inability to pull off such a well-planned murder doesn't prove you did it. That's the tough part because you planned it so well. It must have taken a long time, if for no other reason than to accumulate that much vacuum cleaner dirt."

Perry shifted his weight in his chair. His amiable expression shifted to neutral and disengaged, as if he were watching a bad TV show. He checked his watch.

"You were so close to getting away with it, Perry. When I realized Andrew Fine didn't kill Maggie, I thought we had to start all over again. Maybe that Slim character wrote the letters and he's our killer. Then I had a hunch who Slim was so I came over here this morning. Beth confirmed my suspicion. Slim is Stevey Fine. Then she said Slim and Maggie could have been so happy together and that Maggie deserved happiness and love more than any person she knows. That rang a bell for me. It took me a few minutes to put it together—I've only had three hours of sleep—but while driving away this morning I realized Beth's words about Maggie deserving happiness more than any person she knows, that was in the love letters. Almost verbatim. So I wondered if Beth could have written those letters. And Stevey Fine confirmed that she did.

"I can see from your expression, Perry, that you know what letters I'm talking about." Perry put the pipe in his mouth but didn't let go of the bowl.

"Maggie figured out early on who wrote those letters. Your problem, Perry, is not that Beth wrote them. It's that you discovered them and you didn't factor in the possibility of Maggie saving them. And why would you, the way Maggie rejected Beth? But that's the kind of person Maggie was. She thought the letters were sweet. Even though they were from her best friend. And so she saved them. And their existence unraveled everything for you.

"Because until we knew who wrote those letters, they implied that a secret admirer was out there. Someone we didn't know about. And that unknown person became a suspect. We never would have guessed they were written by Beth if she hadn't quoted one to me."

"Your delusion," said Perry, "is starting to become worrisome. How could I discover the letters if Maggie had them?"

"Excellent question. I wondered the same thing. Beth obviously didn't tell you. She mailed them from all over the city. Then I remembered. Your field is cyber forensics. All it would have taken from you was a little suspicion.

"It must have been sad, Perry. Beth could no longer love you the way she used to. She didn't have the capacity, or maybe 'availability' is a better word, because she was in love with Maggie. And when you love someone so dearly, to the point that they're your reason for existence, it hurts like a mother when they don't love you back. I mean, it's a debilitating pain. And that empty hole created by Beth no longer being in love with you, well, that awful feeling was your seed of suspicion that maybe Beth loved someone else.

"You're an old-fashioned couple. You haven't added on to your house. You don't live above your means. You have one computer. You share one computer. That Dell on that desk right there. And that's how you knew about Beth's love letters to Maggie. You found them on the hard drive, even if she deleted them. Because you know how to do that, Perry. That's your expertise. Even if Beth never saved the letters, you installed a program that captured every keystroke typed on that keyboard. You did something. And I know for a fact it happened at that computer."

Perry sat still and quiet. He swallowed and said, "And how do you know that?"

"Because there was this crazy coincidence that happened when Maggie got killed. See, she has a daughter no one else knows about. Her name is Ansley Bell, and Maggie had her when she was fifteen. Do you want me to stop because you know all this?"

"I don't know any of it," said Perry.

"Maggie gave Ansley up for adoption, and Ansley grew up in California. But she didn't get along with her adoptive parents so well, and when she was still in high school, she met a guy who saved her from them by marrying her. But she'd made a mistake, so she ran away and hid in Minnesota after discovering her birth mother lived here. Maggie and Ansley made up for their years apart by becoming dear friends. Maggie offered to help Ansley obtain a divorce. She wrote a letter to a lawyer and, god-damnit, Perry, she wrote it on that computer, probably so she could get away from her kids for a few minutes to think clearly. And you found that letter when you found the others. It included the contact information for Ansley's ex-husband and the fact that she'd been hiding from him for eight years. So to get back at Maggie for stealing the love of your life, you tipped off Ansley's ex-husband and told him where he could find his long-lost wife."

"I didn't make that connection," said Ellegaard. "Interesting."

"Isn't it?" I said. "That crazy coincidence of Ansley's mother dying and her ex-husband showing up wasn't a coincidence at all. Both incidents were born in that computer. The only coincidence was the snowstorm giving you the opportunity to kill Maggie shortly after you wrote to Ansley's husband telling him where she was."

Perry removed the pipe from his mouth and took a big gulp of beer.

"The stupid thing on our part is we back-burnered the letters when Andrew Fine looked like our killer. But this morning, after we realized Andrew Fine didn't kill Maggie, we came back to the letters. Maybe they were important, after all. Especially because the day I received the letters from Robert Somerville, someone broke into my house. I didn't put two and two together. I didn't know what they were looking for. I know, it makes me look kind of stupid. But I didn't think whoever broke in would be after the letters, that the burglar wanted to intercept them on their way to Edina PD. I didn't consider that possibility because the letters weren't written by a killer. The sender genuinely loved Maggie in the most unselfish way. I don't know if you read any of those letters, Perry, but trust me, they are beautiful."

Perry slouched forward in his chair, his elbows on his knees.

"I hate to sound defensive, but maybe another reason I didn't connect the letters to the break-in is I didn't have them. I went home after seeing Robert Somerville then I took them to Detective Ellegaard."

"I have the letters," said Ellegaard.

"I wonder where Beth is," said Perry. "She really should be home by now."

"Then I wondered if you knew those letters still existed, so I called Robert Somerville. He told me he was going through Maggie's stuff after she died, and he ran into you outside the house. He told you he found a collection of love letters written to Maggie by a secret admirer. He said that—what were his words?—'They just added some weirdness to tragedy.'

"I don't know if you wanted the letters because you were afraid they could incriminate you or because you wanted to protect Beth. Either way, you planned to take them from Robert Somerville's house. My guess is you were casing the place when I walked out carrying the letters in the same decorative box that Robert had carried out of Maggie's house when he told you about them. Then you followed me to my house and waited for me to leave. I'm pretty good at spotting a tail, Perry, but you were trained in spec ops. I'm guessing you're better at that game than I am."

"This is sounding quite fanciful, Mr. Shapiro." His voice was dry and hoarse. The beer couldn't fix it.

"But when you broke into my place to look for the letters, you made a mistake. You took your cell phone with you. And you should have known better. Because my neighbors across the street, Karyn and Alice, they refuse to protect their Wi-Fi network with a password. They invite neighbors to use it for free because they hate the cable company and it's their way of getting back at them. So your phone jumped onto their network. And I'm sure you know how easy it is to see what devices have used a network and for how long. That log puts your phone within a hundred feet of my house for twenty minutes during the time frame it was broken into."

Perry rubbed his chin. "If that were true, that would, at best, make me guilty of breaking and entering, not murder. I didn't kill Maggie Somerville. You have no evidence that proves otherwise. Now, if you'll excuse me, I'm genuinely concerned about my wife. She's been gone over three hours."

"She's running a twenty," I said. "Maybe she's taking it slow."

"Not this slow," said Perry.

"Tell him about the DNA," said Ellegaard.

"Oh, yeah," I said. "Thanks, Ellie. Perry, I had this theory that whoever killed Maggie, their DNA is in the system—that's why they took such measures to hide it in the vacuum cleaner dirt with a billion other people's DNA. So when I found out you and Beth had a key to Maggie's, we ran a check on you two. No arrests. No trouble. Nothing. Your DNA wasn't in the criminal database. So, in my mind, you couldn't be a suspect. But that assumption was premature because you're a military contractor who works in the Middle East. Your DNA is in the military's system in case you were killed or kidnapped and they needed to identify a body part or something."

"And tell him the final piece," said Ellegaard. He was starting to have fun with this. It worried me.

"Right," I said. "The thing I couldn't figure out was how the killer carried so many bags of dirt into Maggie's house without Maggie or anyone else noticing. I was really stumped on that one. Then I learned about the red oaks and how late they drop their leaves. That's a ton of leaves that fall in late November and into December and even January. Leaf pickup is over by then. And Maggie, she wouldn't hire any help to rake up all those leaves. But she'd accept help. From her kids. From Stevey Fine. Even from her ex-husband. And she accepted it from you and Beth, too. That's why she has a garage full of bags stuffed with leaves. Except they weren't all stuffed with leaves, were they, Perry? A bunch of them were filled with vacuum cleaner dirt—maybe a few leaves on top of it in case anyone opened them up—but a lot of dirt. And you had ample opportunity to put those dirt-filled bags in Maggie's garage."

We listened to the *tick, tick, tick* of the grandfather clock for half a minute, then Perry said, "Those are some interesting ideas. But I didn't kill Maggie. If I did, you'd have evidence, not just theories. And you have no evidence whatsoever."

"I'll admit it, Perry. I'm especially impressed by your timing. Waiting for the snowstorm like that so you could use the backyards and frozen ground and creek to flee the scene and get back into your house leaving no footprints, no trail, nothing."

"I'm worried sick about my wife, gentlemen. If you'll excuse me." Perry stood.

"You don't need to worry about Beth," said Ellegaard. "She's safe and sound at the Edina police station."

"What are you talking about?"

"We picked her up during her run," said Ellegaard. "Told her we had a new suspect in Maggie's murder and we were wondering if she could come to the station for more questioning."

Perry sneered at Ellegaard. "You had no right to do that." He sat back down.

I ignored Perry's protest. "The first thing we did was ask Beth if we could take her fingerprints because we didn't have them. She obliged and we compared them to the prints on the letters. It's not easy to lift prints off paper, but we did it. Then we were positive Beth had written the letters."

Perry closed his eyes and took a deep breath.

"Then we gave the letters to Beth. And I have to tell you, Perry, she was touched. She couldn't believe Maggie had saved them. She burst into tears. She didn't even care we knew she had written them. Not even a little.

"And then we asked Beth some questions. Where did she write the letters? She said on the computer in her living room. Did she ever save them to files? No. She didn't want you to see them. Had Maggie ever borrowed her computer? Yes, sometimes, because her kids were always on the computer at the house. Did she ever take something to help her sleep? No. She's never had a problem sleeping. After she and Maggie returned from Beaujo's Sunday night, did they come in for one more glass of wine? Beth's memory of her last night with Maggie had improved. Yes, they did come in.

"Why? Hadn't they had enough wine for the evening? Yes, said Beth. They had. But when Maggie dropped her off, you stepped outside to ask if Maggie could come in for a moment. Beth said you wanted to talk to Maggie about the city planning to put sidewalks in the neighborhood. Apparently, it's quite the hot topic around here, and you've been organizing opposition to the plan. You only wanted a minute of her time.

"That is when, according to Beth, you insisted on pouring them a nightcap. One last glass of wine. Into the kitchen you went. And out of the kitchen you came holding two glasses of red wine. But what neither Maggie nor Beth knew is that each glass of wine contained a couple of dissolved Rohypnol tablets. Within half an hour, Beth had to excuse herself to go to sleep. Maggie was so drowsy—you offered to drive her home even though home was just around the corner. Do you know how long Rohypnol stays in the system, Perry?"

Perry didn't say a word.

"Ten days or so. We just asked Beth if she minded taking a urine test. She didn't mind a bit. And guess what. Even though she doesn't take sleeping pills, she tested positive for flunitrazepam, which is what Rohypnol is. How the hell did that happen, Perry?"

"I think you gentlemen had better leave," said Perry. He stood and waited for us to do the same.

I remained seated. "I can't prove you killed Maggie Somerville. Not today, I can't. But the Edina PD will. They'll go over every cell phone call, every e-mail you've sent, and every credit card purchase you've made in the last ten years. They'll analyze the vacuum-bag contents found in Maggie's house and compare them to the carpeting in your office. Not only will they search it for DNA matching the people who work in your building, but they'll analyze the dye lot in the carpet. That's the problem with wool carpeting, Perry. No two lots are exactly the same because each batch of wool takes the dye differently. And all the little things the police find will add up."

"Like last night," said Ellegaard. "I asked the head cleaning woman how often she changes the vacuum cleaner bags. She got this puzzled look on her face then realized that she's never changed one. Not once in nearly two years of vacuuming over a hundred thousand square feet of carpeting, six days a week, has she changed a vacuum cleaner bag. That's weird."

"That's not nothing," I said. "And more evidence will turn up. It always does. Maybe it'll take a while, but the police will find something that proves your guilt beyond a shadow of a doubt. And even if they don't, Perry, even if somehow you're not found guilty in a court of law, Beth believes you did it. We just went through all of this with her. She knows you killed Maggie Somerville."

Perry Lindquist's face had turned scarlet. "I would like you gentlemen to leave now."

I pulled out my cell and made a call. "Hi, Chief. It's Nils. Perry would like to talk to Beth." I held the phone out to Perry. He took it, ended the call, and handed it back to me.

"You've ruined my life, Mr. Shapiro."

"No, Perry. You've ruined it."

35

Perry sat back down in his chair. A sense of relief seemed to wash over him. "I'm a duck hunter, gentlemen. Have been since I was a boy. I'm a pretty good shot. But even the best of us, sometimes we shoot a duck out of the air but don't kill it. You can tell before they hit the water. If they fold, they're dead. If they don't, you just crippled it. The dog will swim out and get the duck, and it's usually dead by the time the dog drops it at your feet. But once in a while, a duck refuses to be taken. It knows it's no match for a seventy-pound labrador, so it uses whatever strength it has to dive underwater. Down it goes, as far as it can, then it clamps its bill onto a reed or whatever it can find. The duck never lets go of its grip and drowns. But it's never taken.

"I respect those birds. They were going to die either way but they went on their own terms." Perry's eyes grew calm and resigned. "I'd seen people die before. I was in the army for twenty years. I was on the ground during Desert Shield and Desert Storm. I've seen terrible things. And then again over the past ten years as a military contractor. Unspeakable things.

"But to take the life of Maggie Somerville was a horror I wasn't prepared for. I took two shots of Johnny Walker. Just to dull my senses. She was already unconscious. I just had to hold the pillow there. See, it was her or me. Because without Beth's love . . ." He trailed off as if he'd lost his train of thought. Then he came back. "I've done a lot of good things in my life. I hope they count for something."

No one said anything for a minute. Maybe two. Then Ellegaard stood up. "Let's go down to the station, Perry."

He remained seated. "When I was working over there as a military contractor, a lot of people wanted me dead, or better yet, captured. They would've tortured the hell out of me to get intel on how to protect their digital information. That wouldn't have been good for me or my country." Perry put his pipe in his mouth. "I was afraid this day might come," said Perry. "Didn't think it likely, though. Thought I had all my bases covered."

"Can I ask a question, Perry?"

"I don't see why not."

"Was the carpeting a coincidence or did you try to frame Andrew?"

"Both. I've been in Andrew Fine's office park a hundred times on business so I was well aware his building and my building had the same carpeting. I'd been collecting the dirt for over a year when Fine started seeing Maggie. That presented the opportunity to frame him.

And from everything I know about Andrew Fine he deserved it."

Ellegaard said, "How so?"

"Sometimes Beth and Maggie would stay up late and drink wine on the deck. They thought I was asleep upstairs, but I'd crack the bedroom window and listen to their conversation." Perry held the pipe in his teeth as if he were smoking it. "He treated Maggie like a sex slave. Introduced her to sodomy and the whole shebang. Maggie wasn't crazy about the deed but she put up with it because she'd fallen in love with that monster. Beth did not care to hear about it, poor thing.

"It's not so much that she's a prude. No, it bothered Beth because of her feelings for Maggie. I think that one-sided love affair started before Maggie and Robert divorced. It's a terrible thing, divorce, rips a whole family up by the roots and scatters them in the dirt. Maggie leaned on Beth for support. Beth liked having someone who needed her. She and I were never able to have children. We tried. For decades. Saw a fertility doctor. That didn't work. I wanted to adopt, but it didn't feel right to Beth. Her sister adopted a child and had a rough go of it. I said that could happen with a biological kid, but her mind was made up. So we kept trying. Never gave up hope until Beth turned forty, then we just kind of quit.

"Truth is, all those years the sex was more about function than love. We started right after we were married so that's all we knew and it seemed normal. I don't want to speak for all heterosexual men, but a woman can just lie there and the sex can still be pretty good. Does the trick anyway. One of the guys at the office says sex is like pizza—even when it's bad it's good. I have to agree."

Ellegaard looked at me in disbelief over how much Perry was telling us.

"I was in Afghanistan seven, eight years ago. For the first time in my life I slept with a woman other than Beth. Another military contractor. Also married. She initiated it. Said what happens in the battlefield stays in the battlefield. When there's death around you every day, you grab as much life as you can. Kind of like Majors Burns and Houlihan on *M*A*S*H*. I didn't know sex could be like that. Frequent and physical and in all sorts of positions and locations. We were both clear on what it was. We loved our spouses and, if all went well, would be returning to them, not each other. That's just what we did.

"After that experience, I started to suspect Beth might be wired to prefer women more than men. She's a timid thing. Maybe if she were coming into her sexuality today instead of thirty years ago, she'd have the courage to be who she was born to be, but she certainly didn't then. She is no trailblazer, my Beth. Maybe she doesn't prefer women, I don't know. Maybe she just fell in love with Maggie. Either way, my bride stopped loving me. Or being in love with me, at least. I guess she couldn't genuinely love two people at the same time."

Perry moved the pipe from one side of his mouth to the other. "My parents are gone. I had a sister, but she died of leukemia when we were kids. Beth is all I have. She is my life. She *was* my life." He looked around the room, taking it all in, then smiled a melancholy smile. "Please tell Beth there's a letter for her in the attic. It's buried deep in the insulation between two joists, directly under the attic fan. It's a love letter, not a confession. A simple love letter."

Perry Lindquist bit down on his pipe. The stem cracked, then crunched. Perry's breathing grew heavy. Then he collapsed.

"Perry?" said Ellegaard. "Perry?!" Ellegaard pulled out his phone and dialed 911. "This is Detective Ellegaard with the Edina police. I have a male, midfifties who just collapsed." Ellegaard asked me the address. I told him. He told the operator and hung up then made a move toward Perry.

"Stop, Ellie. Don't try to resuscitate him." But the Boy Scout didn't listen. He knelt toward Perry. I dove from the couch, tackled Ellegaard and pinned him to the ground.

"What are you doing?!" shouted Ellegaard.

"It's cyanide. Put your mouth anywhere near his and you're dead."

36

Perry Lindquist chose to die and the master logistician didn't make any mistakes on that endeavor. He had put three cyanide capsules into the mouthpiece of his pipe, well beyond a lethal dose. It took less than five minutes for his heart to stop beating. When the paramedics arrived, they pronounced him dead on the scene. Just as well. Maggie's children, including Ansley, were spared the heartache of a trial and the media fuckery that no doubt would have ensued.

I felt somewhat guilty about lying to Perry. Rohypnol only stays in the system two or three days—there's no way Beth could have tested positive for it. I also made up that bullshit about Karyn and Alice having an open Wi-Fi network and logging his cell phone. But we all use a few tricks, private investigators and everyone else, just to get through the day.

I finished giving my statement to Chief McGinnis at 7:15. We said good-bye with a handshake and wished each other well, though at least one of us had no desire to see the other again. I drove home, took a shower, and made it to Lauren's a few minutes after 8:00. We went to Mill Valley Kitchen on the corner of France Avenue and Excelsior Boulevard and sat at a table for two. The restaurant has heavy white woodwork, white linens, and white-clad servers—all awash in firelight from glass oil lamps.

Lauren absorbed the flames and reflected them back like an opal in a thousand colors from a thousand depths. I found her beauty impossible to ignore. We ordered a bottle of wine. The server asked to see her ID. I thought *oh boy*, and, in my dog-tired state, might have said it out loud. She showed her license to the server, who nodded and smiled and then said, "Thank you." Then we ordered half a dozen small plates, which we agreed might or might not be enough food—we could always order more if we wanted to—there were no rules. The server said she'd return in a moment with our wine and left.

"You must be exhausted," said Lauren.

"I am, but if I went to sleep now, I'd get up at 4:00 in the morning and wouldn't know what to do with myself. So I'm happy to be here, especially with you even though I have no idea who you are."

She smiled. "What would you like to know?"

"Let's start with your last name."

"Brown. Anything else?"

"What kind of nurse are you?"

"Oncology."

"Wow."

"Yep."

"Can I ask you an impolite question?"

"Please."

"How old are you?"

"Thirty-four."

"Bullshit."

"How old do you think I am?"

"Twenty-six."

"Thank you."

"How old are you really?"

"Thirty-four."

"They don't ask a lot of thirty-four-year-olds for ID."

"Flattering lighting."

"She didn't ask to see my ID."

"Are you thirty-four?"

"I'm thirty-eight."

"There you go."

"Ever been married?"

"No."

"Have any kids?"

"No."

"Do you want to get married?"

"Meh."

"Please try to keep your answers brief." She laughed. "Where did you grow up?"

"St. Louis Park."

"What year were you born?"

"I'm thirty-fucking-four. Do you want to see my driver's license?"

"Yes." Lauren reached into her purse and pulled out her wallet. She flipped it open, removed her driver's license, and handed it to me. "This looks like a fake."

The server brought our wine and uncorked it and

poured a splash in my glass. I pushed it over to Lauren
who lifted the glass to her mouth as I told the server, "She's
buying." Lauren started to laugh and nearly spit the wine
back out but managed to swallow it. "That wine made
you almost choke. I think we should send it back."

Lauren said to the server, "Don't listen to him. It's perfect." The server continued pouring and left. "So, any
other questions? Before we start enjoying our evening?"

"Ouch."

"I don't get to joke around?"

"Not yet," I said. "I have something to say."

"I'm listening."

"I'm sorry about last night."

"Why would you be sorry?" The question was genuine. Not a hint of sarcasm. She must have seen the con-
fusion on my face. With kind eyes she said, "Oh, don't
tell me you have one of those good-boy complexes. Because that'll catch up with you."

I laughed, but she wasn't joking.

"Take care of yourself first, Nils. It's the only healthy
way to get through life. And regardless of what you
think happened last night, you were sweet."

"Really? Maybe I do have a good-boy complex."

"Don't worry. With proper nutrition and exercise, you
can live a normal life."

We ate and drank and talked until 11:00. I learned
that Lauren hated most of the same things I hated, and
if that's not a foundation for a relationship, then I don't
know what is. Later, sitting in her driveway, I asked if
she wanted to come over for dinner the next night and
she said yes. Then we kissed good-bye for half an hour
as if we were sixteen.

At 11:45, I stood outside Micaela's building and pushed
the button next to her name on the security system. I

took her awhile, but I finally heard, "Nils. What are you doing here? Is everything okay?"

I could tell I'd woken her. I looked into the security camera and said, "I need to talk."

"Uh . . . okay. I guess."

I didn't expect a warm welcome at nearly midnight on a Sunday, but I didn't expect hostility, yet that's what I heard in her voice. And that said it all. She buzzed me in. I took the elevator to the top floor—it opened into her foyer. "I'm in the kitchen." She was pouring two glasses of the Tyrconnell when I walked in. She said, "What's going on?"

"I wanted to tell you in person that I can't see you again."

"What do you mean?"

"This is the last time we'll see each other."

"Ever?"

"Ever. Or at least for a long, long time."

We took our whiskeys into the living room and sat on the couch. She wiped a tear off her cheek with the sleeve of her flannel pajama top.

"You don't get to cry, Micaela."

"I can."

"No, you can't. I know you love me. But you don't love me enough to put up with the inconveniences that go along with living that love—the responsibility that comes with it. So we're done doing whatever it is we've been doing." She nodded. "I still love you and that's my burden. I can't make how I feel go away. I have tried. I'm just hoping I'll learn to live with it, and it'll get easier over time. Like with a death."

"That's a nice comparison."

"It's an accurate one. Be well. And never, ever, doubt my love for you. Even if I join a cult and marry a dozen women." She managed a smiled. I drained my glass and set it on the table. I stood and walked toward the elevator.

"Nils?"

"Yeah?"

"Can I call or e-mail once in a while? Just to see how you're doing?"

"Please don't."

The elevator door opened. I stepped into it. The door shut, and I descended out of Micaela's life.

In mid-April, I was in Lunds buying fresh-caught steelhead to cook that night for Lauren. After the butcher handed me a white paper package, I turned around and entered the produce section in search of brussels sprouts, baby potatoes, arugula, and lemons. I set out to gather my bounty when I noticed Beth Lindquist, thirty feet away, squeezing avocados.

I observed something on her face I hadn't seen before—I'm quite certain it was happiness. Not giddiness, just a baseline level of joy I hadn't noticed three months prior. She had lost two loves. Yet, a few months later, there in produce, she looked like she'd lost two captors.

I parked in front of the shitbox and carried my groceries up the walk, past the Edina Realty sign with the SOLD appendage hanging below it. In a week, the sale would close, and I'd move into an old coat factory, not in but near Stevey Fine's building. It was on the ground floor, so it didn't have a view. But I loved it because the building had yet to be renovated. It had a loading dock—I could park my car next to the living room. And it had an emergency eye-wash station—you never know when you'll need one of those.

I'd miss my little patch of lawn. The snow had melted. The grass was brown and dormant and, in places, covered by patches of snow mold. Karyn and Alice, across the street, had already raked and seeded their yard. I told them they were foolishly optimistic. It was only April 14—it would snow again. They both sighed in resignation, then Karyn said, "Maybe this year it won't."

I opened my front door and noticed a battalion of last fall's un-raked in the planting beds against the house. A green shoot had breached the half-decayed clump of brown and gray. It reached skyward two, maybe three inches. It might have been a tulip or hosta or even a weed. I didn't know. It was too new to tell. I wished it luck, opened the door, and carried my groceries inside.

Read on for a preview of

BROKEN ICE

MATT GOLDMAN

*Available in June 2018
from Tom Doherty Associates*

A FORGE BOOK

1

I saw Roger Engstrom three times—the second two he was dead. But the first time he sat on a tufted leather chair in the Saint Paul Hotel's Harold Stassen Suite with a Yorkshire terrier on his lap. The dog was the result of neither intelligent design nor natural selection. Man created the Yorkshire terrier, and Man had made a terrible mistake. If your full-grown dog fits in a bag designed to carry keys and a wallet, it's not a dog you're toting around—it's an accessory.

Roger had curly blond hair threaded with silver, was tall and lean except for a soft belly that hung over his belt. He wore a navy long-sleeved polo tucked into khaki pants that rode up his legs revealing socks festooned with images of computer chips. Duck boots covered his feet, protection from Minnesota's March slush.

He scratched between the little creature's ears and said, "Thank you for seeing us on short notice, Nils." His voice was high-pitched and soft. "The Missing Persons unit of the St. Paul police are doing everything they can, but we know about your success in Duluth and then again last year in Edina. We hear you're the best there is, Nils. And our Linnea deserves the best."

Roger referred to murder cases, not missing persons, but I kept that to myself. "When did you first notice your daughter was missing?"

Roger looked to my right. His wife, Anne, sat on the loveseat beside me. I thought it strange Roger chose not to sit next to her but rather in the lone chair. It was his meeting, I supposed, and he was going to run it.

Anne wore hiking boots, canvas work pants, and a plaid flannel shirt of reds and blues. She was dressed like a roofer but was far more feminine than her not-so-masculine husband. Her gray eyes looked out from behind oversize eyeglasses. The lenses were so big I worried birds would fly into them. She had shoulder-length chestnut hair with bangs that brushed the top of her glasses. Her hair color looked expensive and almost real.

Anne said, "Linnea's curfew was 11:00, but we fell asleep in the bedroom, so we don't know if she came back or not."

"What did she do last night?"

"She went to the hockey game. We all did. It's why most of Warroad is here."

Warroad, Minnesota, lies six miles south of the Canadian border. Its citizens and a few others refer to it as Hockeytown USA, a deserved moniker considering the population is fewer than two thousand people, but no

United States Olympic Hockey Team has won a gold medal without a player from Warroad on its roster. The tiny town has sent several players to the NHL and won four Minnesota State High School Hockey championships competing against Twin Cities–area powerhouses and the hockey-centric Duluth schools.

Anne said, "Linnea sat in the student section with her friends. After the game, they all walked to dinner at Burger Moe's to celebrate the victory, and somewhere between the Xcel Center and the restaurant, Linnea disappeared."

"So Linnea never made it to Burger Moe's?" I said. Anne shook her head. "That's not even a two-block walk. No one noticed her leaving the group?"

"We've spoken to Linnea's friends," said Roger. "They all said the same thing. She was there. Then she wasn't. There were over eighteen thousand fans last night and they all poured out of the arena at once. And no one saw anything unusual. That's why the police are treating Linnea as a runaway. That and she's still seventeen."

"But they're treating Haley Housh as a missing person," said Anne.

"Who's Haley Housh?"

"Another senior from Warroad. She's missing, too."

Anne relayed the information as if it were happenstance, as if she were talking about the weather or what they'd eaten for lunch that day. "Were Linnea and Haley together?" I said.

"No," said Anne. "Haley and Linnea aren't close. They didn't sit near each other at the game, and Haley's group wasn't headed to Burger Moe's. All anyone knows is Haley disappeared from the crowd outside the stadium like Linnea did. But Haley's eighteen, so they can't consider her a runaway."

Two girls from the tiny town of Warroad go missing

at the same time. Only insular parents would believe that's a coincidence. The police wouldn't, and I sure as hell didn't. "Do you have a picture of Linnea?"

Anne found a photo on her phone and handed it to me. If Anne had told me I was looking at a picture of her at seventeen, I would have believed her. The same chestnut hair. The same gray eyes. Only Linnea's were playful instead of resigned. Maybe more than playful. Maybe a little wicked. A girl with Linnea's looks would have an array of trouble offered to her. I turned toward Anne. "Do you think Linnea ran away?"

"No," Anne said. "Linnea's a happy girl. Popular in school. The only possible reason I can think she'd run away is to take off with her boyfriend. But he's not going anywhere."

"Why not?"

Anne looked at me with indifference or fatigue or perhaps numbness over her daughter's disappearance. "Luca Lüdorf? He's Warroad's star player."

"Have the police questioned Luca?"

"Yes," said Roger. "We talked to him, too. He's devastated. He has no idea where Linnea could be. Hasn't heard a word from her."

"What happens when you try her cell phone?"

"Straight to voice mail," said Roger. "Texts don't register as delivered. And the police have had no luck tracking it."

There was a knock on the door. Roger got up to answer it.

I lowered my voice and looked at the cold eyes under the chestnut bangs. "How long have you lived in Warroad?"

"Five years. We moved up from Minneapolis so Roger could start NorthTech."

Roger opened the door. A tall man, nearly forty with blond hair and a boyish face, stood in a navy-blue suit he couldn't break the habit of wearing.

"Can I help you?" said Roger.

"I'm sorry to bother you. I'm a colleague of Nils's."

"Of course. Please come in."

"Roger and Anne," I said, "this is Anders Ellegaard. He works with me." I would have said works for me, but that's not how it is. If anything, it's the opposite. Before Ellegaard, I was on my own and worked out of my shit-box house and aged Volvo. But nine months ago, Ellegaard resigned from Edina PD and used his connections to secure start-up funding. Now we have an office downtown and a junior investigator and an assistant and, worst of all, a website. My life, as I knew it, went to hell the day Ellegaard leased us a copier. But I'm making a steady living for the first time, have health insurance, and an IRA. And Ellegaard doesn't complain about me too often, so I try to keep my complaining about him to a minimum.

Roger and Anne said a grave but pleasant hello to Ellegaard, then Ellie asked if he and I could talk in private. The Engstroms made a fuss about stepping into the bedroom, but I insisted Ellie and I leave the suite. We did and walked down the hall lined with silver room service trays piled with mostly eaten breakfasts, empty coffee cups, and spent napkins.

When we were far from the Engstroms' eavesdropping range, Ellegaard said, "Have you accepted the case?"

"Not yet. Why? Did St. Paul PD turn up anything?"

"Yeah." He looked down, shook his head, then looked back up. "The other kid, Haley Housh, they just found her body in a cave along the Mississippi River."

"Jesus."

"It's about to leak. Thought you'd want to know before deciding on the Engstrom case."

"Anybody else in that cave?"

"No. St. Paul PD's forensics people are setting up now to comb through it." Ellegaard and I stood in silence for a full minute. Then he said, "Too tragic." I thought he might cry. "I don't know, Shap. Maybe we should leave Linnea Engstrom to the police."

"What?"

"Hey, I have three daughters. I can imagine all too well what the Engstroms are going through. But this smells like a runaway to me. If the kid doesn't want to be found, it will be hard to find her. Mostly likely, she'll come back when she's ready."

"Or she's dead like Haley Housh. Or has been raped. Or drugged and kidnapped into trafficking."

"Don't do this, Shap. Don't make it seem like I don't care about a seventeen-year-old girl. That's malarkey and you know it."

"Don't say malarkey. That's not a word anymore." Ellegaard never swore. Or drank. Or jaywalked. He looked uneasy. I said, "You want to stick me on BrainiAcme."

"It's a solid case, Nils. It's lucrative. It'll help build the firm's reputation."

I looked up at Ellegaard's blue eyes—they weren't ice blue or gray like Anne's—they were blue like a baby's. The goodness in his veins must have preserved them that way. When he was a cop he could always be the good guy. You would've never seen him on YouTube abusing his power. He wore a gold shield that protected his moral code. Now he wore a businessman's getup, and his code was exposed and vulnerable. He needed me to help defend it. "Give me a week on this, Ellie. If Linnea doesn't turn up by then, I'll work the BrainiAcme case."

A maid pushed a cart of towels and toiletries toward us. We stepped aside so she could pass, and I helped myself to a sewing kit. You never know when you'll need one.

Ellegaard said, "All right. What's your gut?"

I smiled at the tall man in the navy-blue suit, not because I had a gut feeling about Linnea Engstrom, but because Ellegaard asked for it.

2

I took the case. Roger and Anne Engstrom shook my hand, and Ellegaard slipped a check for five thousand bucks in his suit coat's breast pocket. I wouldn't have asked for up-front money from the parents of a missing teenage girl, but my partner has something I don't have, a head for business. I helped protect Ellegaard's moral code. He helped me survive in this world.

We assured the Engstroms of our diligence, said our good-byes, started out the door, then heard an odd thwacking sound. I turned just in time to see the last quarter bounce off the glass dining table. Neither Anne nor Roger Engstrom had thrown quarters. No one else was in the suite. I looked above the table. A mostly crumpled dollar bill was stuck on the fifteen-foot-high ceiling. It was an old bar trick and inadvertent two-dollar tip. Stick a thumbtack through George Washington then place four quarters on George's face and crumple the dollar around them. Throw it up just right, and the weight of the quarters forces the thumbtack into the ceiling. Hours or days later, gravity calls the quarters home, the folds in the bill loosen, and the coins fall out. You've tipped one dollar. But the tack keeps the dollar on the ceiling. When there's enough of them up there, someone who works at the bar knocks the dollars down. You've tipped a second dollar.

I said, "How long has that been up there?"

"I didn't know it was," said Roger.

"I've never noticed it before," said Anne.

We called maintenance. Two men arrived with a ladder. One braced it while the other climbed up and pried the tack from the ceiling with a flathead screwdriver. Ellegaard told the man to let the dollar and tack fall without touching either. My partner grabbed a plastic spoon from a cup near the in-room coffeemaker and used it to lift the quarters, half crumpled dollar, and the thumbtack to the table. He then called the front desk and asked for hotel security.

"What does that dollar mean?" said Anne.

"I've seen that in bars," said Roger. "It could have been up there for days. What a strange thing to find in a hotel of this caliber."

I said, "Don't touch the quarters. The police may be able to get clean prints off them."

A dark-skinned African American woman, about five foot seven, showed up looking like a tourist. She wore jeans, a red Duluth East sweatshirt, and Red Wing work boots. She introduced herself as Rosamond Pinkney, Saint Paul Hotel security. She showed us her ID and badge.

I said, "Nils Shapiro," and shook her hand. Ellegaard did the same and gave her our Stone Arch Investigations card.

Rosamond had met the Engstroms earlier that morning. I explained how we'd discovered the dollar in the ceiling, and that the police should dust the bill, tack, and quarters for prints.

Rosamond said, "I've seen a few things in this hotel. I've never seen this."

She used her cell to call the police. I used mine to photograph the tack and quarters and dollar with my iPhone, flipping the dollar over with the spoon to capture both sides.

Rosamond said a St. Paul detective was on the way. "And just before you called I finished reviewing security camera footage from six o'clock last night to just a few minutes ago. No sign of Linnea entering the hotel. I'm sorry." Anne removed her giant glasses and wiped her eyes.

Ellegaard and I headed to the parking garage, where he hung his suit on a hanger in the backseat of his Lincoln Navigator. I pulled my old Sorels out of my new Volvo wagon, which was the envy of every hockey mom in the state. It had all-wheel drive and nav and smelled like Sweden. Ellegaard insisted I get something new, that as principals of our firm, we needed to make a good impression. Maybe that was true, but I didn't care for it. A car is like a relationship. When it's new and perfect, it causes more anxiety than comfort. You're just waiting for that first dent or a scrape to put you back on nature's well-trodden path to chaos and disorder so you can relax.

We left our new and perfect cars at the hotel and walked over the Mississippi River on the Robert Street

Bridge. It was the first week of March, and the big river flowed swollen and stained with runoff. The temperature had hovered just north of freezing for days, and the snow was mostly gone save for the small mountain ranges of dirt and ice the plows had made in corners of parking lots. It was, no doubt, spring's tease. A warm week for the hockey tournament, then next week, during the state basketball tournament, when athletes wore shorts and sleeveless shirts, the first of the March blizzards would pound the town white.

"You'll have to take the brunt of this case, Nils," said Ellegaard as our feet crunched road salt and sand. "I'll help interview the friends and parents and teachers. I just—"

"You don't like this case—you don't have to explain it."

"It's not just that. Last week, Emma got her period for the first time. It's messing with me a little."

"I bet." I'd known Ellegaard's three girls since they were born. I've watched him change a diaper, bundle a toddler for the sledding hill, placate the three of them in a slow restaurant by having them guess what color packet of sweetener he held in his fist. I made mental notes of Ellegaard's parenting skills because I assumed I was right behind him. But it hadn't happened. Not on purpose. Not by accident.

Ellegaard and I stepped off the bridge then followed a gravel path. A few minutes later, we stood outside the entrance to one of St. Paul's caves. Most are natural. Some are man-made, carved out of the sandstone bluffs along the Mississippi. The caves have been used for growing mushrooms and making blue cheese and housing hundreds of homeless during the Great Depression. During Prohibition, bootleggers made and stored liquor in the caves. They set up a speakeasy and even a dance hall.

When I was in high school, kids talked of exploring the infamous St. Paul caves, but, as far as I knew, it never amounted to anything more than talk. Most of the entrances had been sealed off in the 1970s to discourage exploration. Too many bad things had happened over the centuries, the worst being cave-ins due to the caves' soft sandstone walls and ceilings.

Ellegaard and I arrived before the press. A handful of St. Paul cops and forensics personnel gathered inside the yellow tape near the mouth of the cave. A trio of gas-powered generators roared electricity into snaking cables. St. Paul cops have a reputation for community policing, the only problem being it's based on their definition of community. We certainly weren't included in that definition, and that's the look we got from a heavy-set uniform who stood six foot four and had a face so fat his ears looked like an afterthought.

"This is an SPPD investigation, guys," said the cop, whose name tag identified him as Officer Terrence Flynn. "We're not ready to talk. Go on home." The *o*s in *go* and *home* were harder than calculus. Terrence Flynn was blue-collar St. Paul all the way.

"We're not press," said Ellegaard. He handed the cop our business card.

The cop read it. "Jesus Christ. Privates. You got to be fucking kidding me. Will you let us do our jobs here?" The cop looked us over and seemed to recognize me. I avoided eye contact and let Ellegaard do the talking.

"We have no intention of getting in your way. Until a few months ago, I carried the badge myself. I'm sensitive to what you're dealing with here. It's just we're working for the parents of Linnea Engstrom, the other missing girl from Warroad. As you can imagine, they're a wreck. They know you're doing everything you can, but they hired our firm just to make sure they're doing everything they can. You can't blame parents of a missing girl for that."

Flynn said, "You got any information that can help us out?"

"Not yet."

"So what do you want?" said Flynn. "I can't let you in there. They're still processing the scene."

"Just a quick look around, Officer," I said. "I'll stay out of the way."

"Hold on just a mother-fucking minute. Jesus Christ. You're that guy. That guy from the news. Who solved Duluth and Edina and made all the cops look like idiots. No fucking way, buddy. No fucking way I'm letting you in there."

"Officer Flynn," said Ellegaard, "I'd like to introduce you to my colleague, Nils Shapiro. The police in both Duluth and Edina were grateful for his help. I should know. I was one of them."

"Shapiro, that's it," said Flynn. "Yeah, Nils Shapiro." He smiled, and his fleshy cheeks expanded. "Take a walk."

"Nice to meet you, Officer." I extended my hand to the big man. He didn't take it.

"Turn around guys. I'm not fucking around here."

A March wind pushed from the south. A male cardinal clung to a high, skinny branch in a birch tree and tweet-tweeted the coming of spring. A car behind us on Shepard Road disagreed with the cardinal's forecast, its snow tires screaming on the pavement that winter would return.

Ellegaard stepped closer to Flynn and lowered his voice. "Listen, Flynn. Nils here was all over the news last year. But it wasn't his doing. Did you ever see him interviewed? You did not. Because he wouldn't consent to an interview. Not for the *Strib*. Not on TV. Not even for the radio. But we still get calls every week begging for one. Someone in this town gets killed, the press wants to know what Nils Shapiro thinks. But every time they call, what do you say, Nils?"

"I say no."

"You hear that? Nils says no to every request he gets for an interview. But guess what's going to happen if you don't let him take a peek in that cave." Officer Terrence Flynn looked as if he'd just stepped in dog shit. "On TV, Nils will say the town of Warroad is suffering because teenage girls just disappear off St. Paul streets during the hockey tournament. In the newspaper, he'll say the town of Warroad, which has already lost one of its girls, could very well lose another because St. Paul police bungled the investigation. On the radio, Nils will say that, despite his solving murders in Duluth and Edina, the St. Paul police are so worried about their precious reputation that—"

"I'll run it up the ladder," said Flynn. "Just keep your fucking panties on." The cop walked away.

Ellegaard smiled, quite proud of himself, then his eyes caught sight of something, and his smile disappeared. I looked over my shoulder and saw two police officers escorting a couple about my age toward the entrance of the cave. They wore matching green windbreakers. The woman was red-faced and crying. The man appeared grayish white and walked with a stumbling gait. The parents of Haley Housh seemed to be in separate hells but found each other's hands as a uniform briefed them before entering the cave. The back of their matching windbreakers said CRAIG'S BAR & GRILL.

The mouth of the cave looked like the mouth of an unpleasant person, a horizontal grimace, twisted and

contorted. The police had covered the ground in tarps.
The uniform led the Houshes by crawling into the mouth
first. The poor Houshes had to forfeit the simple dignity
of walking upright to identify the body of their dead
daughter. They followed the officer into the cave on hands
and knees. A few minutes later, the mouth spit them back
out. Mr. Housh's face had turned red and wet like his
wife's. He labored to breathe. His sobs carried in the cool
air. They walked away from the police unescorted, back
toward Shepard Road.

Ellegaard didn't say a thing. We caught each other's
eyes and understood the plan. He raised his voice toward
Flynn, who was on his cell near the entrance of the cave.
"What's the holdup, Officer?! I'm about to make some
calls. And you do not want me to make those calls!" All
eyes turned toward Ellegaard, and I feathered into the
shadows of the birch trees.

3

"Excuse me, Mr. and Mrs. Housh." They stopped and turned and looked at me. Haley's father's corn silk blond bangs danced in the breeze over pale blue eyes. His wife stood short and heavy under a home perm. Her blue eye shadow looked like it was imported from Chernobyl. Cursive stitching over the left breast of their matching Craig's Bar & Grill windbreakers told me their names were Mike and Connie. I said, "I'm sorry about Haley." Connie buried her head in Mike's chest.

"Yeah, thanks," said Mike, a Minnesotan on auto-polite. His voice shook. Then he steered his wife back toward the road.

"My name is Nils Shapiro. I'm a private investigator." They stopped. I saw a vague recognition in their eyes but they said nothing. "I'm working for Roger and Anne Engstrom." If the parents of a dead child can be knocked down even harder, hearing the name "Engstrom" did just that. Mike's face soured, giving him a gestapo-like appearance, and Connie's lower jaw jutted forward like a bulldog's. "I'm sorry. I didn't mean to upset you further."

"Warroad's been shit since the Engstroms moved to town," said Mike. "And now it's a whole lot worse than shit."

"No offense," said Connie, "but we sure as hell ain't gonna help you help them."

"I'm not asking for your help. I'm offering my services. Free of charge. Losing your daughter is tragic. I can't make it any better. But I can help the police figure out what happened."

It was supposed to be a sales pitch, and maybe that's how it came out, but the words felt genuine when I heard them. I wasn't immune to the Houshes' pain. I'd seen it before in the early days of my solo career, taking money parents didn't have to help find their missing kids. Mostly teens. Mostly runaways. The only difference being those parents' anguish was swirled with hope.

The Houshes had just left the last of their hope in a cave. Legally, Haley Housh died as an adult. But in reality, she was a child.

I did want Mike's and Connie's help finding Linnea Engstrom. They knew it, but they welcomed any chance of relief. Learning how Haley spent her final hours *might* provide the slightest bit. They looked at each other. They didn't need to discuss it. Then Connie turned toward me and said, "That's a kind offer, Mr. Shapiro. Thank you."

"I only have one question at the moment." They

didn't object, so I continued. "Did Haley have a boyfriend?"

"She did," said Connie. "At least that's what she called him. Ben Haas. He lives in Woodbury."

"Her boyfriend lives in the Cities?"

"Ben worked at a summer camp near Warroad," said Mike. "They met when Haley was working at the Dairy Queen. They somehow made the distance work, you know with the video chat and all."

"Do you know if they saw each other last night?"

"They were supposed to after the game. I don't know if they did. The police are looking into it."

"Thanks. I'll be in touch after you give your statements to the police." I handed them my card. "And don't hesitate to call. For any reason."

As I walked away I thumb-typed a note on my phone. *Ben Haas: Haley Housh's Boyfriend-Woodbury.* Then *Luca Lüdorf: Linnea Engstrom's Boyfriend—Warroad.* And finally, *Craig Housh: "Warroad's been shit since the Engstroms moved to town."*

When I returned to Ellegaard, Officer Flynn stood next to him. The fat cop said, "No one's fucking happy about this, especially the brass. So here's how it's gonna go. Our PR department is telling the press we've hired you, even though we're not giving you a fucking nickel. And you're going to go along with it or else we'll be giving the interviews and say you're more worried about stuffing your wallet than finding missing girls."

"That's fair," I said.

Terrence Flynn raised the yellow police tape and said, "That's bullshit is what it is." I ducked under. Ellegaard stayed where he was. "What," said Flynn, "the ex-cop too high and mighty to look at a dead girl?"

"Nothing like that, Officer," said Ellegaard. "Just no need for a crowd."

Terrence Flynn shook his head then walked me to the cave and handed me to another uniform. Officer Julia Mason had orange hair, freckles, a pug nose, and big gums that looked like the result of unfortunate genetics rather than poor dental hygiene—her teeth were new sneakers white. Her blue polyester cop pants shined at the hips and knees from wear. She led me into the crooked mouth. I wanted to say something about her taking me in because fat Flynn couldn't fit, but kept it to myself. The story of Ellegaard's strong-arm tactics had spread. I was less welcome at the scene than dead Haley Housh. I had to behave like a big boy if I wanted even a token attempt at cooperation from SPPD.

I slipped into the cave then stood. LED floods lit up the sandstone walls and ceiling. Graffiti was everywhere, not the artistic kind, but the kind akin to what's on the stall doors in a middle school bathroom. I learned "The Packers Suck!" and "Andy fucked Patti in the mouth!" and "Javier is a fag!" The proliferation of exclamation points . . . They just don't have the impact they used to.

Artists had carved into the soft sandstone walls creating images of penises, flaccid and erect, dripping with something penises should or shouldn't drip with. The floor was made of sand and was littered with beer cans, schnapps bottles, fast-food wrappers, spent hypodermic syringes, an overturned shopping cart, underwear, and used condoms.

I live in one of the most beautiful urban environments in the world, seemingly because every bit of its literal and metaphorical ugliness had been swept into that cave.

A dozen crime scene investigators took molds of footprints, sifted sand for genetic material, and collected trash in labeled plastic bags. It was a futile effort. The cave had collected centuries of human DNA. Even if a suspect was identified and his or her DNA was found in that cave, if it wasn't in one of Haley Housh's body cavities, its proximity would be circumstantial.

Haley Housh lay on her side in the sand near the cave wall, a wet mush inches from her head, a phone near her hips. She had long, dark hair and gray skin and wore a black-and-gold Warroad Warriors letter jacket, a scarf and mittens.

The Ramsey County medical examiner knelt over her body. The M.E.'s name was Char Northagen. She stood six two and was prettier than autumn. Fifteen years ago, she was a torn ACL away from making the U.S. Olympic volleyball team. Now, to every straight male cop's dismay, she played for another team.

"Is the kid's phone dead?" I said to Big Gums.

"I wouldn't know," she said.

"Mind if I ask?"

"Apparently, Mr. Shapiro, you can do whatever you want."

"Nils," I said, extending my hand to her.

"Whatever." She walked away.

I stepped to the edge of the tarp and watched a forensics person of Hmong descent sweep the cave floor with a metal detector. He wore headphones and a jumpsuit and looked like the Mine Sweeper Green Army Man of my youth. He passed by without taking his eyes off the cave floor.

No one paid any attention to me, so I followed a taped-off path to Char and dead Haley Housh.

"Nils Shapiro," she said without taking her eyes off

her work. "You probably didn't even have to duck to get into this cave."

"With a tongue that sharp, I'm surprised the ladies let you go down on them."

She stopped and looked up at me. Haley's body temperature must have lowered a full degree before Char smiled. "That was good. That was very good. Except I don't have a sharp tongue. I have a quick tongue."

"I stand corrected."

She refocused her attention on the dead body. "Heard you're working for the Engstroms."

"Small cave. Word gets around fast. Any idea what that one was doing in here?"

"Not yet, but she died between 1:00 and 2:00 A.M. That right there is vomit. Don't step in it."

"Good advice."

"I try. No evidence yet of foul play. Rapists don't re-dress their victims down to the hats, scarf, and mittens."

"Carbon monoxide?"

"That's my guess. I'll know for sure when I run toxicology."

Haley Housh probably didn't know most of the St. Paul caves were connected to others. A fire burned for warmth and light in a nearby cave. The air in her cave grew poisonous, but all she felt was sleepy. A couple dozen people die of carbon monoxide poisoning every Minnesota winter. Five hundred are hospitalized. A faulty furnace. A clogged chimney. Lighting charcoal briquettes inside the home. I'd seen my share of it in my early investigator days when I tracked down prostitutes and drug dealers for even less respectable clients.

Haley wore a boy's letter jacket with a hockey emblem on one sleeve. The name embroidered into the jacket was GRAHAM.

I crawled out of the cave. Ellegaard waited for me outside the police tape. I told him all signs pointed to CO poisoning.

He said, "Any sign of Linnea Engstrom?"

"Not yet."

"Do you think she was in there?"

"I have no idea. But I know who we need to talk to next. By the way, we're working pro bono for the Houshes."

I heard it before I felt it. At least that's what I remember. I don't know if the horror on Ellegaard's face was in reaction to "pro bono" or because he saw the arrow lodge into my shoulder.